MW01165462

. . . Or Perish

Joel Quam

NORTH STAR PRESS OF ST. CLOUD, INC.

St. Cloud, Minnesota

To Vivian, Justin, Cassandra, and Seth—for their love and patience,

with additional thanks to Mary for her editorial assistance.

Copyright © 2009 Joel Quam

ISBN-10: 0-87839-328-5
ISBN-13: 978-0-87839-328-2

Cover art and design by Natalie Sorenson.

First Edition: September 1, 2009

This is a work of fiction. Names, characters, places, and incidents are the products of the author's imagination or are used fictitiously. Any resemblance to actual events or persons, living or dead, is entirely coincidental.

Printed in the United States of America

Published by:
North Star Press of St. Cloud, Inc.
P.O. Box 451
St. Cloud, Minnesota 56302

northstarpress.com

Prologue

Once unsheathed by a warrior, a Gurkha knife must draw blood. By tradition, by logic of battle, and by rigorous training of the soldiers of Nepal, this long knife shall not be drawn casually, but instead only in moments of true danger when blood must be spilt. Nepalese fighting men may have scars on their forearms where they have felt compelled to cut themselves after taking out the knife in an inappropriate moment or at a false alarm. Although out of place geographically in southeastern Minnesota, in this case, too, the knife drew blood.

On that evening in the first month of 1998, the body was viewed by police officers in the study of the Munson estate several miles southeast of Hastings, some miles northwest of Red Wing, both comfortable Minnesota communities. Not far away flowed the Mississippi River serving as a physiographic border separating Minnesota from neighboring Wisconsin. The Queen Anne style home built in 1915 stood in a small elite enclave that jurisdictionally fell within the Whitmore city limits. To call Whitmore a city was perhaps generous, for it only held about 2,000 residents; however, in the 1990s the settlement had grown substantially as a bedroom community. Fine expensive homes were built for commuters, a few going daily to Hastings, but most taking the longer drive to work in the Twin Cities—Minneapolis and St. Paul.

Inside the elegant house—the property being a relic from an earlier era of Whitmore's development—police detective Norm Dafney supervised the evidence collection methodology of patrol officers as they moved across hardwood floors, between antique furniture and past the clear glass panels of built-in cabinetry. Through the glass, the officers glanced at the eclectic combination of displays, including rare coins, African masks, and distinctive knives from across the world. No apparent burglary accompanied the death, for only one item from all the collections was not in its assigned place. This exception was a ten-inch sickle-shaped dagger—the Gurkha knife from Nepal. It was out of place, but, in a sense, was not out of possession of the owner. H. Gordon Munson, owner of the estate, collector, president of the prominent charity Minnesota Mission, businessman, and member of the Board of Regents of Masterton College, was prone on his polished dining room floor with the knife thrust through his back and bisecting his heart. The bloody footprints leading away from the body were distinctly feminine.

1

Who Is Mercator?

I didn't expect to find the body. Probably no one would expect to do such a thing, and certainly not in small-town Minnesota. Of course, people died here like in any other place, but the unusual cases commonly were more mundane—the heart attack while shoveling snow, the booze-induced car accident. Death by violence here was generally limited to the occasional hunting incident. Violent crime in the Twin Cities, while mild by national standards, seemed shocking to us in the rest of Minnesota.

It was a Sunday afternoon when I found Munson's knife—in Munson. It was the day of a semi-annual meeting of the Board of Regents of Masterton College. Ironically, it was my relatively few responsibilities that day which gave me the opportunity to be the first to see H. Gordon Munson dead. Perhaps I should say that I was the first to admit seeing the dead man, for on that Sunday the murderer was not available for comment.

I am Mercator J. Eliasson. My father, a geography enthusiast, named me after Gerardus Mercator, the Flemish geographer, who in 1569 presented a flat map projection of the world. An innovative approach, this projection has been used extensively for map production ever since. More recently though, other maps such as those designed by Robinson or Peters have begun to find themselves on school walls.

As a boy I could take solace only in the fact that my father had not named me Hipparchus, the creator of the stereographic projection, or

Thales, designer of the gnomonic projection. Plenty of teasing about my unusual name accompanied my adolescent years. Most jabs were as juvenile as their creators. "Hey, globehead" was the favorite of Austin Jerveny, who, last I heard, was serving time in the Stillwater penitentiary northeast of the Twin Cities. In our geographically ignorant society, few had the sophistication to devise truly clever insults that might stem from the weaknesses of the Mercator projection. That is, for all the value of Mercator's creation and the longevity of this map projection's popularity, it has a significant flaw in that it vastly distorts the high latitude regions in order to maintain correct shapes of continents and countries. Distortion of land area increases with distance from the equator, thus Greenland erroneously appears to be the size of South America.

As an adult I enjoyed the distinctiveness of the name. I believed that my particular moniker was striking enough to provide name recognition. For some, though, I go by "Merc" and let them speculate as to the source of the nickname.

Along with the gift of my name, my father also imparted to me a vast array of geographic knowledge. In our household, atlases and maps were not merely displayed, but were perused actively. Certainly my father clarified for me the significance of the Mercator projection and its classification as a "conformal" projection where forms on the map were projected to conform to their true shape, even if this sacrificed accuracy of size.

Furthermore, my father took frequent opportunity to drill into my consciousness an understanding that geography is not only a knowledge of place names, but also a study of spatial relationships and interactions between people and locations. It never ceases to amaze me how often such facets of geography turn up in my daily life and work. For a year and a half then I had served as the alumni director of Masterton College, a small liberal arts institution located in southeastern Minnesota town of Masterton, not far from the smaller settlement of Whitmore. At work I occasionally had the chance to talk thoughtfully about geography and spatial interaction. What I hadn't anticipated was that one aspect of the job would be to solve a murder.

Finding the Body

Certainly at the beginning, the police made it clear that they and they alone would be investigating and solving the murder. At the scene of the crime and later at police headquarters, I explained to officers how I had happened to find the body. I had been on campus for the events of the day, focusing on the meeting of the Board of Regents. Although I did not need to attend the meeting itself, I did want to be on hand to greet the regents, all of whom were graduates of Masterton College. Along with President Marjorie Wheelwright, several administrators, and a few faculty members, I was scheduled to attend the Sunday noon luncheon with the board members.

I arrived on campus at 11:30 that morning and mingled in friendly conversation with several regents and others. At noon we filed into one of the private dining rooms adjacent to the large cafeteria dining hall where the students eat. In fact, the rumble of students' voices was background noise, as we awaited our meal. At 12:05 three chairs remained empty around the table. Munson's seat at the east end was vacant, although President Wheelwright sat in her chair at the opposite end. Three seats down on the right of Wheelwright was a chair I suspected was reserved for J.P. Kiick, professor of philosophy, who was serving as the faculty's observer at board meetings. Kiick was notorious for not being punctual, so this surprised no one. To my right an open chair was reserved for the board's non-voting student representative, Sean Lothrow. The young man was the boyfriend of Janie Everest, a student worker in my office.

Ten minutes late, J.P. Kiick bustled in, looking, I thought, a bit more flustered than usual by his tardiness.

"I'm very sorry," he announced to the group as a whole, his arms spread wide in a conciliatory gesture. "I just . . . well . . . I'm just late again." Glancing around, he noticed that all of us lacked plates, so he wondered aloud, "Surely you haven't eaten already!"

"No, no, J.P., we and you still get a meal! You're a late scoundrel, as usual." Shirley O'Flaherty joshed with Kiick.

Indeed Kiick generally got away with being late. At forty-seven and still dashingly handsome, his good looks certainly aided his cause. His flowing brown hair always seemed on the verge of wildness, yet consistently maintained a fashionable part and style, but somehow never ever appeared to get cut. This hair plus a ruggedly endearing face and, yes, even a cleft chin, all combined to catch many a woman's eye. His playful personality and amiable grace appealed to both genders, leaving Kiick a very popular fellow. In some settings I even heard J.P. genially explain away his tardiness as beyond his control, simply a function of his self-diagnosed and self-introduced malady of TDS. Always prompted by a response of "TDS? Hunh?" he would enjoy describing his self-coined definition of Temporal Deficit Syndrome. On one occasion at some now vaguely recalled campus event, I overheard his admission that he devised the definition to tease the attractive receptionist at his chiropractor's office. In this case, however, he skipped the TDS reference. Even without the normal mention of Temporal Deficit Syndrome, no one appeared to be at all unnerved by Kiick's tardiness.

In fact, his entrance and declaration prompted a lively banter between him and several members of the group, lasting until 12:20 when a member of the serving staff interrupted to inquire if we wanted to start the meal, even though two places still remained empty. A quick consensus was reached, ruling that since the board's meeting was scheduled to begin at 2:00, the meal ought to commence. Stepping over to the phone on the wall, Marjorie Wheelwright quietly stated to the group that she would call Gordon Munson to check on when he might arrive. As salad was brought in, I casually noted that she seemed to be doing a lot of number punching, but no talking.

I was halfway through my salad when a student from the campus' main switchboard interrupted to inform us that Sean Lothrow had called to say he was having car trouble. He didn't know what to do to get to campus from his apartment in Hastings, but apologized for missing the lunch. Thinking that my presence wasn't really required at the luncheon and that perhaps I could help him out, I was about to volunteer myself to pick up Sean, when I observed that regent Harriet Johnson was being served beef tongue and peas as the meal's entree and vegetable. I never liked that mushy green vegetable and long lived blissfully ignorant of the flavors of certain animal body parts such as tongue, brains, or testicles. Perhaps I could drive out to Sean's apartment and get a fast food chicken sandwich on the same trip.

"Why don't I go get Sean?" I offered.

President Wheelwright too had now been served tongue and was looking strangely at it. Beneath bobbed brown hair, her eyes puckered in apparent disapproval, before she hesitatingly accepted my suggestion. Giving the events that followed, I never did ask her if she had a fleeting thought of avoiding the tongue too, before speaking a reluctant assent to me.

As I rose to leave, President Wheelwright spoke the words that set in motion a period of drama and danger for me—"Would you check on Gordon Munson too?" I nodded, for I could drive an efficient triangle between Hastings, Whitmore, and Masterton.

Thus, it was that Sean Lothrow sat in my car while I knocked on the door of H. Gordon Munson's home in Whitmore, near Masterton and not far from Hastings. I'd picked Sean up, teased him a bit about not living on campus like most students, and listened to his assertion that a senior needed more flexibility in his lifestyle than that found on campus. From Sean's apartment, I dialed Munson's phone number, but like Marjorie Wheelwright, I got no answer even after many rings. So, Sean and I drove on, swinging by Munson's house on our way back to the college.

At 1423 Old Stone Moor Way, we cruised up the long driveway and parked in front of the striking old home. Only thinking that I would perform a perfunctory rap on the door, I left Sean in the car. After all, I thought, surely Munson would be on campus by now, having only been delayed a few minutes by some business matter or such thing. Knocking on the old wooden door, I noticed that it, like the rest of the house, was striking in quality and design. The front door had two long etched-glass windows. I was admiring this glass, waiting what seemingly might be a short, but reasonable amount of time. I intended to wait long enough to give Munson a chance to come to the door from some distant part of the big house, if somehow he actually was home, but not too long, as I was charged mainly with getting Sean Lothrow to campus.

While trying to measure the time, and still admiring the door, I adjusted my view and peeked in through the etched glass. Perhaps it was that little bit of boredom and discomfort of standing idly on the doorstep. Perhaps it drew from the curiosity latent in humans, ready to spring unbidden when given an opportunity. Perhaps it was the striking perspective that the etched glass proffered. Whatever the particular cause, the result was that I saw the blood. Well, I thought that it might be blood. Some kind of dark reddish liquid had flowed from an adjoining room a foot or two into the next room, a long tongue of thick liquid. Of course, the etched glass wasn't entirely clear for viewing. My hand involuntarily reached forward and tried the doorknob. It turned.

This created an instant dilemma. It seemed that further investigation was warranted. I mean, I could be seeing a decorating accident, a spilled can of paint, but I really didn't think so. Yet, Minnesotans are private people who avoid both mistakes and confrontations. As I stood at the door, pondering whether or not to go in, my mind flashed to a winter street scene several years earlier, when walking along I had noticed that a pickup truck's lights were on while the engine was off. Thinking of myself as a Good Samaritan, I had opened the truck door and pushed in the knob that controlled the headlights. As I shut the door, a man burst from the nearby house, bellowing, "What the hell are you doing?" My explanation of turning off the headlights barely tempered his anger and suspicion enough to allow me to walk away without further incident. I didn't want a similar confrontation, if I walked into Munson's house and it was spilled paint on the floor and he or someone else was already upset by the mess. At the same time, both my conscience and my curiosity were urging me to do the right thing and investigate.

I called Lothrow over for support and to act as a witness to my good intentions. He peered through the glass and concurred with my opinion that the liquid on the floor might be blood. Upon entering the house, it was evident that it was blood, not paint or some other liquid. Glancing at the fine surroundings, I first noticed that a handsome chess set had been disturbed, with several pieces toppled onto the floor. At least a king, a knight, and some pawns had been knocked off the table. I could see two pawns on the edge of a fine Persian rug. I carefully, but with determination, continued forward and looked into the dining room.

Munson was there. Dressed casually in a blue knit shirt and khaki chino pants, he was sockless in Minnetonka deerskin moccasins. There was a horrified look of pain on his normally handsome face, most assuredly not from finding me uninvited in his home, but certainly from the knife that had been plunged through his back. Transfixed, I stared at the body, somewhat taking in the bloody footprints and surroundings, but largely stunned, just stunned. Sean Lothrow, having stepped over the blood in the living room and having taken a look past me, spent the following few minutes retching in a corner of the living room.

3

At the Office

My Sunday afternoon discovery of Munson's corpse obliged me to spend some time with police officers, more than once relating my account of how I found the body. Normal Monday mornings were fairly mundane, often spent going through paperwork and handling other kinds of alumni director duties. Today, however, I was something of a celebrity. Joann Mulgrew, assistant director of Admissions, stopped at my door on the way to her office, asking me what it was like to find a dead man. Financial Aid director Roger Black joined her halfway through my explanation, so I had to repeat some of the story for him. Although I tried to downplay my account of the events, my colleagues seemed extraordinarily impressed.

"It's not like I caught the murderer," I offered, in what I thought was a modest and true observation.

"But, Merc, most of us are lucky to find our own car keys, and here you find a dead man. And not just some old dead guy, but a murdered Gordon Munson! This is, wow . . . this is, wow!" offered Mulgrew.

"It's all in the hands of the police now," I pointed out, making what turned out to be a rather incorrect assessment considering later events.

"Maybe you'll solve the murder too!" quipped Black, clearly in a joshing tone, but somehow in a way that lingered in the back of my mind long afterwards.

Back in the office, my efforts to do paperwork were largely foiled by the nearly steady stream of passersby mixed with frequent rings of the telephone. The *Minneapolis Star-Tribune* newspaper had reported on the murder, mentioning that a college employee had found the body. Though my name was kept out of the article, on campus the news of my identity as the unnamed finder of the body spread rapidly. Those who phoned from off campus didn't have this knowledge, but several graduates called to ask about the case, expressing concern for the state of affairs at the college upon the murder of the head of the Board of Regents. To the first caller, Cassandra Katrin, of the class of 1981, I admitted that I was the employee who found the body. This prompted great curiosity on her part and extended the call by at least fifteen minutes. After that I did not disclose my secret identity to callers.

Only one phone call was regular alumni business, not related to the murder. Erle Justinius (Class of 1947) called to inquire about forthcoming travel programs that the alumni association would be offering. Having recently sponsored a trip to Norway that drew an impressive forty-four grads and spouses, the association was eager to try another foreign outing. I explained to Nettleton that in a year and a half, the association intended to sponsor a trip that would feature Baltic seaports such as St. Petersburg, Tallinn, and Helsinki. Apparently he knew of St. Petersburg's location in Russia and Helsinki's nearby site in Finland, for he only asked about Tallinn.

"The capital of Estonia, former Soviet republic and now an independent country," was my response. Given that I find Estonia in general and Tallinn in specific to be fascinating, I offered a few encouraging comments before saying good-bye.

For a few minutes before lunch, there was a lull in the concerned phone calls and in the friendly pauses at my door. This gave me a few minutes to review the flyer that would be sent to the Class of 1973 inviting them to their twenty-fifth annual reunion. In the quoted comments of the '73 class communicator, I found a misspelling of the word "its" which she had spelled "it's" even though she did not mean "it is" but was using the possessive pronoun form. I fixed the mistake, wondering if anyone else would have noticed this commonly misused piece of punctuation.

Noontime brought lunch with associate registrar Sherri Stringfield. Having only been at Masterton College for eighteen months, and being in the unusual position in the alumni field of not being an alum of my institution, I was making a consistent effort to get to know others on campus, those who were alums and those who had been around for a long time. Their impressions and feelings about the college helped me gain further insights into the nature of the school, its history, and its lore. Given that I had scheduled the lunch two weeks prior, I chose to keep the arrangement, even with the unusually busy morning. Unfortunately, although Sherri Stringfield was a perky grad of 1992, I found her to be a relatively shallow conversationalist. Undoubtedly I was distracted by the Munson murder, but this attractive brunette stirred no interest within me.

Given the woes of my love life, one would think that I would have been more responsive. Still, her hearsay account of how her cousin June once knew a man who found his grandfather's long undiscovered and decomposed corpse melted into a leather couch neither helped my appetite nor my disposition. She did ask questions about the Munson case, but seemed much more interested in recounting this tale told to her by a relative. Even this description was done in a way that was damn perky. In contrast to her increasingly annoying perkiness, I was feeling a bit nauseous having this new image of couch and old man merging together added to my very clear memory of how Munson looked bloody and dead on a finely polished wooden floor. Quickly, the cafeteria's vegetable medley in front of me became inedible. Miss Stringfield, though, kept talking and talking, her energy wearying instead of invigorating.

Upon my return to the office, I found a phone message from police detective Norm Dafney asking me to stop by police headquarters Tuesday morning. I phoned back indicating that I would be there at nine. This was the first that afternoon of many more calls about the murder. At the time I didn't realize that responding to phone calls would be the least of my concerns.

4

Cold in Minnesota

Leaving the administration building at the end of my Monday afternoon, I exited onto the northern edge of the grassy expanse in the center of Masterton College. At other colleges and universities this central square might be called "the Square" or "the Green," but here most everyone calls it "Vinstrom's Veldt" or in brief "the Veldt." Unofficially that's the name, though on college maps it's only an unlabeled "grassy area." Haakan Vinstrom was the original landowner who sold some and donated some of the acres that became the grounds of Masterton College. Although Vinstrom was Norwegian, the apparent appeal of alliteration allowed the interesting alias, even though the term "veldt" is a South African word, really an Afrikaans word for "plains." Students took curious pleasure in the rarity of the name. To my knowledge the only other use of the word "Veldt" in the toponyms, the place names, of Minnesota is Veldt Township in Marshall County in the northwest corner of the state, far far from Masterton College.

"Hey, Mercator!" I looked around to see sophomore student Pete Putnam approaching with a wave of his hand.

"Oh, Pete." His obvious enthusiasm was inversely matched by the eagerness of my response.

Pete Putnam was a wannabe math major and a definite dork. Today his red plaid jacket did not cover his entire knit shirt—yellow with purple horizontal stripes. The untucked portion of the shirt spilled over green plaid pleated pants, which extended downward to visible paisley socks and wingtip shoes.

11

"How ya doin', Merc?" His lips a snare drum, the words came in rapid-fire percussion.

Pete's older brother Frank was a 1993 Masterton graduate. I met Pete when Frank brought him to campus to start Pete's freshman year.

"I'm fine, Pete." Looking to go home, I tried to sign off with a "Just now ready to get in my warm car and go home."

"Oh, yah! Well, you know, it's that whatchmacallit thing."

I took a deep breath as I fingered my pocketed car keys. Did I really want to inquire into the nature of "whatchmacallit" as Pete stated it? My Minnesota manners got the best of me. "The what, Pete?"

"Oh, you know. What's the dadgumit thing called? I saw it on TV. La Plata? I think that's it. La Plata."

"Pete, La Plata is a planned provincial capital in Argentina."

Running his hand through already mussed short brown hair, Pete looked back at me with twisted lips.

"Pete, could you mean 'La Nina?'"

"That's it! That's it!" Reaching out, Pete pumped my hand up and down, as I wondered if it was possible to speak any faster.

Reclaiming my hand, I explained, "'La Nina' is a meteorological or weather phenomenon more or less the opposite of the more well-known 'El Nino' effect."

"Yep, that's why it's cold."

"Now, Pete, I think it's cold now because this is January in Minnesota."

"Yah, but not always. In 1981 it got up to sixty-nine degrees in Montevideo in January. My uncle, ah, Whatisname, um, Harlen. That's it. My uncle Harlen lives there, and he tells this story, see, that he couldn't play out-door broomball then because all the ice melted. All the ice melted in January! Should have been loads of ice, but no. Hey, he tells that story every darn year."

"But Pete, the average January high temperature around here must be about twenty degrees. It's normal to be cold here in January."

"Then it must have been that La Nina thing that makes the days shorter. They said something about that, I think."

Shaking my head, I continued to contend with him, "I'm pretty sure that this winter is an El Nino year, not a La Nina year."

"Shorter days, shorter days. La Nina makes shorter days."

I tried for several minutes to explain that the angular relationship between the Earth and the Sun determined most broadly the seasons and quite particularly the hours of sunlight each day, but Pete would have none of it. He was beginning to switch into his explanation that the Mississippi River always flows downhill because it flows southward, when he spotted Monroe Wilder about thirty yards away. With an abrupt end to his commentary and a swift, "I'll see ya, then," Pete trotted off in pursuit of the math professor. I saw Monroe try to duck, but it was too late. Pete called and waved at him.

As I turned toward my car, I saw Wilder make a furtive glance toward Pete, and then focus on the sidewalk in front of him as he began to walk very determinedly toward the science building. I left without waiting to see whether Pete caught him or not.

5
Detective Dafney

Police detectives were not commonly found in small town Minnesota. Certainly police officers, police chiefs, sheriffs, and deputies were in appropriate number, but detectives generally were found only in the larger cities. Due to ever-growing wealth from its well-to-do commuters, Masterton and Whitmore had cooperated to hire their own police detective. It was common knowledge in Masterton that Norm Dafney was this police detective only because of his wife, Della Rhodes, who was born and raised in Hastings and had graduated from Masterton College (Class of 1962). Right after graduation, while working at a Lutheran summer Bible camp in Ohio, Della Rhodes had been accused of petty theft by one of the other camp counselors. Officer Norm Dafney had been sent to investigate the case. The vivacious young blonde, vociferous in her protestations of innocence, had impressed the young, unmarried policeman. After a short investigation Officer Dafney found the missing items, a bit of jewelry and a pocketbook, hidden among towels in the laundry room. A brief questioning of the laundrywoman, newly hired that summer, produced a confession. Further questioning found even more damning evidence—the culprit was in fact a Methodist! The camp hired only Lutheran laundrywomen for many years after that.

Crime had thrown Norm Dafney and Della Rhodes together. With young Dafney being immediately smitten and Miss Rhodes being grateful, a romance soon swelled. Eventually the only difficulty for the couple was geographic; the policeman had been offered a position on the Cleveland force, but the young woman adored her Minnesota homeland. Love created a compromise: they would begin their marriage together in Cleveland, but at least retire in Minnesota. Norm Dafney rose through the ranks in the Cleveland Police Department. When an opportunity for early retirement in 1995 coincided with an opening in the joint Masterton/Whitmore Police Department for a detective, the couple made the move. But, until the Munson murder, no one locally really knew the extent of his skills, for few serious crimes had been committed in that jurisdiction since the now gray-haired Dafney's arrival.

The next morning Detective Norm Dafney discussed the case with me, citing one circumstance as his key piece of evidence, "If the shoe fits—well, in this case the footprints! When Patrolmen Arness and MacPherson arrived at the scene, they found bloody steps leading away from the body of H. Gordon Munson. You may have seen this information in the *Star-Tribune*."

I had mixed feelings about Dafney. True, he appeared generous in his willingness to review the case with me. Perhaps this could be attributed to overconfidence or perhaps he already had adapted to Minnesotan courtesy—"Minnesota nice."

I'd met the detective once before the murder, but in my official college position and at an alumni function. At that event he had seemed uncomfortable. My surmise was that he felt out of place without his uniform, being dressed in a sports jacket that clearly could not be stretched far enough to button over his shirt, the tails of which kept tugging past his belt. I assumed his wife's status as an alumna gave me an easy way to approach Dafney for information on the case. What I had forgotten was that he had invited me to the police station. I had not asked for an interview.

Thus, not yet having that realization, I continued the conversation casually. "Detective, one of my first thoughts upon finding the body was 'No, Bond—James Bond—can't be dead.' Is it common for those finding bodies to think odd kinds of thoughts?"

"It can happen. I suppose you're referring to the common observation that Gordon Munson looked something like Sean Connery."

"Yes, in fact, on campus I heard, well perhaps you would call it gossip, but I heard that Munson himself liked this comparison, even knowing that it helped him as a ladies' man."

"Yeah, well."

"Detective, it certainly was no secret that our dead regent was a dashing figure, a successful player on the board game of love. I'm told that Munson thought himself to be more charming than Bill Clinton. Could it be that the murder was the result of a love affair gone bad?"

"A female stalker? Perhaps a so-called 'black widow'? Obviously, we do know that her shoes," the stocky lawman consulted his notes, "a pair of simple pumps tracked through blood near the body. She may have used a handkerchief to wipe blood from her hands, maybe her shoes. We're sending the hankie in for testing."

"But, Detective," I interjected, "did anyone actually witness the crime? Perhaps someone simply came in, found Munson dead on the floor, stepped in the blood and—"

"Listen, Eliasson," he noted in an impatient tone, "they all say that. I've yet to find a perpetrator who didn't claim to be as pure as the wind-driven Minnesota snow."

I noticed the venom in the way he spat out the word "perpetrator," but I persisted, "You said 'she.' Are you really sure it was a woman?"

He chuckled confidently, seemingly at my foolishness. "You think we can't recognize a woman's shoe print? C'mon, give us *some* credit. Although, there is the handkerchief."

"Of course," I conceded.

His eyes squinted at me. "Even so, Marcus . . ."

"Mercator," I corrected.

"What?"

"My name is Mercator. You said Marcus," I added, trying to be polite.

"What kind of name is that?" I couldn't tell whether he was annoyed with the interruption or genuinely puzzled.

Over the years I'd developed a lengthy set of explanations for my name—the short version, the long version, the scholarly version, the something-in-common version when dealing with a "Zandria," a "Brick," or a "Binaca." I chose the short version. "My father's a geography enthusiast. He persuaded my mother to let me be named for the creator of the most famous world map—the Mercator projection."

Dafney grunted in some sort of comprehension. "Anyway, Mer-Ca-Tor," accenting each syllable, "there is the handkerchief. It's possible that there was an accomplice. The woman, or maybe someone with her, was sufficiently agitated to leave behind a blood soaked handkerchief."

"What! There may have been two killers! Detective, do you have any suspects? What assurances can I give to the college alumni?"

Dafney's eyes narrowed and his brow furrowed. For a surreal moment, his squint reminded me of my high school English teacher, Bob Brisket. Mr. Brisket always stared intently at my classmate Austin Jerveny whenever Austin would ask one of his typical questions—"Mr. Brisket, I spilled ketchup on my essay. Can I turn it in tomorrow or do you want it all bloody like this?" The teenager Austin certainly never confided in me regarding his emotions when subjected to Mr. Brisket's stare, but Dafney's peering gaze jarred me, impelling me to the belated realization that he had summoned me, not the other way around.

After a short pause Dafney said, "We're narrowing the list down fast. The hankie was monogrammed." When he paused after this revelation, I understood that the conversation was over. Rising to leave, I was interrupted.

"Mer-Ca-Tor, what is your middle initial?"

"Ah, J for Jonah." I blithely declared. "My mother was perhaps overly pious and gave me a middle name for Jonah, the man who failed to follow God's wishes, ended up in a whale, but later repented his sin."

"Well, sinner, the letters stitched into the handkerchief were MJE. Perhaps your sin was murder?"

6
Carole's Plea

She walked into my office on one of Minnesota's typically cold winter afternoons. As her shoes tapped up the stairs to my second-floor office, I knew it was she. You can't be married to a woman for four years and not recognize the pace and rhythm of her step.

"I need your help," she asserted in an urgent tone that still somehow belied her natural zest.

I started to rise from the corner chair, where I sat away from my desk while reading a few reports. "Carole, it's good to see you!"

Her lips pressed together. "I'm not here to make up."

Slowly I glided back into my overstuffed chair. Normally this seat brought comfort, but not today. My estranged wife was here and clearly her frustration with me had not lessened.

"You look lovely, Carole," for she did and always had. At only two inches short of six feet in height, Carole was tall enough to be a model. Actually she was almost slender enough to be one too, but the curves of her body arched more widely than those of the typical willowy model. Not that I was complaining—I liked curves. In fact, it was this sensual form that first prompted me to approach her for a date six years earlier. I suppose that her naturally wavy shoulder-length brown hair framing a classically oval face didn't hurt either. Soon I came to adore the way her eyes crinkled when she smiled with glee, to revel in the quickness of her mental calculations, and to rest in the compassion of her soul. Even in brief moments of reflection like this, I wondered how I could have gone so wrong to wound this wonderful woman. I was determined to win her back—by subtle flattery, plaintive honesty, quick humor, or anything from my array of masculine charms. Thus, I thought that the combination of honesty and flattery through, "You look lovely, Carole," would be a simple approach to begin to seek her favor today. Certainly this observation should introduce some warmth to the preliminaries.

Instead her face flushed, and her temper flared, "You're not listening."

Admittedly, that was one of my flaws. In fact, the trials and tribulations of our marriage largely had been centered on my minor failings. I had committed none of the major sins—no affairs, no money troubles, no falsehoods, or deceits. Instead the repeated irritations of the little things of daily life and my ineffectiveness or perceived ineffectiveness in dealing with these matters had alienated the love of my life, creating our current legal separation. Listening, or rather, *not* listening to her, was one of these failings.

Of course, there had been the restaurant ruckus that had served as the catalyst for the current cessation of our marital cohabitation. In St. Paul, we were enjoying a meal with two other couples at one of those restaurants where the customer purchases a gourmet hamburger and then personalizes the burger at a toppings bar—tomato slices, grilled and raw onions, sautéed mushrooms, four types of cheese, three brands of mustard, and more. We sat down at one end of the establishment, with Carole across from me and with me facing the length of the seating area, both of us toward one end of the table. Soon Carole was leaning into an intense conversation about Las Vegas. It became evident that I was the only one at the table who never had been there. I was soon left on the periphery of the anecdotes about various travels to Las Vegas. I tried to listen politely, but my attention wavered and my eyes wandered around the restaurant. Six or seven tables down, there was a beautiful young woman facing me. Her classically oval face was framed by curly brown hair that tumbled past her shoulders. I stared briefly at her, but shortly she was joined by a burly fellow I took to be her husband. Returning my attention to our table's conversation, I noted that Carole's friend Sally was recounting her rendition of the time that she had seen Julia Roberts in the ladies' room at Caesar's Palace. First, I doubted it really was Julia Roberts and second, it didn't really interest me.

My eyes flickered to the lovely face of the brunette those several tables away. Her gaze caught my own, so I quickly looked away. I am loath to admit it, but I glanced at, peeked toward, observed, peered at, stared toward, gawked at, and eyed the brunette's lovely face another ten or twelve times, in between bites of food and bits of conversation.

I once heard a scholarly argument that the human eye and brain inherently are drawn to attractive images that deposit a moment of chemical pleasure in the brain. Perhaps my brain and my eye biologically couldn't help it. Indeed, the general typology of the woman's hair and face matched Carole's features; certainly I ought to find those features appealing. Yet, perhaps I shouldn't make excuses. Anyway, it was unfortunate that the attractive stranger noticed at least six of my glances. I should have stopped looking or something. Eventually, I rose from the table to refill my beverage at the soda fountain. There I was accosted by the beauty's husband, who belligerently demanded that I stop staring at his wife. Although I tried to calm the man, soon his outrage was sufficient to draw the attention of most diners. So Carole got wind of the situation and was hurt and befuddled by my behavior. She was irate with me at home that night, leaving me to sleep on the sofa. A few days later she left.

But this day she was here to see me. "Jill's in trouble. I need you to help her."

A dilemma instantly formed. Not that I wouldn't help, I had been striving for weeks to regain Carole's favor, but Carole knew at least three women named Jill, including a high school classmate, now a hooker turning tricks on Hennepin Avenue in downtown Minneapolis. I could offer the response "Jill who?" but this might or might not prompt another strident "Aren't you paying attention?" reaction that I had heard all too often.

Now partly rising from my chair, so that my body language wouldn't be submissive to Carole's downward gaze, I guided her to the chair next to me. Cautiously I chose what I hoped was a safe reply, "Tell me about the situation."

"A regent of Masterton College was killed—somebody named Munson. It's in the newspaper." Flinging the *Minneapolis Star-Tribune* onto my lap, she continued, "Jill's scared she'll be accused of the murder. You've got to help her."

This time my cautious approach worked. I could fill in the blanks myself. Jill Moreland, assistant professor of geography at Masterton College, was my wife's friend from their college days. I knew Jill. She had socialized with us on occasion, when there was an "us." Carole naturally had continued their friendship alone since our separation. I had not even considered linking this Jill with trouble.

"Carole, that's preposterous . . ." I started.

"I knew you'd resist," she shouted, pounding a fist of otherwise elegant fingers onto the arm of her chair. "Damn it, don't you care?"

"Honey, that's not it. Of course, I'll help Jill. I was trying to say that it is preposterous to imagine that Jill could kill anyone."

"Of course, it's impossible," she raged, equally loud as she agreed with me, "but she thinks the police might arrest her. You know that policeman, Detective Dalfreen."

"Dafney."

"Mercator, this is not daffy!"

Her anger was building, and only from a misunderstanding of pronunciation. As I thought about it, one of our troubles was that, for her, a display of anger or other strong emotion was cathartic. She was better off emotionally afterwards. In contrast, for me an expression of anger, especially toward my wife, was foreign to my nature and seemed to imply a lack of love. Perhaps though this is what I got for marrying a foreigner. Don't misunderstand, both Carole and I are Americans, but my heritage is entirely Norwegian—stoic, outwardly cold, slow to show almost any emotion. Carole is third generation Ukrainian—fiery, passionate, stubborn.

So, on the one hand I was feeling great pleasure and a sense of opportunity to have her here in my office, but on the other hand this budding conflict evoked in me a strong sense of discomfort. I needed to stop her from creating an argument.

"No, no, Carole, the policeman's *name* is Dafney."

"A police man is named Daphne?"

"Well, yes, but it's *Norm* Dafney."

She looked unconvinced but accepted this with a brief "Whatever."

At this point for someone else I might have ventured, "The police generally know what they're doing" or "Is there some evidence against her?" or even "How does my knowing the police detective give me crime-solving skills?" With Carole I knew better. I accepted the challenge, unclear as it was. Inwardly, I hoped that my time and a successful resolution of the case would reap me the benefit of reconciliation.

"Okay, but I'll need to talk with Jill soon then."

"She's waiting at home."

"At our . . . I mean, at your place?" I said, even though my heart knew that it was the house where we had shared part of our marriage years.

And so, the task presented to me by Carole was to reveal whether the spatial interaction between Jill Moreland, the geography professor, and H. Gordon Munson, the regent, was one of murder.

Thus continued Tuesday, with the dramatic arrival of my still technically wife Carole and her questionable request that I help Jill Moreland. A key complication in completing this task successfully lay in the fact that I wasn't a policeman. I wasn't a lawyer. I wasn't a private detective. In fact, I had no particular connection with the law or the legal system. The closest I'd come to the legal system was several years before at my job at an athletic club. I helped a patron, actually a judge in the state court system, avoid detection on what would have been a trumped up marijuana charge. Or perhaps I could count the time driving in Pennsylvania when I managed to elude a speeding ticket because the police car, flicking on its flashing lights as I passed its hiding place behind an overpass, couldn't break into the heavy turnpike traffic before I had undetectably blended into a mix of other cars, vans, and eighteen-wheel trucks.

At most levels, I suppose that my quick decision to agree with Carole to help Jill appeared to be a foolish choice. In terms of addressing my love for Carole, my loneliness, and even my sexual longings, the decision wasn't made by the logical or practical realms of my brain, but was chosen by my heart.

7

Jill Moreland

She wept nearly inaudibly. Conflicting emotions moved through me. On the one hand, I felt sympathy for this woman. Jill Moreland was an acquaintance, someone who could become a good friend, or, in another circumstance, perhaps a lover. Now she sat, overwrought in front of me. It seemed appropriate to lend emotional support.

On the other hand I was a stoic Norwegian Minnesotan, so I reserved display of my kinder emotions, as I did also with my stronger ones. I rationalized that I needed to maintain an even emotional keel, for a biased view based on Jill's tears could lead to an ineffective evaluation of her situation. I stretched for a compromise to lead to a trusting dialogue without the skewed perspective of a wrenching emotional scene.

"Jill, I'm here to help you. Carole asked me to come see you. Both of us care about you. Can you tell me what's going on?"

Emotion and tears clouded the smoothness of her normally mellifluous voice, but she responded, "Mercator, thank you, but everything's ruined. Gordon Munson was going to pull me out of the hell that has been this past year. I was going to keep my job. Now he's dead and they're going to think I killed him!"

"What the hell is this hell, Jill? I've only been here at Masterton College for a year and a half, but I've heard that students adore you."

It would be easy to adore her. Jill had red hair, which for as long as I could remember had created an automatic attraction for me. Perhaps this was because, in general, red is my favorite color, whereas most people cite blue or green. Whatever the reason, I find nearly all redheaded women attractive. Women, who would not draw my attention at all if they were blonde or brunette, rivet me with their red tresses. Jill Moreland, I think, would have been lovely in any hair color. In the end, however, I was confident that features like her cute nose, long legs, and milky white complexion would draw notice from most men. Even during the happiest times with Carole, I still noticed. Now trying to get her back, perhaps I shouldn't notice so much. My focus returned to the question at hand.

She was answering. "Mercator, the students do appreciate me. They take my courses in hordes and give me outstanding evaluations. Every term several students request to join my already full classes as overloads. I take a few, but," she paused with a puff of breath, "I have to say 'no' to some. Oh, I hate it when they look so sad, but I can't have more students than chairs in the classroom. Can I?"

I assured her that she couldn't take every student who asked. Still, I remained baffled about her main problem. If superior classroom performance wasn't good enough, then what was the point of having professors? I'd even heard about professors at major universities who taught little and poorly, yet retained their positions. Masterton, though, openly valued teaching, promoting this as its strength, key for a liberal arts college with only about one thousand students. I said as much to Jill.

"You know that many professors at the big schools have their graduate students teach courses. Professor Ph.D. Big Title at Brand Name University has few committee responsibilities or campus obligations either. But, Masterton College publicly cites excellent teaching as its greatest asset."

"Jill, is that the problem? Does the college feel that you haven't contributed to the campus community? I don't recall hearing complaints."

"No, I've chaired committees, attended events—okay, some were boring as all get out, but I liked being there for my students. I participated in outreach programs like that thing the college did with the Lions Club. Even got a couple of small grants. I've done the routine."

"What's the problem? You've performed well." I was really puzzled now.

24

Abruptly the tears evaporated, seared away by a fire that blazed in her eyes. "Mercator Eliasson, performance is not the relevant factor in education today. Any ass with a doctoral degree can get a job and get tenure, but my petition for tenure has been savagely reviewed for months for the sole reason that I don't have a Ph.D."

Perhaps I'd been isolated from some college issues, while holding the hands of alumni, yet ignorantly I stumbled on, "But Jill, everyone knows that professors have doctoral degrees."

As she responded, I thought for a moment that her eyes had flickered red nearly matching her torchlike long hair, "Why? What does the degree do to qualify the professor to teach students? What? Hunh? What does the Ph.D. degree do to elicit from them a yearning to master the material, to stimulate them to want to come to class?"

"You need a Ph.D. to know the material."

"Half right," Jill acknowledged, making some sort of hand signal apparently to show the concept of half full or half right. "Technically though, someone could on their own volition and initiative learn the material through self-study. Well, surprise! Most people take courses. The coursework in graduate study and particularly in doctoral study does provide the depth of knowledge proper for the career of teaching undergraduate students."

"So, what's the problem?"

"The problem is that a Ph.D. requires a dissertation. The dissertation is a massive tome of research that," she raised both hands two fingers forward on each, "quote 'investigates' an unexplored topic or aspect of a realm of study in the field. Ha! Supposedly so! Really three trends are going on.

"First, there are those few scholars who really do write a valuable scholarly tract dealing with a meaningful subject. Their work is noted or even eagerly studied by many other scholars in that particular discipline. I applaud them.

"Second, there are, and these are most of them, those many doctoral candidates, who choose topics of some possible interest, marginal to modest, and spend years of their lives cranking out drafts, crunching numbers, expounding theories all in order to produce a voluminous text that will be read by a notable few. Who would want to read the thing? Their doctoral committees, their parents—ha!—and an obscure scholar once every few years.

"And third, we have those who are desperate to obtain a Ph.D., probably to keep their jobs. They go to the," again she used her fingers as quotation marks, "'less discriminating' universities, where they produce a load of crap. It turns out to be little more than an undergraduate's senior paper, but these universities will grant a Ph.D. for it. Do more car accidents happen when it is raining? Damn. Throw statistics at it. Get a Ph.D.

"Find Harold Peabody Rothschild's 1948 dissertation that showed that more babies were born in Boise, Idaho, in October than in July. Repeat Rothman or Rothschild or Rothmaker or whatever name I made up here, when he asserted that it was cold in January in Boise, thus more babies nine months later in October. Paste in similar data for Rapid City, South Dakota. You're a genius! Get a Ph.D."

I couldn't see how this related to murder, but she was revved up and certainly had my attention. "Whoa, Jill, I had a number of great college professors. I don't like to think they were frauds or incompetents."

"Mercator, were those professors outstanding teachers?"

"Yes, they were," I blurted, a touch uncomfortable now.

"Were they good people who cared about you as a person and not passively as only a face in a crowded classroom?"

"Yes." I almost raised my voice.

Her voice dropped to a quiet yet somehow penetrating tone as she tapped her finger twice pointedly on the table, "But you granted them great respect and honor, simply and only because you once saw framed Ph.D. diplomas on their walls?"

I stared at her for a few seconds as her quiet sarcasm echoed in my ears. Her eyes met my gaze and then sparkled with the slight pleasure of knowing that she had made her point.

In the same voice she hammered it in further than she knew, "Your father, who named you for a mapmaker, is a mailman. Could he teach an introductory geography class? Or would the lack of a Ph.D. disqualify him in your mind?"

It was a shot to the center of the target. "You've got me there, Jill. Dad is a geography enthusiast who easily could teach an entry-level geography course. Okay, Professor, you may be teaching me something here. But hey, Jill, why not do the dissertation anyway to assure that you would keep the job?"

"Mercator, in truth, I don't have the research interest to be the first and best type of dissertation writer. For the second type of dissertation, the obscure and nearly meaningless research, I simply refuse to waste such a large chunk of my time—years!—to do it. Oh, by the way, Mercator, a common strategy is to pledge that you *will* do the dissertation, then get tenure, and then never write the dissertation after all.

"My conscience won't allow me into the last category, the crap Piled Higher and Deeper. Get it? Piled Higher and Deeper. Ph.D."

"Okay, Jill, I think I understand. Nevertheless, you're facing a murder charge. We need to talk about the case and why the police think you killed Gordon Munson."

The passion abruptly drained from her, and the bright twinkle in those enchanting eyes faded into a black hole. "My tenure case has been a major issue for months. After much discussion, argument, and attempted negotiation, the resolution of the case was to be decided Sunday. Finally! The Board of Regents would have taken a vote on granting me tenure Sunday evening, had not Munson died. What kills me is that on Saturday, Gordon implied in an email that he'd vote for me and that his influence was sufficient to produce a majority!"

"Jill, if Munson was going to give you a victory in this battle over tenure, then why would the police think that you killed him!"

Her now baleful eyes took in mine as she suggested, "Probably because they're my footprints outlined in his blood."

27

8

Who Found the Body?

hose were your footprints!" I exclaimed, with both mouth and eyes widening.

"Well . . . yes," she acknowledged.

"I had no idea those were your footprints, when I saw . . ."

". . . the report," she interrupted, "in the newspaper. I'm the mystery person described in the article as the . . . oh," she gasped, pausing with apparent reluctance to say the words. Finally she intoned, "the killer."

In most other settings, I wouldn't have been able to hear her final two words. In this tense setting, her faint intonation was quite clear.

"But surely you didn't kill him?" I asked, somehow unable to raise my voice above a whisper.

"No," she harshly whispered back.

Without my conscious realization of the movement, my left hand had reached up and started massaging my face. Carole had seen this habit before, a common adjustment for me in the face of stress. In fact, sometimes she had been the cause of such stress.

Carole inquired, "You're still with us here, Mercator?"

"Yes. Yes."

Eyes closed now, hand still on my face, I tried to focus my mental energies on this horrible admission—her bloodstained footprints. My mind skipped to another gut wrenching realization—her initials were similar to mine. Jill—J, Moreland—M; two out of my three—MJE. The handkerchief too? But her initials weren't quite the same. How?

Before my brain could sort this out, my tongue had spoken. "Jill, what is your middle name?"

"Mercator!" This was Carole interjecting, unhappy with my seemingly apparent non sequitur, diverging from our ominous topic.

"Erica," Jill quickly answered, though in a tone that suggested the she too was puzzled by my inquiry.

J-E-M for Jill Erica Moreland, a permutation of my M-J-E. Could it have been her handkerchief in Munson's blood? Or was that sort of mixed up thinking?

"Jill, do you have any handkerchiefs with your initials on them?"

"Mercator, what are you doing?" It was Carole again, unmistakably exasperated at my pointless inquiry. "What are you doing?"

"Hold on," raising a hand in my defense.

"Why, yes," Jill responded, with a facial expression that transparently combined mystification with apprehension. Quite apparently she didn't understand the basis for my query.

"Do you have one with you?"

Stretching her single word response out for three seconds, she said, "Yeesss."

Opening her purse, Jill extracted a folded white square of cloth and handed it to me. "Here it is."

Taking it from her, I explained, "The police found a handkerchief, bloody, next to Munson's body."

Both women audibly inhaled a fearful breath. Carole was the first to speak. "With initials, monogrammed?"

"Yes, Jill, how many of these do you own?"

"Six, well really five now. I lost one of them years ago."

Detective Norm Dafney told me that a bloody initialed handkerchief . . ." I started to say, as I unfolded the hankie.

"With my initials? But Mercator, you don't know," Jill slipped in, "about my initials."

I had unfurled the hankie and was looking at the initials MJE on it. Not JEM for Jill Erica Moreland, but MJE. Why were my initials on Jill's handkerchief? Jill had admitted being at the scene of the murder. Now her initialed hankie apparently matched that found with the corpse.

"M-J-E." I looked at her. "Aren't you J-E-M, Jill?"

"Yes, Mercator, that's what I started to explain. Actually, it's kind of a long story."

"Shorten it," I tersely commanded.

"I got them after my grandfather died. My mother's father. He was Maurice Jacob Evers. M-J-E. My grandmother thought it was cute that M-J-E was a twist of my J-E-M. I was only eight years old at the time, so I took them as her gift. I still find them somehow touching. They're little bit masculine, I suppose," she chuckled, but with what I found to be irony, "but I have lacy ones of my own too."

"The police found a bloody handkerchief with the initials M-J-E on it," I stated bluntly.

Carole tried to add a hopeful tone, rapidly noting, "Then the police won't suspect Jill, because the initials are in a different order."

"Unless they match the footprints," I observed, "but they may match the hankie too. For now, though, Detective Dafney has proposed that I killed Munson."

The women jointly half rose from their seats with an exclamation of shock both in words and body language.

After the outburst, I quietly noted, "I'm M-J-E."

"Oh, my." Jill's shock now was turning to a somber realization.

"But why?" asked Carole. "Why would the police think you did it?"

I had already realized that neither Carole nor Jill knew about my role in the discovery of Munson's body. The news reports had only stated that a college employee had found the body. Nevertheless, much of the campus community knew that I was this unnamed employee. The fact that Carole didn't know this served as another sad example of Carole's separation from my life. If things were normal between us, she would have been one of the first to know.

Causing both women to look at me wide-eyed and speechless, I clarified, "I found the body and reported it to the police. The detective wonders if, like some criminals, I returned to the scene of the crime."

Only a few hours earlier, Detective Dafney had asked me whether or not I had killed Gordon Munson. My negative response along with a denial of any motive for such an act had seemed to satisfy the policeman, though Dafney had warned me that my innocence had not been proven.

Finally, the two women chorused, "*You* found the body?"

"Yes, I did."

"No, I found the body," claimed Jill in a matter-of-fact tone.

"Jill, I found the body. I'm the unnamed college employee mentioned in the media reports as having found the body."

"No, Mercator, please . . . listen . . . my footprints in blood . . . I found the body."

"Carole, did you find the body too?" I queried.

"No, thank goodness. The two of you are quite enough."

"Jill, the police understand that I found Munson's body. I reported it. I had a witness—student Sean Lothrow. The newspapers, the radio—they're talking about me." I spent a couple more minutes recounting how Sean and I found the dead man.

"But Mercator, when I found the body, it was still warm."

Carole, listening intently, shuddered at this. I grunted a gruff acknowledgment.

The silence that followed allowed, maybe prompted, me to continue. "All right then. I'll grant that you found it first. Sorry, but no prizes for that. Why don't the police know this?"

"I . . . I never called them.

"Yes, I understand that, but why didn't you?"

"My first instinct was to run over and see if he was alive," she explained, speaking rapidly now that she could tell her story. "I suppose that was foolish, obviously he was dead. Given the wound, obviously dead. But when I did check the body, that must have been when I walked through the blood."

31

God, but Carole is gorgeous. I thought to myself. If only I could kiss her, I would feel so . . . but then Jill's words brought me back to reality from my not-so-pertinent thoughts. Strange how my passion for Carole is so forceful.

"Finding Munson dead and clearly murdered, I was just . . . just . . . well just . . . I don't know."

"It was unexpected, shockingly so, to find the body. I know. I found the body, um, too."

"Yes, but the thing was that after I checked the body, I heard a noise."

"From Munson!"

"No, Mercator. I heard a noise from another room in the house. You know how in psychology they say 'Fight or Flight.' I didn't think about it. I didn't calculate any odds. My brain suggested that the murderer was still in the house. I started to leave, but slipped. I realized that my heels were wet. I quickly took off my shoes and ran. I rushed out the front door, closing it behind me to slow down the murderer, if I was being followed. When I got to my car, I looked at my shoes and saw the traces of blood. I know that I left shoeprints in the house."

"Are you sure that it was a person you heard in the house?" I wanted to know.

"No. I considered going back in to try to clean up the footprints, but I was too scared."

"Why not call the police and explain?" I asked, while Carole had fallen silent, still only listening now.

"I suppose that was a mistake, but I feared that the footprints would suggest that I'd killed him." She had a forlorn look now, a look that asked—did I blow it?

"And a motive for that? Was it the tenure case?"

"Yes, the conventional wisdom on campus has been that Munson would vote against me, thereby dooming my case."

"Would you have killed him to prevent him from casting that decisive negative vote?"

"I suppose not, but anyway he sent me an email asking me to come to his house, implying that he had decided to vote in my favor."

I had been expecting that her answer would be, "NO, I WOULD-N'T KILL HIM!" so I was caught off guard by her somewhat meek "I suppose not." I nearly missed the rest of the response, but asked, "He said what? In your favor?"

"Um, that seemed to be the flavor of it. That's what I took it to be."

"So you were there upon an invitation which you perceived to be favorable to your tenure case, but upon seeing the corpse and hearing a sound, fled fearful for your safety. But now, upon reflection, you wonder if the evidence of footprints, flight, and conventional wisdom about your case would place you under suspicion."

"Yes. That's it. Yes."

"Did you have a monogrammed handkerchief with you at Munson's house?"

"I don't know. I don't really think so."

Later, reflecting back on this conversation, I thought she might have hesitated in that answer. Had I made it too easy for her to agree? Was there something else in the mix that she hadn't told me?

We stayed and talked for some time, agreeing that Jill would go about her normal business, trying not to be conspicuous. I told her I would try to find out more information. I asked her to go home and find all her MJE handkerchiefs. If she originally had six, but lost one of them some years ago and I held another one, there should be four more at home. I gave her instructions.

Should I have demanded that she find a lawyer? Go to the police? I admit that I didn't want to lose my chance to win back Carole's favor, so I didn't suggest it. Still, maybe speaking of a lawyer at this point would have avoided some of the events that came later.

9

Professor Covington

The next morning I drove the streets of Masterton over to the college. A true small college town, it was dominated by the school that took its name. Of the roughly three thousand people residing there during the school year, one thousand were students and virtually everyone else worked for the college or provided for those who worked for the college. Masterton had no manufacturing plant. No commercial entity existed which did not do the majority of its business with the college or its employees, although certainly the college had external suppliers as well.

The college itself was a handsome campus with most of the buildings having been constructed from fine quality stone masonry. Founded in 1901, Masterton College strove to compete with many colleges in the region, but primarily with St. Olaf College and Carleton College, both located in Northfield not so far west of Masterton.

I strode up to the York Social Science Center. This new structure featured a facade of shimmering mirrored windows. Exuding modern style, the facility stood in dramatic contrast to the adjacent classic style of Old Main. The stately building was a strikingly handsome stone structure of arches and towers. As I mounted the stairs, a stunning image of Old Main appeared, reflected in the mirrored exterior of the York Center, offering a visual balance between the age-old quest for knowledge and the modern technological world. Inside the double door entryway a bronze plaque honoring J.R. York, the school's first president, was paired with a glass-encased list of professors, offices, and classrooms within the building.

I suppose that I should have gone back to my office first, but I wanted to avoid being bogged down in trivial tasks when I had Jill Moreland on my mind. Even the single act of checking my e-mail at the office could end up being an hour-long task. Logically, at least in the reasoning of not beginning my day in my office, it seemed wise to start at the secretaries' office. Even in my own college days, it had become apparent to me that the absentminded professor was not a myth, but commonly was an accurate description. Thus, I learned that the secretaries' office frequently developed into the focal point of order and organization in a building. Additionally, in my college days my girlfriend Kristine had performed work-study duties in such an office. At the time, she told me that gossip was rampant in such areas, that anything personal known on campus, certainly was known and probably was known first to the secretaries.

With this motivation, I went to see Elsie Norris. Elsie reminded me of my mother's friends. She was the right age (about sixty years), with the correct demeanor (a kind face and a quick smile). I knew that she had worked at Masterton College in various capacities for thirty-five years.

"Can I help you?" she offered in a friendly but a let's-get-started tone. We had met but were not on personal terms yet.

"Yes, I'm Mercator Eliasson, the alumni director. I think I've seen you around before, but perhaps we haven't been properly introduced." It seemed the cautious approach.

"Oh, yes. I know who you are. You're still in the south-side office, next to the treasurer, Sebastien Kroon, aren't you? Room 207, the Gilmore T. Nasby Memorial Room, isn't it?"

Obviously caution was unnecessary. It was apparent that she knew plenty about me or at least about my whereabouts.

"Yes, exactly right," I replied with what I hoped was an endearing smile. "Sometimes I like to wander through the buildings. As alumni director, my dealings directly involve graduates, but it seems logical that I might benefit from knowing students before they become graduates. So, I try to get out of the office some." All this was true, although my presence in the York Center today was not for that stated reason. I wondered to myself whether that was a lie or rather an omission of the truth.

"Fine then," she said. "Oh, would you like some coffee?"

"No thanks. I've never developed the habit." Realizing after a moment that having a beverage would offer a time for conversation, I ventured a halting request for tea.

"Oh, certainly." Disappearing into a small workroom, she called back. "Do you want regular or decaf?"

"Regular."

"Sugar."

"No thanks, regular."

She came back with a Styrofoam cup containing hot water, the tea bag, and one of those plastic stir sticks.

In thanking her, I mentioned that I had developed a taste for tea on a trip to Russia a few years previous. "But you know," I added, "Back here I haven't been able to match the flavor of the Russian tea or, for that matter, the rough sugar cubes that they add. I did purchase two of the pewter glass holders and long glasses that the Russians often use for tea, but I still feel shortchanged on the tea itself."

"Gil Nasby used to mention the same complaint. I think he eventually found some at a tea shop in the Mall of America."

"Really? The same Gilmore Nasby for whom my office plaque is hung?"

"Yes, of course. He was quite a figure on campus, you know. A long-time professor of music, he traveled to the Soviet Union in the '70s. Later of course he was on the Board of Regents."

Her comment gave me the angle of approach, a chance to change the direction of the conversation.

"The Board of Regents! My gosh, obviously you heard about H. Gordon Munson, the regent who was murdered?"

She snapped, "I'm not going to say anything about that. It's ridiculous that anyone might think Professor Moreland could have anything to do with such a horrible crime."

"Wait, wait, wait," I softly calmed her, raising my hands palms open in a defensive posture, "What does Jill Moreland have to do with this?"

"That's the rumor!"

"My wife and I know Jill personally and also find it inconceivable that she could kill anyone."

"Oh, my goodness! Well, that's a different story! Why didn't you say so in the first place?"

Seeing a cleared path, I pushed forward, "Can you tell me about Professor Moreland's situation here at Masterton College? What would suggest the rumor that she has killed Munson?"

"We adore Jill here, that is, most people do, but she has had a difficult time. If Munson went against her on the tenure case, she'd lose her job."

"Some alumni have called me, concerned that Munson's death might somehow reflect badly on the college. To address alumni concerns over this, I'll need to have a better understanding of Jill Moreland's life here at the college. Good or bad—I need to know. Could we start with the positive side? You used the word 'adore.' Why do colleagues or students care for Professor Moreland?"

My question prompted a fifteen-minute harangue, positive but intense, on the personal assets and professional qualifications of Jill Moreland. Good words to hear, but at times such as this, my listening skills were challenged. At the nine-minute mark of this testimonial, I unconsciously massaged my scalp as a means of physical relief to my mental state, but regrettably this prompted a prolonged yawn. A look flashed over Elsie Norris' features, the look that a cat hater might present when seeing a scruffy alley cat scarf down a pair of fish heads from a garbage can. Given the "I love my Jack Russell Terrier" bumper sticker on her bulletin board, she probably loathed cats. Not wanting her to loath me for failing to listen to her commentary, I had to restate my interest in this testimonial. As a result I suffered through an additional several minutes of commentary. In the end though, I got from her a list of names to contact in the campus community. I would begin with Professor Philip Covington, one of those individuals cited by Elsie Norris as favorable to Jill Moreland.

Following the secretary's directions, I headed down the tiled hallway, moving past closed classroom doors. I could hear the muffled voices of lecturing professors, yet not the words. As I walked along, a young man rushed into the corridor. Clad in ubiquitous jeans with a T-shirt poking through a partially zipped jacket, he appeared to be late for class. Tugging on the brim of his baseball cap and twisting an unruly strand of hair under the band, he paused momentarily to collect himself. As he then spun into the room, I heard a droning lecture pause, then continue anew. The classroom door swung behind him, but it popped the latch and drifted open about a foot.

The murder case already had made me curious about professors and teaching, so I paused outside the door, angling my body to gain a view of the instructor, but also to present little distraction. As it turned out, this concern was unnecessary. Not seeing me at all, the professor, a burly man with a trim white beard and close cut graying hair, stood before the class clad in a blue blazer and tan slacks. Occasionally his bulging eyes focused through small European-style lenses onto a student, then the gaze scattered nervously across the back wall. More commonly the professor stared intently at his own handwriting on the chalkboard or at the adjacent screen illuminated by the overhead projector. The more I watched this presentation, the more I realized how uncomfortable this professor was in front of his class, distinctly so, preferring to avoid the inquiring gazes of the students.

The professor's discomfort exaggerated his mannerisms while I could hear his tension in his speech patterns. Soon I realized that even though words spilled from his lips like water through river rapids, he filled every momentary mental pause with various verbal tics. This nervous pattern, so obvious to me, yet apparently unheard by the professor, became the dominant element of the lecture, effectively obscuring any useful information that might be imparted. I spent several minutes only counting the seconds between each verbal tic, but never got past the count of eight. Eventually though, I got weary of this and proceeded down the hall, wondering what it would be like to be a student in that class. No wonder that one had come in late.

Somewhat farther down the hall, I found room 112, the office of Professor Philip Covington, longtime fixture in the History Department.

Finding the door ajar, I knocked and, poking my head into the room, heard a gruff, "Come in." It was a command, not a request. I obeyed.

I introduced myself, "Professor Covington, my name is Mercator Eliasson, alumni director here at the college."

"Oh, yes, yes." Covington had met me before and certainly could have seen me at college functions, but I wasn't sure he'd recall my name.

"Elsie Norris," I said, offering my hand and twisting my head to indicate that I had come from the direction of her office, "sent me this way, after I spoke to her about the murder of regent Munson. I understand that you knew H. Gordon Munson."

With an athlete's firm grip, this angular, tall, and scholarly looking fellow responded, "Surely the police are handling that."

"Indeed they are, but the college is drawing some attention. As alumni director, I catch some of that interest and have something of a public persona. Certainly it's not often that our part of the state has a murder. And now there's a rumor that purports that Professor Moreland might be implicated in the matter."

"Then you'll be pleased to know that Jill is innocent."

"You can prove that?" I replied, thinking with surprise and enthusiasm that Covington was offering an alibi.

"Sadly, no. However, I am certain, beyond any doubt, that she could not commit such a crime."

Hopes for an alibi quickly dashed, I sat down on the wicker couch set against a short wall next to the door. Most of the other walls were covered with books and papers overflowing from narrow bookshelves. A poster of the Warren Beatty movie epic *Reds* filled a rare open space. A few of the bookshelves were tidily organized, but others showed evidence of a hasty stuffing together of papers and books. Light streaming in from a small window highlighted the dust in the air.

"You know her well?" I continued.

"She's a colleague and, I would like to say, a friend, although I don't often see her outside of campus."

"Why do you say that she's innocent? An impression?"

"Mister . . ." he paused, apparently not knowing my identity quite as clearly as he first had pretended.

"Eliasson. Mercator Eliasson." I contributed, filling the void.

"Mercator, what a striking geographic name. So, hmm," he paused. "What is the capital of Latvia?"

This, the geography quiz, was another common response to my name. I had been asked to name rivers, mountains, states, borders, population size, and many other geographic features. However, very, very few of these inquirers asked to know about geographic understandings of how any particular part of the world worked. For instance, Covington was asking about the capital of Latvia. He probably didn't realize that Latvia had a declining population, an unusual situation explained by way of Latvia's geographic features in the Soviet Union and in post-Soviet Europe.

"Professor Covington," I sighed, "surely as an academic you understand that the study of geography is more than simple memorization of place names, although knowledge of place location certainly is useful."

"Yes, of course," he demurred, perhaps pretending to know this.

"Riga."

"Hunh?"

"The capital of Latvia is Riga. But we were talking about Jill Moreland."

"Oh, yes," he said. "Jill Moreland is a trusted professor here. Students love her, faculty colleagues admire her, even administrators respect her. Although certain parties did stir up this nasty controversy over the issue of tenure and the Ph.D., Jill has behaved in a thoroughly professional manner throughout. I cannot imagine that she would act with such integrity and then commit a slaying."

"Certain parties?" I queried. "Can you give me names?"

"What? Jill Moreland had parties? At her house? I wasn't invited." He reacted with puzzlement and definitely with sagging shoulders.

"No, no. You said that certain parties caused trouble for her tenure chances."

"Oh, yes," he noted, regaining his more confident demeanor. "The Dean of the College, André Sholé, is Jill's primary adversary in the administration. I don't know how great a supporter President Marjorie Wheelwright is, but at least she's not openly antagonistic. Additionally Monroe Wilder of the Math Department and Les Peck in Religion are known to oppose tenure for anyone without a Ph.D. Both serve on the Faculty Personnel Committee that sends powerful tenure recommendations to the Board of Regents. Others here may harbor similar beliefs, but these are the opponents who possess particular power. I understand that the faculty committee was deadlocked, but that Sholé, in the manner of the vice-president in the U.S. Senate, as convener of the committee cast the tie-breaking vote against tenure. So the committee sent a four-to-three split recommendation to the Board of Regents for final action."

I jotted these names down and looked across Covington's desk for any hopeful information. "Do you know of anyone who could help me prove Jill Moreland's innocence?"

"I know of no witnesses to the murder, but in general J.P. Kiick—um, he's in the Philosophy Department—is a prominent supporter. Also, you could talk with Theo T. Sar of Information Technology and Rhonda Woodson in Education."

"Thank you for your time," I ventured, rising from the couch to leave. "Oh, out of curiosity," I added, my hand on the doorknob. "Who is the professor teaching down the hall? Glasses, short gray hair, beard? I don't know all the faculty yet."

"Sociology class?"

"He was talking about population patterns," I noted, unsure whether or not that could be sociology, although I recognized at once that geographers could study population.

"Yes, that would be Grizzly Bear, or more formally Orson K. Baer. Why do you ask?"

I let out an embarrassed little chuckle in admitting that I had eavesdropped for several minutes outside the classroom door. As I explained my dismay over Baer's teaching style, I watched Covington's head bob in agreement.

"Yes, old Baer is infamous on campus. That class meets a general education requirement for graduation, and Baer is known for giving out an easy A, so the course always is full."

"Even when he lectures in that annoying and distracting fashion?"

"Many students will tolerate poor teaching for an 'A.' No student will suffer lousy teaching if a good grade is difficult to earn."

"But what about excellent teachers like Jill Moreland?"

Agreeing that Jill was an excellent teacher, Covington indicated that professors who excited students about the subject matter, whatever the subject, would draw large classes even if the grading was challenging.

"So Baer is kept on because he gets enough students in class," I suggested.

Covington leaned his head back, pointed his sharp Adam's apple forward, and guffawed so loudly that momentarily my mind flashed back to childhood visits to Uncle Clarence's Iowa farm and its braying donkey, Ralph. "You don't get it, do you? Good or bad, professors aren't really evaluated for their teaching! Are you kidding? We're judged for our so-called scholarship. It's publish or perish, and Baer has published plenty. It's drivel, but it's published."

Publish or Perish. Gordon Munson perished while Jill Moreland hadn't published or even written her dissertation. Had she twisted this academic axiom to try to avoid her own peril? The police might think so. Had "Publish or Perish" become "Jill or Kill"?

10

Dallas Blundin

I felt the need to consult my friend Dallas Blundin. Besides being the noteworthy partner at the firm of Crumby, Zon, and Blundin, Dallas was my personal lawyer and my friend. Calling his St. Paul office from my office phone, I reached his receptionist, Caitlin Lenz. About my age, Caitlin was ideal for her job. Gregarious enough to present a friendly introduction to the firm, pretty enough without being too distracting, and uncannily skillful at regulating the office flow of clients, attorneys, witnesses, and even private investigators, Caitlin more than earned her salary.

"Crumby, Zon, and Blundin. How may I help you?"

"Hi, Caitlin, this is Mercator Eliasson. Is Dallas in today?"

"Hey, Mercator. How are you?"

So often in our current society, this inquiry is not actually an attempt to determine physical, mental, or emotional health, but is offered as introductory conversational filler.

"I still suffer from the heartache of not being able to see you more often, Caitlin."

"You flatter me, Mercator."

"In fact, I was thinking of committing some sort of crime, so that I would have to come see Dallas, and see you too."

"Now, now, I know you have eyes only for Carole."

"Well," I drew the word into a long stretched, "weeeellllllll, I would like to check in with Dallas, anyway."

"Okay, it's back to business, Merc. Dallas is in a meeting now. After that he plans to play basketball at the club, before being in court this afternoon."

I first met Dallas on the basketball court at the Ramsey Athletic Club in St. Paul. At one time I'd done some administrative work for the club. By being in the wrong place and the wrong time, I'd stumbled onto a scandal in the making. Fortunately, I was able to block the intrigue and save the club some embarrassment. Suffice it to say that club officials were less than happy to learn that one of their waitresses had accepted a bribe from the spiteful ex-wife of a municipal judge and had treated him to marijuana brownies with his evening meal at the club. The subsequent appearance of the judge, up for re-election of course, in a half-dressed manner at a private meeting of officers of a local credit union had narrowly avoided public exposure. My discreet intervention and investigation had been so appreciated by the club's leaders that one of the perks I secured as a bonus for services was permanent access to their facilities. Although I no longer worked there, I still could use the facilities anytime. While I played basketball at a variety of courts, including at the gym on campus, I frequently come over to the club for a game. The judge, a Masterton grad and happily reelected, also had been thankful for my work and later was helpful in my getting the job at Masterton. His influence overcame the disadvantage that my lack of a Masterton College degree held for me.

So Dallas soon would be at the gym. "Excellent, Caitlin. I'll catch him at the club. That should do."

"Make it so, Merc. Say, you're a Trekkie, aren't you?"

"I prefer the term 'Trekker' implying fan but not fanatic."

"That attractive counselor on the show, what's her name?"

"On *Star Trek: The Next Generation*, you mean?"

"That's the one, Merc."

"That would be Deanna Troi, half-Betazoid, with heightened empathic abilities."

"Yes, but, I mean, what's the actress' name?"

"Marina Sirtis."

"That's it. That's it." The words came more rapidly now. "I was reading that she's married to a rock star."

My heart skipped a beat as a wave of inexplicable panic briefly swept over me, before a ray of hope appeared in the possibility that Caitlin might be kidding me.

"Wait a minute." I protested, "That can't be."

"Yes, I recently read it. Was it Friday? Or the other day? Whatever the guy's name was. I dunno. But, yeah, he's a guitarist in a rock band."

I both liked and disliked this passage and Caitlin's now more informal tone. Was she teasing me?

Not immediately sure why this was bothering me, I persisted in my objections. "That can't be."

Seeming to sense that she had hooked me, Caitlin went on, "Yeah, yeah, she's married to a rocker. Does that upset you?"

"I know that rock musicians are 'babe magnets,' but to marry one?" The unnamed musician obviously could not prompt name recognition, so my mind provided a stereotype of the longhaired, tattoo-engraved, half-stoned guitar banger. I gave an involuntary twitch at the thought. Of course, Marina Sirtis's husband might be a great guy, with or without these characteristics.

"But, Merc," her pitch now moved in a singsong, "should Counselor Troi be saving herself singly for you?"

"Of course not!" I blurted, although my heart silently contended that this option would be highly appealing. "But a beautiful starlet ought to leave the illusion that she's available to her male fans, not some rock star."

"What's wrong with a rock star?"

"Nothing, I suppose." I was getting myself into a corner here. "I don't know anything about this musician she married, but so many rock stars are scraggly-haired sinners with drug or alcohol problems."

"I see, so since some rockers are less than model citizens, your actress must pass on *all* musicians, and then remain virginal so she can appear available to you and other hormonally charged Trekkies. Or Trek*kers*. I know, I know."

"Yes!" I offered before her obvious sarcasm fully reached my distorted logic. "Well, no . . . or maybe."

"Oops, another call. Good luck with basketball. Bye, Mercator."

45

I had a bit less than an hour to reflect on the philosophical ramifications of rock stars' love lives, before reaching the athletic club.

Located on several stories of the Griffin Bank building in downtown St. Paul, the Ramsey Athletic Club was a brief drive from the Minnesota capitol building and a short walk from the Ramsey County office building. If I left Masterton in the next few minutes, I could reach the club in time for a noon game of basketball or "loonball" as the club members call it.

Dallas once told me that the term "loonball" was created when several state officials were the most regular, if not crazed, basketball players who came to play during the lunch hour.

Crazy = loony
State officials = state birds = loons
Lunch hour = noon
Basketball = ball

Thus "loonball." "Loony loons at noon for ball" obviously didn't work as a catchy phrase, so "loonball" was coined.

Having a bit of alumni business that I also could transact in the Twin Cities, I decided to go up and join that day's games. After winning the first game on a jump shot that hit the rim four times before dropping through the hoop, I took some good-natured kidding from my teammates. I did take a hit, knocking my right knee onto the floor, after being fouled by Paul Sturm, a manager at the Science Museum, as I drove to the basket.

Overall, it was Dallas who was the star, exerting his famed intense demeanor on the court. Not surprisingly, he turned in the play of the day to cap off his performance. At game point (leading thirteen to ten, going up to fifteen by twos and threes) our team was defending. Stan Freiberg, a state senator from Bemidji, attempted a shot from the wing but missed the mark. Lutz Ingermark, assistant district attorney for Ramsey County, rebounded as Dallas and I released for the fast break. Ingermark, an armchair quarterback at best, went for the touchdown pass, sending the ball arcing over Dallas' head downcourt.

The ball sailed way beyond my friend, heading for the far right corner. With only one opponent back on defense, Dallas raced after the ball. I sped toward the basket from the other side. Reaching the ball after a bounce left it suspended high in mid-air a foot beyond the out-of-bounds line, Dallas made his move. Recognizing that the defender would hang back a few feet and not pursue him to the boundary, but would let him save the ball, Dallas instantaneously calculated that a simple flip of the ball inbounds would only return it to the possession of the opponents. Having no direct passing angle to me, Dallas produced the unexpected, like his trademark cross-examination query that left the witness off guard.

Not looking back, he leapt over the line. While airborne he extended his right hand to the ball, and in one swift motion flung the basketball behind him and down. As the bounce pass hit the floor several feet in front of the opposing player and ricocheted over his head, the defender was caught flat-footed. After its bounce, the basketball leisurely floated down to my awaiting hands underneath the basket. I converted the uncontested lay-up for a fifteen-to-ten victory. Actually I almost celebrated the pass too early, for my casual lay-up rolled around the rim before dropping through. It was my game-winning basket, but it was Dallas' play.

Our teammates crowded around to offer congratulations, and a couple of opponents, regular loonball players, teased Dallas about his "lucky" play. One of them, a downtown pharmacist, chose that time to offer an added jab in the form of a joke.

"Blundin, have you heard this one? I read it in a magazine the other day," razzed N. Tenzio Matthews. "A guy calls his lawyer's office, the receptionist answers the phone, and the fellow says, 'Can I talk to my lawyer?' The receptionist mournfully replies, 'I regret having to tell you this, but he's dead.' The guy says, 'Oh! I'm sorry, I didn't know,' and hangs up."

Matthews, not a great jokester, already was giggling at his own joke, but continued. "The next day the same man calls again asking, 'May I talk to my lawyer?' The receptionist with puzzlement in her voice asks him, 'Didn't I speak with you yesterday? Your lawyer is dead.' He says, 'Oh, okay,' and hangs up. This same pattern goes on for week or so.

"He calls once again and asks to speak with his lawyer. Finally the receptionist has had enough and shrieks into the receiver, 'Look, I told you over and over that your lawyer is dead! What part of it don't you understand?' The guy responds, 'Oh, I understand he's dead, I just so like to hear you say it!'"

Matthews roared loudly at his silly joke, and Dallas convivially chimed in. Lawyer jokes had become a fact of life for him. This was a feature of Dallas's personality that had endeared him to me. He had his own set of lawyer jokes that he eagerly shared. Given my own concern about the profession, I like a lawyer who could laugh at himself and his career. And a basketball player to boot!

After showering, I walked out to the parking ramp with him.

"Dallas, did you hear about the murder down my way."

"Yes, interesting. Someone connected to Masterton College, wasn't it?"

"That's right! H. Gordon Munson was the chair of the Board of Regents at the college."

"Yes, yes. So you must have known him then."

"I found the body!"

Dallas' torso didn't stop its forward motion quite as quickly as his legs, so his quick halt caused him to lean forward. Grabbing my shoulder for support, Dallas pivoted and pulled me around to face him.

"Whoa. You. You found the body."

"Yes, I did. What's more, the police think that I might have killed him."

Dallas' single raised eyebrow reminded me of Star Trek's Mr. Spock. I took some time to explain the situation to him—how I found the body, the monogrammed handkerchief. I didn't think the police's interest was that strong, but I listened carefully to my attorney's advice. Perhaps I should have explained the involvement of Jill Moreland, but I safeguarded that information, for I needed to preserve my opportunity to please Carole. But perhaps I should have told Dallas.

11

The Funeral

On Thursday the funeral for H. Gordon Munson was held at St. Ansgar Lutheran Church in St. Paul. The top administrators from Masterton College attended. Expecting that some number of faculty also would wish to be present, perhaps even joined by a few students, President Wheelwright announced that classes would be cancelled for the day. Given that this was Thursday and that Friday already was reserved for spring registration, and thus no classes, for those students with completed final exams in the January term, this created an early start to the week-long break before the spring semester.

St. Ansgar Lutheran Church, a marvelous old stone church built in the 1880s on a small rise in northern St. Paul, held perhaps two hundred mourners that morning. Of course, family members took their seats in the front pews while prominent officials also sat near the front of the church. Though I was not familiar with Munson's family, the service bulletin I received in the narthex listed surviving family members. With this as a guide, it was simple to pick out son Allan N. Munson, accompanied by his wife, Gloria, and their sons, Nathan and Glen. Sitting with them was Gordon Munson's ex-wife, Helen Contini Munson, mother of Allan. Alongside her was a gentleman whose gray pinstripe suit closely matched his neatly trimmed hair and metal eyeglasses. Given no mention in the bulletin of a surviving brother, I assumed that this fellow either was the ex-wife's brother or her new paramour. A few other people sat in the first two rows, apparently family too—cousins or the like.

In the third row Marjorie Wheelwright was the most prominent representative of the college. She had marched down the center aisle with Sebastien Kroon, the college treasurer, who sat beside her. Kroon, in a dark gray suit with a solid black tie, faced forward so that I could see but an edge of his face, undoubtedly having the same dour look that so typified his personality.

Kroon's eyes never seem to be fully open, perhaps some ten percent short of the mark. His mouth always seemed frozen in a slight downturn, so that his lips looked like a never-savored croissant. Stansfield Gezelig, one of the college's art professors, once remarked that Kroon truly looked the part of a financial manager never quite comfortable with the balance sheets and assets he supervised. Indeed, Masterton College, though financially solvent, was not blessed with a substantial endowment, and certainly was never flush with cash. Partly to Kroon's credit, the college functioned with modest extra income to keep its programs going, its professors adequately though not extravagantly paid, and its students not overly burdened with current tuition costs or future loan payments. Masterton wasn't competing with Stanford on faculty salaries, nor with U.C. Santa Barbara on geographic location and scenery, nor with Williams College for elite students, but the college did balance its budget while drawing mainly good to very good students from the Midwest. Due to it geographic location in Minnesota only a few miles from Wisconsin, Masterton claimed most of its students from these two states.

In the row behind Wheelwright and Kroon, other Masterton officials sat, including academic dean André Sholé, registrar Stella Horton, and several of the regents. I did not presume myself to be a high-ranking college administrator, so I was content to sit toward the back of the church. This vantage point allowed me to scan the crowd, recognizing a number, though not all, of the faces. I saw at least twenty faculty members, including professors J.P. Kiick (Philosophy), Roe L. Spellenko (Economics), Monroe Wilder (Math), Virginia Loop (Theater), Callie Bosson (Physics), Goren Eidechse (Philosophy), Roxy Gannon (Psychology), Nicholas Roberts (History), and Jill Moreland sitting with my wife, Carole. By the time I arrived, Jill and Carole were already seated in a crowded pew, leaving me to find other accommodations among the other members of the college administration and staff and family members comprising the mourners.

With a minute before the scheduled start of the memorial service, I absently looked through the crowd. From my vantage in the third from the back row on the right side of the sanctuary, I caught a flicker of movement out of the corner of my left eye, as someone quickly flitted into the far left corner of the last pew on the opposite side. A trim woman all in black had joined the gathering. Accepting her as yet one more mourner, my eyes moved back to glance idly among the crowd. However, these same eyes, as I'd already shown, had a tendency to take a second and even third look at an attractive woman, so they flicked back to gaze at the new arrival. Like most of the women, she too wore a black dress, but this one was neatly tailored and, even in apparent mourning, showed off the fine curves of this lithe woman's body. My evaluating eyes observed a smoothly shaped face partially obscured by dark sunglasses that the woman had failed to remove, even inside the church. What could have been attractive shoulder-length, light-brown hair was pulled into a severe bun and topped with a black scarf. My eyes started to leave her, but then flashed back to her profile, as a glint of recognition tugged at my memory. While trying to identify her, I assured myself that she did not work at Masterton College. How then did I know her? I projected her to be in her mid-forties, so while she could be a graduate of the college, she wouldn't be one of the recent graduates I would be most likely to recognize. Might she have attended a reunion event?

Before I could identify this woman, Pastor Lars Anderson began the memorial service, drawing my attention to the front. Anderson proceeded through the designated funeral liturgy as found in the green hymnal, with the congregation participating at highlighted sections of the service. In the eulogy the pastor praised Munson's good works, especially through his charity, Minnesota Mission. Anderson then reminded the audience of the Lutheran theology that it was not through the balance of works and good deeds versus the sum of sins that people earn their way to heaven, but instead it was through the acceptance of God's grace that heaven became a gift. At the very word "gift" a sparkling array of colorful light burst in an angled display though the sanctuary's multiple stained glass windows as the sun chose that moment to come from behind clouds. A few in the crowd gasped at the startling effect. As I glanced toward the light, I again saw the woman in the back corner. Seeing the other parishioners' pleasure in the streams of reds, blues, greens, and yellows crossing the sanctuary, she had removed her sunglasses for a clearer view herself. In this way I recognized Aimee Forbes.

Aimee Forbes, a prominent local actress, appeared in numerous live theater performances in the Twin Cities and often shilled products for local television, billboard, and print advertisements. Occasionally, she garnered minor roles in Hollywood films. Her publicist claimed that she had almost been nominated for an Academy Award for best supporting actress for one of these roles. Nevertheless, Forbes seemed happiest with life in Minnesota and, in any case, did most of her acting work here at home. So why was she at Munson's funeral?

I had little time to ponder this question, for the service moved forward. The eulogy ended and immediately was followed by the hymn "A Mighty Fortress Is Our God." Unlike some services, this funeral did not include communion, so the remaining liturgy was quickly concluded. The bulletin indicated that the interment would follow thirty minutes later at St. Paul's prominent urban cemetery, with a catered reception an hour after that at the Landmark Center, downtown St. Paul's classic structure.

As I left the church, my peripheral vision glimpsed another person in black I had not noticed. This time the figure was male, large, and authoritative. Detective Dafney stood twenty yards outside the flow of the exiting crowd, calmly perusing people's faces and demeanors. Curious, I strode over to him.

"Detective Dafney," I stated, accenting the first syllable of his last name, so that the introduction appeared to sound like an invitation for conversation.

"Ah, Mercator Eliasson. Joining the mourners?"

"Yes, Detective. You too? I didn't see you inside."

"Didn't go inside. Can't say that I'm mourning. I didn't know Munson. Why are you mourning, Mercator?"

"It's true I hardly knew Munson," I admitted. "I'd met him at college functions but had never had more than a few sentences of conversation with

him. So, really, I'm here in an official capacity as the college's alumni director, symbolically representing the college's alumni at their loss of a key board
member."

"I too—official capacity."

"But no uniform, detective?" I queried.

"Privilege of rank today, though I usually do prefer the uniform. All
those years, you know. And I'm not here to represent grieving citizens. Just
trying to find the murderer."

"What! Could the murderer be expected to kill someone at the
funeral?"

"Nuts, Mercator." After all this conversation, Dafney finally actually looked at me, one eyebrow raised. "Sometimes police officers attend funer-
als and wakes. There's sociological evidence that murderers actually are
drawn to these events in order to satisfy some deep-rooted emotional need.
In crimes of passion, the murderer may feel remorse. The funeral—a secret
form of penitence. In similarly heated killings, sometimes the murderer finds
enjoyment in seeing the suffering of others at the funeral."

"Really."

Now turning to bore his eyes into mine, Dafney asked, "So again,
why is it that you came to the funeral?"

"Strictly official business, detective," I stated as coldly as I could,
realizing that this was not entirely true, for I was there partly in my effort of
helping Jill Moreland.

Not sure if the detective could perceive my partial deception, I
watched as he turned away and called out, "I haven't entirely eliminated you
as a suspect, geography man. I suppose the crowd is heading for the cemetery. You coming, Mercator?"

I didn't answer, for I didn't know my answer. I hadn't planned to go
to more than the funeral, but now given Dafney's assertion about murderers,
I started to consider going to the cemetery and maybe to the reception as
well.

12

The Cemetery

I went to the cemetery. There were no emotional tugs and I didn't think my official responsibilities should include my presence at the gravesite, but the detective had stirred my curiosity. Had the murderer been at the church? Would the murderer be at the grave? Should I also go to the reception?

I managed to join the funeral cavalcade to the cemetery, being one of the last of perhaps thirty-five cars following a police car escort that cleared a path through the traffic. Each of the trailing cars bore a small flag tethered to a magnetic base, as provided by the funeral home. Cross traffic stopped to allow the motorcade to wheel freely to the cemetery grounds.

Although many cemeteries in rural Minnesota are plotted conveniently adjacent to small countryside or village churches, this wasn't feasible in the metropolitan area. Thus it was that this large cemetery took in churchgoers of many denominations, plus non-believers too. Though the parking lot was ample, it still was a five-minute walk to the gravesite. I walked past elaborate marble tombstones etched with names and dates and stepped near simple stone markers. I couldn't help but think about my own forebears, though not buried at this cemetery and certainly not murdered. Many of my ancestors were buried next to small rural churches on the hillside slopes of Norway.

Munson's plot stretched in what looked like one of the more expensive sections, near a pond adjacent to a copse of small birch trees. For those

54

who aver that the deceased should rest comfortably, this met the description of a cozy scenic setting. Not being in the family group, I chose to stand at a polite distance, some thirty yards from the open grave. A much smaller number of mourners were present here than had been at the church.

Obviously, the family was present. Following Detective Dafney's sociological analysis, could one of the family members be the murderer? I knew almost nothing about Munson's family, save that his widow wasn't technically a widow, rather an ex-wife. Had there been lingering animosity between these former spouses? Could Munson's son bear resentment from the breakup, feeling that the father had caused the marriage to fail and the family to fracture? Maybe, but even so, their presence at the gravesite was normal, drawing no particular suspicion. In fact, absence from the interment might be considered more suspicious, inferring a lack of caring for the dead man.

Also standing at a polite distance from the family was Marjorie Wheelwright, still accompanied by Sebastien Kroon. Near her I saw professors Monroe Wilder, Virginia Loop, and Lindey O'Barnes. I hadn't seen O'Barnes at the church. Had he only come to the interment or had I simply missed him at the service? Admissions director Morris Townsend stood nearby too. Neither Jill nor Carole had come to the graveside.

Additionally, there were a couple dozen people unfamiliar to me. That is, while I believed that I had seen them at the funeral, I didn't know who they were. Relatives? Colleagues? Employees? Deciding to be snoopy, I tried to appear to amble aimlessly along, while in fact striving to hear bits of conversation.

". . . odd at work without Munson watching over us," remarked a young man. He looked to be recently out of college, wearing a tweed sports jacket with no tie, covered by an unzipped down jacket. I presumed that he worked at Minnesota Mission, Munson's charity.

Next to him, a woman of forty or so, a mousy looking lady, bespectacled and with an amorphous, yet trimly cut twist of brown hair, neither slim nor chubby, more shapeless than anything, responded, "Bob, you shouldn't speak ill of the dead," looking at him with slightly contracted eyes and a barely raised accusatory index finger.

"Oh, Lyn, I don't mean anything bad. But, you know, he did want us to keep at it."

"Every good businessman wants his business . . . or charity to succeed, Bob."

The words came out in a monotone, as if an automatic response from a distracted mind. Perhaps she was repeating words Munson had used at work.

This Lyn said something else, but I was out of earshot as I slowly ambled through the crowd. I had come close to three men who appeared to be businessmen, clad in similar suits and ties and Burberry wool coats.

"Stupid bastard, Mun. He'd cheat his mother at pinochle, to be sure to win," said the tallest of the three.

"Ha, I once heard him say that he spiked his golf partner's lemonade to make him a bit too tipsy for the eighteen holes. Beat the guy by twelve strokes, he bragged," said the middle man.

"What a jerk! I hate his guts." The short guy added his thoughts, in agreement.

I was mentally locking in their faces for later recognition, when the middle guy continued, "So, will that philistine run the thing now Gordon's dead?"

The trio abruptly moved from suspects in the murder to mourning or at least respectful business colleagues. They weren't talking about Gordon Munson, though they might have been talking about Munson's son Allan. I angled my path slightly right past them. Trying to sound absently casual I threw out a few words, "A sad day, huh?"

This elicited only a couple grunts of acknowledgement from them, but gave me the chance to add another comment. "At the college—by the way I'm the alumni director—we didn't know much about Munson's business life. Are you fellows business colleagues?"

"Sort of," responded the tallest one. "We're not employees, but we had dealings with Munson."

Sticking out my hand and saying, "Mercator Eliasson, alumni director" prompted three handshakes and introductions—Jay Rayfield from Portlake Paper, Morton Jerrold Emory from Field Business Wholesale, and Gil Dennison from the Mandrake Company.

"So, now without Munson," I asked, "who'll run his charity?"

After a pause, Rayfield said, "See the guy holding the rose up front? Acting so morose? That's him. The son, Allan N."

"What's the 'N' stand for?" pondered Morton Emory.

With a touch of a smirk, Gil Dennison asserted, "Nimrod."

We all chuckled quietly so as not to appear inappropriate, then I nodded in acknowledgement and moved on. The next knot of people was from the college.

"Hey," came from Morris Townsend, the admissions director, somewhere in his fifties, balding and short.

With an upward bounce of my head, I returned the greeting, trying to make it apply to the whole group. Others nodded back.

"So," I tossed out an empty syllable.

"Making an extra effort, are you, Mickey?" continued Townsend.

"Mercator." I corrected. O'Barnes looked a bit embarrassed for Townsend, while Wilder's face twisted into a slight smirk.

"Oh, yes. Sorry. What did I say?"

"You said 'Mickey' but my name's Mercator."

"Right! So do you know lots of stuff about maps then?"

"Sure."

"I've always been confused about small scale and large scale maps."

"Oh, yes! You and lots of people. You see, a large scale map, perhaps with a scale of one to one hundred, can't show much of the Earth's surface but *can* show its features in relatively large detail."

At this point the pastor reached a small podium with the funeral home's name emblazoned on it. In a whisper I rushed to continue my explanation in a lowered voice. "But a small scale map, perhaps with a scale of one to one million, can show a substantial area, but with small detail." This sentence overlapped with the pastor's words, "Let us join in prayer," and the beginning of that prayer. Townsend looked at me with half-closed eyes, but with folded hands, I hoped getting my explanation.

This ended my pre-interment perambulation. Afterwards it was comfortable to walk back with the Masterton group to our respective cars.

No one in the group seemed particularly broken up or emotionally upset. Monroe Wilder was the gruffest of the bunch, but he always put forth a gruff demeanor. Marjorie Wheelwright caught up to us and politely thanked us for coming. As we passed the small group of people that included the mousy woman and the young man she had lightly reprimanded, the woman raised a hand in acknowledgement toward us. As she was to my right and all the rest of my college colleagues were to my left, I could not tell if anyone responded to the wave of her hand. When I turned my head toward my own group, no one made any motion or comment. Perhaps the woman was politely noting our group as it passed.

"Anyone going to the reception?" asked Townsend.

"I don't turn down free food," I replied, but only Townsend agreed, the others indicating plans to go home.

So, I went back to my car. The parking lot was emptying. Thus, as I edged my car backward, I carefully watched my rear view mirror. Far in the background, I could see the equipment next to Munson's grave. Someone in a black dress and scarf was bending over the grave, dropping a flower. As I focused on her, a car honked. Braking abruptly I averted a collision. When I looked back again, the woman was gone.

13
The Reception

The reception was catered at the Landmark Center, near the downtown core of St. Paul. This marvelous old stone building with castle-like turrets had originally been built to house, surprisingly, a post office, in addition to a courthouse. In these capacities, the structure stood as the Old Federal Courts building in St. Paul for several decades. Scheduled for demolition after the federal government moved out in 1967, the building was saved by a public outcry. Extensive renovation inside created a popular first-floor venue for large gatherings. In fact, I had previously attended my college roommate's wedding reception there.

The reception after the funeral was not intended as a festive occasion, though with good food and a large crowd, the decibel level of conversation soon rose and not in such a somber way. Even here the capacity of many to enjoy the company of others came out. My own personality didn't work that way. I didn't enjoy the seemingly random and meaningless conversations of chit chat, but I recognized that for many people such conversations were enjoyable and a means of connecting to others in the world. Psychology professor Roxy Gannon once suggested that my personality type is INFJ. I responded with, "What? I'm an F-ing jay?" She explained that on the well-respected Myers-Briggs Personality Inventory, she thought I would register as an INFJ, the rarest type, with about 2.7 percent of the population sharing this category. I asked if this was bad or good. She said, "Neither. It simply is what it is. But you might find it interesting to look it up." Probably I should sometime.

At first glance at the reception, I saw only Townsend from the college. Expecting to find no one else familiar, I decided to try to combine eating with mobility as much as possible. Perhaps I could manage to eat while secretly working on my task of helping Jill and the murder case.

Maybe it was the free food, maybe more so the timing, but there were many more people at the reception than at the cemetery. In fact, I felt sure that some of these folks also hadn't even been at the funeral service. I estimated three hundred people at the reception, sampling from various platters of meat, trays of cheese and crackers, and glasses of punch. After filling my own plate, I meandered through the crowd toward an empty table. This path yielded little interesting snippets of conversation as I passed by.

". . . heard that there'll be snowstorms during the next two weeks."

". . . and my wife bought these blinds for the house. Very expensive and not . . ."

". . . the Vikings. It was cool that they beat the Giants in that wild playoff game, but of course they couldn't handle San Francisco. They don't have a high draft pick this year, so they're going to need a miracle to get significantly better."

". . . yesterday they got back from the Bahamas and you should see their tans."

I wanted information about Munson and the murder, but these were everyday conversations, useless. I munched on slices of turkey breast and cubes of Muenster cheese. A few people sat at the other end of my table. I smiled a faint greeting as they sat down. After some minutes I finished eating. Draining the last drops of punch from my glass, I rose from the table and proceeded back across the hall. I deliberately took obtuse angles and indirect routes toward the food line, but again encountered no interesting conversations.

I reached the food line, standing behind about twenty people. Of course, this would be my second time through, but my own personal rule was that free food had no limit. Looking at the crowd, I was surprised to observe that the mousy looking woman whose comments I had overheard at the gravesite was sitting with a small group of Masterton people. Morris Townsend was there, along with administrative assistant Michelle Hayes and three classified staff members whose faces were familiar to me, but whose names escaped me. I heard the shuffle of feet behind me that indicated a couple of additional people in line.

"So odd to be here," said a quiet female voice behind me.

"Yes, but we didn't have to walk far, the food's free, and we know the ex-wife," replied another whispering female voice.

I wanted to turn immediately to see these women, but endeavored to be subtle. In the inching of the line forward, I began progressively turning my body, so that my angle of vision moved ever so slightly toward them.

"Yes, and we also know that Helen loathed Munson."

"In the later years, yes, but she did show up for the funeral."

My gradual turning motion was getting closer to providing an angle of vision allowing me to see them.

"I'm sure she did that for the family."

I had reached the trays of food. I gathered up some more turkey slices and cheese cubes. Then I intentionally dribbled a few roasted peanuts off the edge of my plate. In that momentary pause to pick them up, I glanced directly at the two women trailing me. Both were in casual business attire, which suggested that they were office workers. Though different in appearance—one five-foot-nine at least and plump with short brown hair and glasses, the other five-foot-four maybe and slender, with somewhat long blonde hair and hoop earrings—they appeared to be pals. At the moment, they were the last ones in line.

"Did I ever tell you that Munson once made a pass at me?" remarked the shorter woman.

This caused me to start slightly, so that my beverage almost sloshed over the rim off my plastic glass. My near slip up went unnoticed, for the taller woman was also surprised by this question.

She leaned down, bringing her head inches from the blonde hair of the other woman, "What! When?"

"It was at one of those office parties. It must have been before you started working in the office. Helen had been divorced from Gordon for some time . . . a long while. Anyway, mid-party Gordon arrived to discuss some business with Helen. She stomped off, leaving Gordon standing alone in the center of the room. So he walked over to the punch bowl and food table to help himself. I was standing nearby. He first asked me for permission to take food, then started flirting, and eventually asked me to go out for a drink later on. At that moment Helen came back in the room, thrust some papers into his hand, and sent him out the door."

"Oh my gosh! Was Helen angry with you?"

"No. No. She really didn't notice anything. She didn't stay after that, just walked away too."

As the taller woman completed her gathering of food and began to walk away to a table, I was still handling my plate and glass. Thus it was that I heard the blonde quietly under her breath note, "I would have said 'yes.'"

14

Registration for Spring Term

*T*he following day was registration for the spring term at Masterton College. From seniors looking to include at least one slack course their final semester to freshmen often still undeclared in their majors and unsure of even the most basic requirements, students would parade through the college gymnasium stopping at tables staffed primarily by faculty. Although I myself was not a faculty member, I had volunteered to assist with registration, for it gave me the delightful opportunity to interact directly with students. In my role as alumni director, I mainly saw graduates of Masterton College. Of course, this was natural given my job, but registration and other campus events offered the chance to mingle with the students still packing an effervescence for life, yet unencumbered by the responsibilities of career, mortgage, and children. These were exciting times to share, and I savored my chance to do so. I hoped the college would continue the hands-on aspect of registration and at least delay the advent of the impersonal efficiency of electronic registration.

Thus, with a zealous bounce in my stride I arrived at Rønnevik Sports Center for spring registration. Arriving some twenty minutes early to assist with final preparations, I found many faculty already busying themselves arranging the long folding tables that ringed three sides of the arena.

Chantelle Hicks, choir director and associate professor of Music, and Guy Rankin, professor emeritus of Education, stood near my usual station.

Rankin, at six feet in height and with an ever-growing paunch, could see over the much shorter Hicks and observe my approach, but neither he nor Hicks paid any attention to me, focusing instead on their lively conversation.

I heard Rankin comment, in his Texan drawl, "Aw, darlin', look at this from a practical viewpoint. She's got a temper like a dust devil in the West Texas desert. She might have done it, and you shouldn't allow some misguided sense of sisterhood to blind you to the facts."

Chantelle Hicks, a thirty something African-American woman with a powerful, silky smooth singing voice, didn't like to be called "darlin'" or even "darling" by anyone but her husky husband, Ervin Braxton. In a bit of locker room talk, offered by Ervin after a session of pickup basketball on campus one day, he had recounted a tale that Chantelle once had nearly broken a solicitor's arm between the front door and frame, after he had called her "sweetie" when entreating her to contribute to some environmental fund. The door swinging shut coincided with "I ain't *your* sweetie." The door and the retort were faster than his retreat.

"Listen, Guy," she spat in rapid breaths, her ample chest moving in a way that I thought Ervin would admire, "First, I'm not your darlin'" sarcastically exaggerating his Texas accent. "And second," moving closer to Rankin so that she had to tilt her head more sharply to look up to his weathered face, "this woman is smart enough to know that even if her temper blows like that hurricane now and then, she's innocent of this ridiculous charge."

I could imagine Guy Rankin offering some other colorful metaphor, comparing Chantelle to the spouting of a North Texas wildcat oil strike or some such thing, so I attempted to intercede.

"Actually, Chantelle, a dust devil is more like a tornado than a hurricane, but caused by locally excessive surface heating. But hey, what's going on?"

In unison they intoned, "Jill Moreland."

"The Munson murder?" I queried, now that they had my full attention and I had theirs.

"Of course," Guy proclaimed casually, the obviousness of my question apparently being of some smug amusement to him.

Chantelle, though, hooked my elbow with her hand and tugged me to her side. Yanking my arm downward so that my ear came close to her lips, she whispered in such an urgent tone that any premise of secrecy seemed utterly pointless to me. Nevertheless she explained that Guy had heard a rumor that Jill Moreland had been arrested for the murder of H. Gordon Munson.

"A rumor, Guy?"

He answered me with a half smile and a quick tilt of his head.

"Guy, murder's an extraordinary charge. It's scandalous that you would spread such gossip."

"It's from a reliable source." He countered, with emphasis on "reliable."

"Who, Guy, who? Who is this reliable source?"

This, however, brought only a pursing of Guy's lips and a small shake of the head.

"Oh, no, Guy," interjected Chantelle with a sigh of apparently great dissatisfaction, "it's not Tom Burdown, is it?"

Tom Burdown was a retired court reporter, one of Guy's fishing buddies. I knew him to be something of a lonesome widower who latched on to anyone who even remotely appeared available for a conversation. I wasn't sure I would trust him as an authoritative source, even with possible courthouse connections. Chantelle, it would seem, had a similar disinclination.

Guy Rankin blankly denied Chantelle's guess, seeming a bit offended at her undisguised disregard for Tom Burdown. As she refused to accept this simple denial, his attempts to persuade her became more and more vociferous. Eventually he came to notice that indeed other people had begun to pay attention to his conversation. Unhappy with this attention, he leaned his head toward the space between Chantelle and me, and in hushed tones blurted, "If you must know, it was Monroe Wilder who told me."

"Speak of the devil," Chantelle indicated, nodding toward the south entrance of the sports center. Having entered the building a moment ago, Monroe Wilder, math professor, was scanning the arena, apparently looking for his place among the numerous tables set up for registration.

Without a word I broke away from Guy and Chantelle. Although I realized that the two of them might be constrained either to awkward silence or to further argument, my interest now lay in confronting Wilder. I took a diagonal path across the basketball floor, the open space that soon would be full of milling students. I had reached the center circle when a voice over the sound system caused me to slow my pace and turn.

André Sholé, academic dean, had the microphone. "Colleagues, would you please take your places. The students soon will be allowed to enter the arena momentarily, and we must be prepared for them."

Given little choice, I made my way back to my assigned place, a table three down from the registrar. Four tables farther down, Chantelle Hicks caught my eye and offered a sympathetic smile, but also sat down to prepare for the forthcoming task of registration. Quickly the arena quieted, and Dean Sholé gave what I had learned from a previous event was a standard template for the registration process. I listened to the dean, giving him only the same level of attention I'd given my father when I was a twelve-year-old and he was telling me how to do plumbing repairs. I knew my task, as usual, was to assist the registrar and her minions in addressing any errors or complications that might arise. As the students entered, I absentmindedly watched them scatter to the various tables and corresponding professors. Something about the pattern of movement caught my eye, and I realized that one small section of the U-shaped arrangement of tables remained unoccupied. Leaning to my right to see past a cluster of students at the table adjacent to this gap, I could only make out the last letters of the sign marking the departmental designation. ". . . phy."

Geography! Jill Moreland, as the only member of the Geography Department, should have been at the table. My thoughts quickly scrambled for an explanation. Where was she? I considered the chance that maybe she was merely late. Given the proclivity of some professors such as J.P. Kiick for being late, I recognized that a behind-schedule arrival was a possible solution to the mystery. Jill Moreland, though, rarely was late; in fact, promptness was a virtue she emphasized.

Registration had only started, so as yet there were no problems for me to address. This gave me the opportunity to rise and cross the floor again, this time headed for Jill Moreland's table. This was the familiar basketball court where I was accustomed to running. I wanted to run now, to reach the other side, and somehow to find Jill Moreland there, inexplicably obscured from my earlier line of sight. Instead, faced with an increasing crush of students, I could see little ahead of me. I dodged past a tall fellow and around a petite blonde. Literally pushing on, I moved past other familiar students. After what seemed like a long time to reach the other side, I broke through a final tangle of students to reach the ". . . phy" table. At the same instant Professor J.P. Kiick lurched into the chair behind the table, with an audible "Ooof."

"J.P." I breathed in surprise.

"Hi, Mercator. Were you looking for me?" replied Kiick, smiling up at me.

"What are you doing here?"

Kiick must have perceived a sense of agitation in my manner, for his winsome smile dropped, being replaced by a quizzical look. Slightly turning his head, eyes narrowed, he answered hesitatingly, "The same thing you are? Registering students?"

"No, no! What are you doing *here*? At the . . ." and looking down to point at the sign attached to the front edge of the table, the sign which students had blocked from my vision the whole time, "the Ph, the Philosophy table?"

The drop in my tone conveyed to Kiick a change in my attitude, so that he looked into my puzzled face with a quizzical look of his own. "Isn't this the right table? Philosophy?"

"Oh, yes, J.P." J.P. Kiick taught in the Philosophy Department, so of course this would be his table. My mistake was evident. Both "Geography" and "Philosophy" end with "phy." The Geography table must be somewhere else. Sheepishly I muttered some excuse to the good-looking Kiick and started to move away.

"Looking for something?" a voice ventured from nearby.

Glancing over I saw Monroe Wilder grinning from behind the table to the left of Kiick's. The Math Department's paperwork was spread in front of him. Wilder's attention was focused on me, in spite of the trio of students queuing in front of him. Wilder was absentmindedly signing a student's form, while using his right elbow to try to nudge Kiick into joining Wilder's view of merriment.

"No, no. It's nothing." I attempted, seeking to get away.

"We're happy to help out," Wilder noted, seeming to enjoy my embarrassment.

Waving my hand to indicate that nothing was needed, I moved away, but not before noting quietly questioning looks from professors Lindey O'Barnes and Roe L. Spellenko seated at tables nearby.

Sufficiently embarrassed, I again crossed the gymnasium floor back to my table. Soon I was occupied with a myriad of students' registration woes. Susan Wilkins, a freshman, had registered for English 101A and for Psychology 101B. These were reasonable choices for her first year of study, except for the fact that both courses were offered MWF from 9:00 to 9:50 a.m. When the registration computer rejected her schedule, she was sent to me for assistance. Her case was simple enough. I suggested that she switch to Psychology 101F, like 101B also taught by Professor Benjamin Hunt, but listed as MWF 1:00- 1:50 p.m., a time slot that did not interfere with her other classes. She had to return to the Psychology table to note this change with Professor Reuben Schwartz, a bearded Boston Jew who each year was expected to return to his home city, but now had been at Masterton College for eighteen years.

Other problems were solved quickly too. Becky Brown, a pert sophomore from Milwaukee, needed to add one credit in order to remain eligible for her scholarship. I gave her a PE class on archery. Roman Giovanni was required to take more remedial English this term, but somehow had forgotten to write this on his schedule. Writing did not seem to be his strength.

When I had a moment or two of calm, rare occurrences once students began to reach my table, I glanced around the faculty tables for some glimpse of Jill Moreland. This was difficult through the crowded gym, but two or three times I did note some red hair on the far side, which I assumed belonged to Jill.

While most of the proposed solutions brought no arguments from the students in need, William White, a junior from Minneapolis, presented a greater challenge. A mild-mannered music major, White had registered for Biology 102, a lecture and lab combination of introductory biology. The lab portion of the course conflicted with Music 203, Music Theory, which was a requirement for his major. White adamantly refused to change his biology section, even though a switch would enable him to take Music Theory. My efforts to explain that he did not need to take Biology 102, for his previous coursework in chemistry and physics satisfied his graduation requirements in natural sciences, fell on deaf ears. In addition to this, his selection of Geography 107—Human Geography—and Music 303—Advanced Composition—along with his participation in Concert Choir, meant that on Mondays with biology lab he would be in class from 11:00 a.m. to 6:00 p.m. When I was so bold as to suggest that Mondays could be a bit too challenging, he responded with a simple shrug. Actually, he wasn't even paying attention at first, instead looking fixedly toward something or someone to his right. Eventually I acceded to his wishes. After all, he would be taking the courses, not I. I supposed that he'd take Music Theory next year. After his departure, there was a brief lull. I looked over at the angle of his earlier stare, but only saw a few young women chatting, seemingly conferring over their schedules. Mona Schaeffer happened to look up and granted me a smile and a wave. As I waved back, a thought occurred to me. I punched her name into my computer keyboard. Mona Schaeffer, a lovely long-legged brunette and a rare sophomore entrant as a soprano in the concert choir, also happened to be registered for both Biology 102 and Geography 107. My bit of detective work gave a rather sufficient understanding of the academic motives of young Mr. White.

When all of my tasks of scheduling were completed and registration was winding up that afternoon, I passed by registrar Stella Horton to indicate that I would be leaving. In her late fifties and possibly nearing retirement, Horton had served in her position for fifteen years at Masterton College. She kept her job because of her efficient and capable skill in handling the detailed matters of record keeping, academic regulations, registration, and scheduling. She kept her job due to these qualifications, for otherwise she was widely disliked. After years and years of smoking, her voice was rough, deeper than the tones of most men and especially gravelly in quality. Like the harsh-toned collisions of unpolished stones tumbling through the barrel of a rock polisher, words ground from her mouth. Adding a feature like the whine of the tumbler's spinning motor, her voice leaked a subdued scream of dissatisfaction as she clung to a fascination with sophistication and wealth that few others shared. Her years of prior living in what she called "the City," injected remnants of a New York accent that only aggravated the mix further.

"Stella, I'll be leaving now. Always a few problems, but it seemed to go pretty smoothly today."

"Smoothly!" she half screamed, half growled. "These pathetic professors know nothing of efficiency. Bert Jordan from Psychology misplaced the departmental roster of registering students for over an hour. He was writing down students' names on the back of a takeout menu from the China Doll restaurant where he expects to have supper tonight. He had no clue as to whether classes were full or not. Now that I found the roster, there are thirty-seven people in Abnormal Psych. That pauper Herb Flintridge will blame me for having seven students over his limit, but it's Jordan's fault. So don't tell me it went smoothly."

I mumbled something apologetic and began to drift toward the exit.

"Of course, the worst thing was Geography," continuing in the same abrasive tone, but a bit louder.

It served to stop me dead in my tracks. "Geography?" I reluctantly queried, not sure that I wanted an answer.

"Yes, didn't you notice? No one staffed the Geography Department's table the whole time. That is, if you can call a one-person department a department at all."

My head swiveled to look for the red hair across the gym. Most of the crowd was gone, and I easily focused on the long curly red tresses of Roxy Gannon, psychology professor. Jill Moreland had not been there.

70

15

Lemmings for Dinner

I nearly forgot that I had pledged to join my brother and his family for Friday dinner. Perhaps this near omission stemmed from exposure to the rarefied air of academia and the corresponding absentminded professor syndrome. However, more honestly, I suspected that I was reluctant to suffer another quizzing over the separation from Carole. Although Daniel and his wife, Stephanie, expressed their questions in tones of concern, I still sensed an underlying notion of disapproval. I didn't approve of it either, but like most people, I didn't relish accepting the judgment of others. As I drove through the Twin Cities metropolitan area on my way to their White Bear Lake home, I endeavored to think of ways to twist conversation out of the personal realm.

In the end these mental gymnastics proved unnecessary, for as soon as I entered the front door, I met the rush of a hug from my eight-year-old niece, Holly, and then a leg clamp grip from three-year-old Mason. In addition to my sister Savannah's brilliant only child, Drake, these two were my only relatives of this next generation.

This warm greeting quickly lapsed into the scampering of feet and Holly's call, "Follow me like a lemming, Uncle Merc." Her brother chimed in with a "No, like a Tlingon!"

"Mason, not like a Klingon, like a lemming," retorted Holly.

A bit puzzled, I decided that a wise and caring uncle simply would follow. I did so, even while not knowing whether this would lead to some example of this family's avowed exuberance for Star Trek (Mason's trouble with the "kl" sound aside) or to the products of my niece's fertile imagination—lemmings after all!

As I stepped gingerly past scattered toys and other flotsam on the stairs to the basement family room, musical tones increased in volume until I could detect their origin as a Macintosh computer posted amidst an array of software books and CD cases. Avid Macintosh users, Holly, and to a lesser extent Drake, loved to tease Carole about her use of a Gateway PC at her office. Before our separation, they even asked why I hadn't married a Macintosh user, but this teasing showed an underlying affection for Carole, so the frequency of the Macintosh/marriage joke declined as the length of our estrangement had grown. They missed their aunt.

On the computer screen, small animated figures marched across a landscape of mixed natural and manmade structures. "They're lemmings, Uncle Merc!" declared Holly. She went on to explain that the computer game was entitled "Lemmings" and that the purpose of the game was to guide these creatures through the proper portals to safety. If unguided or misguided, these bouncy beings would follow each other one-by-one off a cliff or into watery depths or to some other deadly fate. The game included numerous levels of difficulty and many varied terrains. Although not a particularly intellectual pursuit, "Lemmings" clearly posed an entertaining, if not addictive, form of delight for Holly and in a somewhat less involved way for Drake. My polite observation of their play soon changed to active interest and then to my own attempts to guide the lemmings. Forty-five minutes evaporated, only to have this spell broken by Holly's mother's call of, "Suppertime."

At the dinner table, I glanced with embarrassment at my brother and offered an apology for ignoring them, but Daniel waved this off with a brush of his hand and a knowing grin. Apparently he had experience with the game too.

"Now we have your attention anyway, so you can tell us what's new," he noted.

Thinking quickly so as to avoid any forthcoming discussion of marital woes, I launched into an explanation of the campus news. "Well, there's the Munson murder . . ." I began.

Interrupting me, Stephanie exclaimed, "You mean the philanthropist killed by that professor?"

Taken aback, I hastened to clarify my status. "Actually, that would be Jill Moreland, a Masterton College professor. I've spoken with her and believe her to be innocent."

"But Merc, wasn't she having s—" Pausing Stephanie glanced at Holly who was eating her potatoes and gravy in apparent oblivion to our discussion, before she continued, "having an affair with Munson?"

"What?" I burst out, bringing a quick look from Daniel. "What makes you say that?"

"The newspaper inferred that she was trading favors for his key vote in her tenure case. Normally news from beyond the Twin Cities isn't featured prominently on the front pages of the metro paper, but this strumpet caught the reporters' attention."

"Steph, just because I admired her red hair when I saw her picture on the news doesn't mean she's a tramp," countered Daniel, finally entering the conversation, but further muddying the waters in doing so.

"I said strumpet, not tramp," scoffed Stephanie, drawing a confused look from me.

I began feebly, "But Stephanie . . ." but my weak attempt was cut off by Daniel's elevated tones, "A whore by—"

"Daniel!" Stephanie's tart rasp interrupted, "watch your language," tilting her head toward young Holly.

". . . any other name," Daniel's words floated by, ending the sentence, but Holly had moved to her pork and applesauce, paying the adults no heed.

In the silence that followed, I found a chance to gather my thoughts in rebuttal of my sister-in-law's contentions. "Jill Moreland is a demure, sensitive professional. I can't imagine her being involved in a compromising relationship with H. Gordon Munson. True, she needed Munson's vote to offset the votes gained by her campaigning colleagues, but I'm confident that she'd bend over backwards to show her best side."

"Maybe her best side is on her back," Stephanie suggested.

"She didn't have an affair with the dead man!"

"Not while he was dead, you silly!"

Pausing while being unsure how blunt to be—she was my brother's wife after all—I allowed her to continue.

"She wore a wet T-shirt in class, you know."

Eyes wide and head swiveling to look at Holly, who had progressed to her pudding but remained in a world of her own thoughts, Daniel harshly whispered, "Where did you learn that?"

"One of her former students is our neighbor's cousin's friend's son and she knows . . ."

"She?" I interjected.

"The cousin. He told . . ."

"The son?" I extrapolated.

"No, no—her friend. He told her that this Professor Moreland wore a wet T-shirt to class and acted suggestively."

Dan fixed me with a look that meant, "Wow, I never had professors like that," but offered only words that questioned, "What does she teach—Human Sexuality?"

Now I was getting rather exasperated, "No, she teaches Geography and, listen, I can't envision a situation where she would act provocatively in class, much less have a tryst with Gordon Munson, even given his reputation for charming women. Stephanie, can you give me the name of this young man who claims to have seen Jill Moreland act this way?"

"Oh, he didn't see her."

"But you said he was her former student and that—"

"Aren't you paying attention, Merc? I said he was her *former* student. His girlfriend was in the class where this tawdry display occurred."

"The uncle's neighbor's fiancé's adopted son's girlfriend?" I queried, my words expressing my skepticism.

"Nooooo," she followed, missing my sarcasm entirely, "our neighbor's cousin's friend's son's girlfriend."

Giving up, "Okay, could you find out her name for me?"

"Sure. It's Ginny Parker."

"You know that too!"

"Of course! She lives next door."

"B . . . b . . . but! Wait a minute. The neighbor's cousin's . . ." I couldn't keep it going.

She recited it slowly as I echoed her words, "our neighbor's cousin's friend's son's girlfriend."

"And she lives next door?" I finished.

"Yes, on the other side."

"So, she told her mother . . ."

"How would I know? I'm not a busybody."

"Stephanie, did you talk to the daughter?" I inquired.

"Oh, goodness, no! Her type doesn't have time for me." Then looking over toward her daughter, she whispered behind a raised hand, at best a porous sound barrier, "She sunbathes nude on their roof, you know."

While this revelation did catch Daniel's attention, when I hastened a furtive look at innocent Holly nearby, she was still inattentive to our conversation, instead preoccupied with spooning her cup of pudding. My stomach betrayed me. The pudding looked delicious. Without looking away from the conversation, I extended an eager hand out to enclose my cup, but instead simply pawed a vacant spot on the table. Now more distracted, I searched for my serving, locating it among a trio of empty and toppled cups in front to Holly's plate. A contented look on her face, my niece was devouring her fourth portion of pudding. We were not paying attention to her. She seemingly was ignoring our dialogue. She pilfered our pudding.

With a sigh at having lost my dessert and an understanding of this conversation too, I tried to salvage the latter. "Perhaps I'll speak with the daughter next door, but I simply can't envision this particular professor sleeping with that particular regent."

"Then why did she kill him?" The good will toward her gender ungraciously vanished.

Trying to remain tolerant, I explained, "While she asserts her innocence, Professor Moreland does acknowledge that regent Munson's vote was crucial to her keeping her job and being granted tenure. He would cast the tie-breaking vote, yet up to his death, he had not publicly revealed how he would cast that vote."

"My wife's assumptions aside," Daniel added, "what's the controversy?"

"Jill Moreland had not written a dissertation to complete a Ph.D."

"But I thought that all professors had to have a Ph.D.," as I had originally thought too.

"That's a common perception, Daniel, but some don't. In fact, Moreland contends that this very assumption shows that the public and students can't discern between professors with a doctorate and those without, thereby indicating that a lack of the degree shouldn't disqualify professors from performing marvelously."

"Why doesn't she at least *promise* to do the dissertation?"

"No, her point is that she already *is* teaching splendidly and that the dissertation becomes merely an obscure piece of research that doesn't benefit her teaching at all."

Enlightenment flooded Stephanie's face. "I've read about that!"

Startled, I watched her with new interest as she elaborated. "Graduate students keep writing dissertations in order to prepare for the job market, even though research actually doesn't improve their teaching skills. Universities offer more and more doctoral programs to satisfy this high demand. Colleagues require that new candidates for tenure have the Ph.D. because it was demanded of them. Once upon a time they did the dissertation, so now everyone else must too. So everyone marches to the incessant beat of the research drum, even while no one stops to analyze the real value of the destination."

Agog at her unexpected show of wisdom, I just sat there. My face must have revealed my astonishment, for she reacted with a brief giggle and a verbal response indicating that she too could read.

"Lemmings," a quiet voice added.

Adult heads spun toward Holly.

"Yes, it's a fun game, Holly," I noted in a patronizing tone.

"Nooo . . ." she responded, matching my patronizing tone, "those people you're talking about—they're lemmings. It sounds as if they follow right along, like in my computer game."

As the three adults fumbled for a response, Holly curtsied to us, then scampered away to the basement.

"Is there any more pudding?" Daniel and I asked simultaneously.

76

16

The Doorbell

*A*rriving back at my apartment at 9:15 that evening, I collected the day's mail from my box. A bill from the electric company. An opportunity to subscribe to *Mother Jones* magazine. My chance to get some sort of free prize, but if only I attended a promotional session about condos being built in Fort Lauderdale, Florida. In short, nothing of importance.

At 9:28 the doorbell rang. One of my childhood friends had a doorbell that played a sequence of six harmonic chimes. That was really neat. This bell simply went "*ding*." Since I had moved in here, or rather moved out of what then became Carole's house, this *ding* had rarely been heard. Once the thirty-something blonde divorcee Donna from four doors down the hall had rung the bell in order to borrow a cup of sugar. Surprisingly I had it, for my pantry held little of such baking items. Later that day the bell had dinged again and it was Donna bringing me a pair of chocolate chip cookies. It happened that I was in the middle of watching an episode of *NYPD Blue*, so my thanks for the cookies were politely concise. As I was getting into bed alone that night, it occurred to me that perhaps what Donna really wanted was for me to ring her bell.

I'd never been very good at catching female mating clues. Oh, I'd done fine in dating, but I also had missed some opportunities. Or had I? It was hard to tell. I particularly remembered an encounter that occurred during a college summer when I worked for the downtown St. Paul health club. During my lunch hour, I was walking through the skyways that connected many of the downtown buildings. In winter these skyways provided an excellent way to get around downtown without having to go out into the cold and snow. In the summer heat, the skyways offered a cooler alternative. Anyway, that particular day, a pretty college-age woman approached me saying, "Aren't you Warren Waterman?" I answered with a polite, "No," and a very slight smile, then turned to go on my way. Since then I'd wondered if the young woman's actual goal was to gain an introduction to me, in which case I completely cut her off. Or not, for perhaps she really was looking for Warren Waterman.

The doorbell rang again, this time with two long insistent pulses. Could it be Donna looking for some bell ringing? Indeed, who would come by at this time of night unannounced?

I crossed the room and peered through the door's peephole. Carole! It was Carole! Running my fingers through my hair, I hoped that I looked presentable. Shirt tucked in, collar straight. As I reached for the doorknob, the bell rang again.

"Carole!"

"Merc, where have you been? I've been calling you all evening." She brushed past me, her flat soles clicking on the lightly patterned linoleum of the kitchenette.

"I was at my brother Daniel's house for dinner."

Carole's shoulders curved and head bobbed. No matter how busy or tense, she loved that family. "Oh, how are they?" she asked with affection glistening from each word.

"They're great. But, you know, an odd thing happened."

"Yes?" with a bit less affection now.

"Somehow we got started on the Munson murder . . ."

"That's why I'm here," interrupting me, "Jill's gone." And off Carole went, preventing an easy response from me. "She's not at her house. She's not answering her phone. She's not at her favorite table at the coffee shop. She's not anywhere."

"But, Carole, she might just be out for the evening. Like I was."

"Merc, I've been calling her all day. All day! I even went by her house tonight. Her mailbox hadn't been emptied. We've got to find her."

"I only got my mail a few minutes before you arrived. Surely, she's fine."

"There was a man outside her house."

"What?" A single bead of sweat formed on my neck, at the nape just above my shirt collar.

Volume increased, "There . . . was . . . a man . . . outside . . . her house!"

"Where? Did he look dangerous? Are you okay?" Three questions, three newly formed beads of sweat.

"Of course, I'm okay. I'm here now, aren't I?" Carole's eyes had narrowed and not in the crinkly way that accompanied glee.

"Okay, okay." I didn't want Carole to become frustrated with me. The sweat became a trickle. "What can you tell me about this man?"

"He was in a car across the street. I walked up to ring the doorbell at Jill's house. I rang and waited, rang and waited, rang and waited. When I finally gave up and walked down the steps, I noticed the man across the street. He actually looked suspicious, like he had nothing to do."

"Carole, I think he was staking out the house. Could he have been a policeman?"

"He didn't have a uniform on."

"If *The Rockford Files* are anything to go by, the police don't do stakeouts in uniform. Uniforms blow their covers. But, darn it, without a uniform it could be anyone sitting in that car. But would Jill have anyone else looking for her?"

"The real killer?"

"I suppose. But we don't know who that is. It doesn't register."

With the word "register" a small flame seared my throat, a reflux of acid rising with warning of alarm. Sometimes I carry a roll of Rolaids or Tums in my pocket for this occasional annoyance. This time the cause of the heat was the word "register."

"Oh, no." My hand moved to massage my down-turned face.

"What? Merc, what is it?"

"Jill wasn't at her assigned place at Masterton's registration today. In fact, she wasn't there at all. Stella Horton was really ticked off that Jill was absent and hadn't called her."

"Who?"

"Stella Horton, the registrar. But who Horton hears doesn't really matter. What matters is that Jill's been missing all day, even after our plan had been for her to maintain her regular work habits."

I barely heard Carole's harshly whispered, "Oh, no," and saw the shimmering watery reflection in her eyes, but standing right next to her, I was aware of both.

Taking her into my arms, I quietly reassured her, "We'll find Jill. We'll find her." I wanted to sooth her and calm her trepidation, yet I also felt the swell of her bosom across my chest and smelled the soft scent of her rich brown hair.

"We'll find her, Carole. I'm sure she's okay."

After trying once more to reach Jill by phone, Carole and I agreed that we would drive by Jill's house. Leaving her car at the curb, we got my Toyota out of the apartment building's garage.

Some people feel a very strong sense of consumer loyalty, in some cases toward automobiles. Every car that Carole's brother Andrei had owned had been a Saab. Most recently he'd been driving a 1993 Saab 900, which was the last model that had Saab's classic distinctive shape. It even was a bit of a family tradition. Carole's father once owned a 1967 Saab Sonnet sports car. While we were married—technically Carole and I still were married—she owned a Ford and I a Toyota. Maybe sometime I would enjoy owning a Saab too, for I could appreciate Saab's distinctiveness, safety, turbo power, and Scandinavian heritage.

As we drove toward Jill's house on the other side of town, a silence fell over us, undoubtedly as we both dwelt on our own nervousness about Jill's situation. Fortunately, the small size of Masterton brought us to Jill's street within six minutes.

"Carole, I'm going to drive past Hamden Street, and when I do, I want you to look down the street and see if the man and the car are still there by Jill's house."

Carole turned her head and peered down the street. "I see two cars parked at the curb and one looks like the same car as before."

"Which way is the car facing?"

"This way, umm, is that north?"

"Yes, north. Okay, I'm turning to go around the block, but circling so that we'll come from behind the car. I don't want him to get a good look at us."

Quickly I cornered three times to the left.

"Now, Carole, I want you to face Jill's house as we go by. Do not let the man see your face."

As we approached, I could see a Ford Taurus parked in the middle of the block. Moving alongside it, I angled my profile slightly away, while still watching the road. I could tell that Carole had followed my directions and was peering directly at the houses on the other side of the street, thereby looking directly away from the man in the tan car. Through my peripheral vision, I saw the man in the vehicle.

"Carole, what about the house?"

We drove the rest of the block, passing a parked blue Chevy. As we went by this car, the Toyota's headlights reflected off a circular shiny surface inside that car. Before I could identify the object there, we had driven past, and Carole turned to me and started to answer my question.

"Merc, when I was there today, there was a newspaper on the front step. It's dark, but I think the paper's still there."

"Have you tried her office number?"

"I've tried all her numbers. And why would she be at her office at this time of night on a Friday?"

"I suppose she could be grading papers," but even by the time I finished the sentence, I knew that this was a weak response. Not on a Friday night. Sure, a professor might stay late at the office on a week day, but with time for grading on Saturday and even Sunday, the odds of Jill being at her office now were very slim.

"Let's swing by there anyway," I suggested, and I turned the Toyota toward Masterton College.

Before I could hear Carole's response, klieg lights exploded in my rearview mirror. The Toyota rocked slightly in response to our startled reflex response to the flashing lights and the authority that it represented. Cautiously, I pulled the car to the curb and watched as the police cruiser parked behind me. A burly officer exited the cruiser and came to my window, which by now I had rolled down in expectation of his approach.

81

"Officer, what happened? I think I signaled for that turn," I appealed into the darkness.

"License and reg . . . What the hell? Eliasson, what are you doing here?"

"What? Oh, it's you, Detective Dafney."

"Yes, and what are you doing here, Marcus?"

"Detective, remember that my name is Mercator."

"Damn it, Mer-Ca-Tor, what are you doing here?"

"Detective Dafney, this is my wife, Carole. We're out for a pleasant evening drive."

"Listen, Mer-Ca-Tor, first of all, I thought that you and your wife were estranged."

"Oh, detective, you know, everybody's marriage goes through tough times. Tonight we're plainly having a pleasant evening together."

"And, second, what are you two pleasant lovebirds doing circling past Jill Moreland's house?"

"Jill Moreland's house?" I queried back, hoping that the questioning uptick in my voice wouldn't break into quavering nervousness.

"Yes, Professor Jill Moreland. She lives down that street."

"Honey," smoothly turning to address Carole, I inquired, "does Jill Moreland live over there?"

"Why yes, dear, she does." Carole answered, though in a tone a half octave higher than usual, a tone that I hoped the newly introduced Detective Dafney would not recognize as different from her normal voice.

"Mercator," it was Dafney again, "why did you circle the block? You know that Jill Moreland lives here."

"Detective, we decided to reverse directions. I mean, one can only go so far in little old Masterton, you know. So, we circled to go back."

"Listen Mercator, you'll be wise to stay out of the way of police business. Jill Moreland is a so-called 'person of interest' in the Munson case. I've placed officer Determan in an unmarked Taurus in front of Moreland's house to await her return home. Now you blundered into the situation, circling her house. Let me be succinct: get out of here."

"But Detective, surely you don't suspect Jill Moreland in the murder?"

"Mercator, she has the best motive. I repeat: get out of here."

"No, no, she couldn't have done it," I continue to bluster.

"Mer-Ca-Tor, get the hell out of here before I bring you back as a suspect."

"Okay," raising my hands, fingers outspread in protest, "okay. I didn't do it either."

"But, Detective," this time it was Carole protesting, but I drove off, leaving Dafney to walk back to the police car in silence.

"Merc, when I told you there was a man watching the house," she began.

"Yes, now we know that it's officer Determan in the tan car. I saw him too."

"Merc, when I told you a man watching the house," she repeated, "the man I saw was in the blue Chevy."

I nearly hit the curb. "What!"

"You never asked me about the kind of car. It was a blue Chevy."

"We need to tell Dafney," I ventured before abruptly changing my mind, "No, we can't."

"If we tell him," Carole agreed, "then we'll have to admit we were looking for Jill and that I was here earlier today."

"We can't do that, but I want to know if the Chevy's still there."

"The detective will catch us," she spoke urgently while pulling on my arm, apparently to emphasize the catching part.

"I'm watching his car in the mirror. He's turning off. If we circle back the other way, we might get by."

Again that evening we drove in a brief but tensely thoughtful silence. I brought the car back around in a careful and, I hoped, surreptitious path to intersect with Hamden Street, while still three and a half blocks from Jill Moreland's house. Stopping the car a bit back from the corner, I directed Carole to get out with me. I knew we were in trouble if Detective Dafney spotted my car. We tread cautiously and only far enough to see down the street toward Jill's house. The blue Chevy was gone. Detective Dafney was standing in the street, talking to the officer in the tan Taurus.

Carole and I quickly backed away and returned to my Toyota. Firing it up, I backed up and reverse pivoted into a nearby driveway. We headed toward my apartment. I carefully watched for cars in my wake, but no one followed and we reached my parking area without further incident. On the return trip, I considered suggesting that we drive to Jill's office and look for her there, but the possibility that a police officer might be waiting there dissuaded me from making that suggestion.

"Here we are, Carole."

"Merc, I don't want you to misunderstand, but I wonder if I could stay here tonight."

"Of course, Carole. I'd be delighted to have you stay here."

"This isn't for sex. This has been a nerve-wracking day. I'd rather not be alone tonight."

What I said was, "That's fine, Carole, whatever you like," though my thoughts were lingering on the word "sex."

Minutes later, inside my apartment I swept my arms wide, saying, "This is all I have, Carole. You can stay, but we'll have to sleep together. I mean, there's only this loveseat besides my double bed. Only a child could sleep on the loveseat. So we'll have to sleep toge—I mean, sleep in the same bed."

"Okay. We'll both sleep in the bed, but again I'm not here for sex."

We spent another thirty minutes on small talk and small tasks, letting the nervous tension of the evening wane. Eventually Carole declared herself ready to go to bed, asking for a couple minutes of preparation. She wandered into my bedroom, returning in one of my button down office shirts.

There is something inherently sexy about a lovely woman wearing a man's shirt. The shirttails flaired downward barely far enough to cover her bottom, leaving it open to speculation—panties or no panties? The number of buttons undone determined the cleavage that showed.

"Is it okay if I wear this for sleeping?"

My loins were saying, "Yes, oh, yes!" but I simply said, "Ah, sure."

We each had our few minutes in the bathroom and then met at the bedside.

"Do you want the left side, Merc?"

"I'm used to it," I said, having spent our married nights on the left side.

"Okay then."

I usually slept in only my boxer briefs, but tonight I wore a t-shirt too, though not the one that read, "Alumni Directors do it annually." It was a free handout at a professional conference that I attended in Boise, Idaho; but, I thought, a weak attempt at sexual humor.

Smaller than Carole's queen-size bed, my double bed put us in cozy proximity. Ruffling my hair, Carole thanked me for letting her stay. I had a glimpse of pink panties, as she ducked under the covers. I turned off the table lamp and moved beside her in the darkness.

Sometime later I awakened, for a second frozen in puzzlement, before, in a drowsy state, realizing that Carole was with me. I noted with a calm bit of pleasure that we were snuggled neatly together. Carole often liked to sleep crookedly on her left side. I was tucked right behind her, matching every twist and turn of her sleeping shape. As I nodded off, I realized that my right arm was draped over her torso, my hand under her shirt, the arc of my right thumb and index finger spread to match the curved underside of her left breast. Contentment warmed me.

After having already once recognized Carole's presence through half-opened eyes in the middle of that night, the second awakening did not confuse me about Carole's presence. What I did not know was how my mouth had reached her mouth or when her hands had started tugging my t-shirt off. But, I didn't care. Pausing the kiss, I let her guide the shirt over my head.

Being with Carole that night was exotic. The warmth of contentment changed to the heat of passion. After these many weeks without her in my bed, making love to her was like being with someone for the first time and yet being with someone familiar. As hands explored bodies, words weren't needed.

I swung my right leg over Carole, pivoting both our bodies to straddle her. The need to unbutton my office shirt became foreplay. Letting my hands play across the single layer of cloth over her breasts, I slowly undid one button at a time. Between each unbuttoning, my lips kissed the newly exposed neck, then cleavage, then belly, as Carole softly purred her pleasure. With the last button undone, I pulled back both sides of the shirt to display her full breasts. She was beautiful, and I whispered an acclamation acknowledging this beauty.

As each line of skin and curve of flesh became exposed, I recognized them completely, yet somehow each revelation brought new arousal. Soon our complementary nudity was complete. Positions shifted and pleasure continued. Later, spent, we nestled together, eventually returning to our previous side-by-side, front-to-back locations. We fell back to sleep together that way, again with my right hand at the underside of her breast.

. . . chocolate chip cookies. The sweet moist aroma was intoxicating and . . .

This pleasant dreamy sensation was interrupted by the hard pounding beat of the "We Are the Champions" tune by Queen. I had set the alarm on my clock radio to the music setting. The classic rock station WAND, one of my favorites, played many of the seventies' songs that I liked. For wakeup times, something loud regularly broke my slumber. The station saved mellow tunes for evening hours. Thoughtful of them, or perhaps the results of marketing surveys.

The necessity of waking today was an unpleasant alternative to the stimulating dream that the alarm had terminated. I had been invited to Roxy Gannon's house for supper—in the dream, but never in real life. She had prepared not only a meal, but even then was in the process of baking chocolate chip cookies. Even awake now, I could still smell them. She had a female friend present, whom we both seemed to know, yet now awake, I couldn't manage to identify her. A man had appeared out of her basement, but Roxy's unidentified female friend then had rushed to my side and advised me whispering, "It's okay, he's nothing more than the college doctor." She then announced loudly, "We're leaving right now," pulling the arm of the "doctor" to lead him to the door.

I looked over to Roxy as she bent to open the oven door, thereby offering my senses two strongly pleasing enticements. First, the door released that sweet moist aroma of the cookies that made my mouth water. Second, as she leaned down to release the door, her skirt rode several inches up the backs of her legs, providing me with a complete view of the full length of her milky white legs. These legs, these shapely beautiful legs, were as much of a visual delight as the cookies were a delicious scent. As she lifted the cookie tray from the oven, she turned her shoulder, tossing her long red hair back to reveal a broad welcoming smile. It was exactly at the rising of all these sensory stimulants that Queen made its royal interruption.

I imagine that Roxy Gannon, as Psychology professor, had some familiarity or even skill with dream interpretation, but it seemed judicious on my part not to seek her counsel for this dream. The symbolism was clear enough to me. Undoubtedly the food represented sex, and the delicious cookies great sex. After all, both food and sex satisfied cravings in a pleasurable manner. The neutralizing of the other man as the "doctor," made it clear that no boyfriend or husband stood as an obstacle to the affections or, apparently, to the carnal delights of Roxy Gannon.

With a foolhardy smile on my face, I lifted my head to look at Carole. How odd that I would dream about Roxy Gannon or for that matter about any other woman, after that middle-of-the-night passion with Carole. I looked to her with a smile, the smile of morning after sex. But to my disappointment, Carole was not there.

Deflated, literally, I gathered myself out of bed, flipping the sheet and comforter into an untidy pile on the bed. Noting the faint aroma of coffee in the air, I hoped that Carole could be found at the kitchen table with breakfast. This hope proved to be fainter than the scent of the coffee. Carole was gone. A coffee cup with a dash of brown in the bottom remained. On the table next to the mug was the book *Magnetic Poetry*. A few weeks ago I'd purchased it on a whim for $1.50 at a used bookstore. Included with the book were several dozen words, in very small print and magnetized, each like a tiny refrigerator magnet. The inside cover of the book was a blank metal page, set for poetry creations. On the metal page was my first effort.

Fully Staggered

The smell of my skin is a summer shower wildly
Evenings when she has love for me.
I, the man, see through her telling dark glass
And run not in secret over her slender build.
For how not sisterlike an offer this is, if wanting
By red lace and blue bouquet,
Then only as sounds to song said after.
I am fully staggered.

17

Detective Dafney Again

7he next day the handkerchiefs arrived in the mail. Technically I didn't know who sent them. The postmark indicated that the package was mailed from a post office in Anoka, a northern suburb of the Twin Cities. I believed that Jill Moreland had mailed the hankies to me, for this was what I had instructed her to do. Although my possession of the handkerchiefs monogrammed with my initials MJE could be mildly problematic for me, if the police found them at Jill Moreland's house, they would be damning.

Therefore, on Tuesday during my huddle with Jill and Carole, I directed Jill to return home and gather and launder all the remaining monogrammed hankies. While wearing gloves, common enough in Minnesota's winter, she was to buy a mailing envelope. Then using a scale at one post office, she should purchase enough stamps to cover the postage. After that, her next step was to address the envelope to me, and seal and stamp it without using her saliva, then mail the package in the drive up area of a different post office. Apparently she had chosen Anoka for this last step.

So, on this Saturday I found a manila envelope stuffed into my mailbox. I tore it open to find five handkerchiefs monogrammed with my initials. As a concerned citizen, I immediately drove to police headquarters in Masterton.

"Detective Dafney, this package was sent to me today," I explained as I tossed it on his desk.

Dafney reached out to catch the manila envelope after it bounced, but before it slid on the desktop. "What? What's this?"

"Are these the same handkerchiefs as the one in Munson's blood?"

"What!" Dafney immediately dropped the envelope back onto the desk. "Damn it, Mercator, now I got my fingerprints on it."

"Oh, sorry." I tried to look apologetic and simple. "I didn't think of that."

Rolling his eyes at me, Dafney used the outside edges of his hands to drop the hankies on to his desk. Extracting a tweezers from his desk drawer, the detective then picked up the corner of one square of cloth, unfurling it.

"Detective, why would anyone send me these? And, in fact, are these the murder hankies?"

"This one appears to be identical to the one we found at the murder, though the bloody one had a loose thread. How many of these are here?"

"I counted five."

"Plus the bloody one makes six. I imagine six might be a typical set to purchase for this kind of thing."

"Okay, but why me? I told you that the bloody one wasn't mine, so now someone sends me more."

"Got any enemies out there, Mercator?"

"Not really anyone since Austin Jerveny in middle school."

"Really?"

"I'm a pretty mild mannered guy."

"You're estranged from your wife."

Pent up tension burst from me. "Carole wouldn't have done this!"

"Maybe it was the murderer then."

Picking up the tweezers, Dafney flicked them in a lazy arc toward me. Reaching up with my right hand, I easily caught them.

"Right-handed, Mercator?"

"Yeah, so what?"

"The angle of the knife's thrust shows that the killer was a right-handed person. We're having trouble judging the height of the assailant because it appears that Munson may have been bending over or rising from a bent position."

"Most people are right-handed, something like ninety percent of the population, I've heard."

"So, Mercator, that means you remain in the pool of suspects."

"With all the world's other right-handed people with my initials?"

"Know anyone else?"

"Detective, surely everyone must! Let's see. Well, you know me. That's one. Ah yes! At Munson's grave I met businessman Morton Jerrold Emory— MJE. Did Emory commit the murder too? Ooo, sorry I really didn't notice if he was right-handed."

18

Pete Putnam Redux

After finishing my business at the police station, I decided to make a brief stop at my office. A few cars were in the employee parking lot. I recognized Sebastien Kroon's red Ford and Soren Timicin's SUV. A few students were traipsing across campus, but it was a quiet and cold Saturday afternoon. I expected a simple walk to my office where I would take care of a few tasks.

"Mercator! Mercator!"

I turned to find Pete Putnam approaching in something more than a brisk walk, yet not quite a full run.

"Hey, Pete," I replied, with only about ten percent of his zeal. No one had his energy.

Saturday being a day without classes, Pete appeared to be dressed casually, not nearly at his sartorial extreme. His red-plaid jacket, which today completely covered his shirt, topped red corduroy pants. His socks and shoes were black and white—a white sock with a black tennis shoe and a black sock with a white tennis shoe. Wow.

"Mercator, did anyone ever tell you that you look like 'Angel'?"

"I look like . . . an angel?" My left hand reached up to massage my forehead. I sure didn't need this now. "Pete, I'm not sure I like having a guy tell me that."

"No, no. Not *an* angel. Angel."

"I don't look like an angel? I look like *an* angel." Now both my hands extended, palms up. "Pete . . ."

"No, you know. That actor on that whatchamacallit show."

"Pete, please tell me that you don't mean Bosley on *Charlie's Angels*."

"Whose angels? No, that show's too old for me. I mean Angel on the whatadingdong show."

"*Hell's Angels? Fallen Angels?*"

"No and no again. The show with the actress with three names."

"Farrah Fawcett Majors? Now we're back to *Charlie's Angels*."

"No. Whatshername, you know."

"Sarah Jessica Parker?"

"Yes! Wait, no. Anyway, she's really pretty."

"Most actresses are."

"Actually, Mercator, I been doing my own survey on attractiveness. In fact, only ten percent of people are better than average looking."

"Hold it, Pete. You want to be a math major. You must know that the definition of 'average' is fifty percent. Half of the population is better than average looking."

"Not so. Not so. Look around. Let's take twenty-year-old people. Lots of them are good looking, especially women, of course. At age thirty, fewer people are pretty or handsome. At age fifty, barely anyone. And after that no one. So you take all those people together and really only about ten percent are above average looking."

"Pete," but he kept going. He always kept going.

"For instance, go to an airport sometime. Watch the people walking by. You'll see a wide range of people. Take a count of the people who are attractive. You'll see."

Looking a number of yards past Pete, I saw Professor Monroe Wilder getting out of his car. "Pete, perhaps you should review those calculations with a math professor," and I pointed towards Wilder.

"Okay, I will." Pete took off like a shot toward Wilder, who abruptly looked up, reminding me of a deer caught in headlights.

That Pete Putnam. An airport, hmm. As I walked the remaining yards to my office, I couldn't help reflecting back to my trip to Detroit two weeks prior. Could Pete be correct, after all? And, damn it, I didn't look like any angel.

19
Find Jill

hy do my thoughts return to you, Carole? I pondered this as I paced through the corridors of the Social Science Building, empty this late Sunday afternoon. Although the immediate challenge was finding Jill, with the broader task of protecting her from a murder charge, my mind frequently reverted to the hope that my efforts on Jill's behalf would translate into fulfillment of Carole's request, and then ultimately to a return of Carole's full favor toward me. Her absence on Saturday morning, the so-called "morning after," confirmed for me that the relationship had not yet returned to where I wanted it to be.

Her absence the next morning at St. Sophia Church, a Ukrainian Orthodox Church in the Twins Cities, one of few such in that denomination in all of Minnesota, was perhaps less telling. One of our marital struggles was trying to reconcile our religious faiths. Though both Carole's Orthodoxy and my Scandinavian Lutheranism were significant steps away from Roman Catholicism, this similarity sometimes was not enough to mask various differences between these two Christian denominations. That Sunday morning I attended the 10:00 a.m. service at St. Sophia Church in the hopes of seeing Carole, but without luck. Perhaps she had attended the 8:00 a.m. service or perhaps she hadn't been at church at all. How ironic it would have been if she had been at St. Hallvard Lutheran Church, my church, looking for me while I had been looking for her at her church.

In any event, while I approached the Social Science Building at Masterton College, I was thinking of Carole and Jill Moreland. As I reached the corridor of Jill's office, the dim lights illuminated only the most salient or prominent elements, essentially the large print, of professors' office door postings.

Asst. Professor of Anthropology
Bertrand Stracken

This much was printed in clean large letters, but I was not interested in perusing a number of fine print items, listed over a small poster depicting ancient Greek ruins.

Professor Seamus MacPherson
Political Science
On sabbatical leave
Academic Year 1997-1998

Numerous three-by-five photos cluttered the door, a couple of which perhaps might have been postcards from France, another a lightly forested scene which had no label to identify the location.

A variety of items also adorned the next door. Along with a small card listing office hours and contact information, a single white sheet of paper simply noted:

Jill Moreland
Geography Department

The office window was covered by a poster labeled "Trakai" which featured a classic towered fortress, not, however, from England, France, or Germany, but from Lithuania.

Scattered all over the door were such a variety of clippings that they only could be called miscellany: a worn Doonesbury comic strip lamenting Americans' geographic ignorance, a stunning photograph of an Alaskan glacier, a customized map of the Twin Cities, a table listing the ten largest lakes in Minnesota, a postcard featuring a pencil drawing of Niagara Falls, even a matchbook cover from the Double Indemnity Bar and Grill in Big Whiskey, Wyoming. Like all the other offices along the corridor, Jill's office was dark.

Even so, I tapped lightly on the door, even still lighter sounding out, "Jill. Jill, it's me, Mercator."

No response. Mentally I began to acknowledge that this had been a foolish errand, hoping to find Jill at her office. I tapped on the door again but had no hope of an answer. I simply had no idea where Jill could be.

Walking back out of the building, I turned toward my car in the parking lot between the Social Science Building and the Science Center. Two other cars were there—a tan Nissan with Professor Roe Spellenko standing keys in hand and a silver Ford Taurus from which Professor Nora Thorsgaard was exiting. A casual wave from me brought similar acknowledgements from them, but no conversation followed. I got into my car and drove away.

Along the main drive in town, at the intersection of State Highway 316 and County Road 7, my stomach growled as I sighted the local McDonald's. Personally I preferred Wendy's, but McDonald's was Masterton's sole fast food burger joint. When saving time, it was a good alternative to Gurt's Grill, the local diner. Not in a hurry, but now hungry, I chose Gurt's.

Masterton co-ed Sara McFadden took my order of a burger with lettuce and tomato, plus onion rings, and a root beer float. From my high-backed wooden booth, I scanned the room. Seated at a small table with Arthur Ringwold, the local computer repair shop owner, was Mac Johnsrud, my auto mechanic, who gave me a wink and an index finger point of recognition.

McDonald's. Sara McFadden, Mac Johnsrud, and maybe Mac computers. Funny, I thought, how the mind links coincidences together. Yet there was something else too. What was it? I'd eaten a bowl of Sugar Smacks for breakfast, but did that count as a Mac reference? Nah, didn't think so. The British term for "raincoat" is "mackintosh," but so what, it wasn't raining. Was there a Mack truck outside? I looked. No such truck. Of what was I thinking? Mac and cheese for lunch? Maybe I saw it on the menu, even though I ordered a burger.

Satisfied, I pulled a crossword puzzle from my shirt pocket, unfolded it, and began with the clues. I had some success before I hit 6-Across: *Lifetime award for electro-acoustic music*. No idea. 6-Down: *Capital of Bulgaria*. Knew that one—Sofia. 7-Down: *Ornamental fossil resin*. Knew that one—amber. I continued to work on the crossword as the food arrived. I had read that eating while doing something else was not so healthy. It was better to savor the food, eat more slowly, and probably eat less. Nevertheless, when I ate alone, more common now without Carole at my side, I tended to eat while doing something else—watching TV, reading the newspaper, or today doing the crossword puzzle. 23-Across: *Cordon* ____. Okay—bleu. 6-Across: *Lifetime award for electro-acoustic music*. Oh yes, back to that again. S _ A _ _ _. Still no idea. What else? 8-Down: *Prefix for more than two*. Five letters. 9-Down: *Consume drugs regularly*. Three letters. How about—use? 6-Across: S _ A _ U_. 10-Down: *Stinker*. Maybe—fetid. I'll keep that in mind, while I eat the onion rings. 16-Across: *Popular perfume fixative*. Four letters, starting with M— Musk. 37-Across: *Worldly board game*. Got it—Risk. Now back to 8-Down: *Prefix for more than two*. _ UL_ I —Multi. 6-Across: *Lifetime award for electro-acoustic music*. S_AMU_—Samuel? No, silly, doesn't fit. 10-Down: *Stinker*. I have two letters k and plus the letter u. Okay—Skunk. S_AMUS. Must be E for electro. SEAMUS. The SEAMUS Award. Still never heard of it.

I did see the name Seamus today. Seamus MacPherson. Aha! There was my missing Mac reference. I knew there was something else. So, what did all that mean?

And why was my brain still prompting me for more? Elle Macpherson. "The Body." Love that model/actress. But no, that couldn't be it.

Seamus MacPherson. What did I know about him? Perhaps a descendant of the Scottish clan MacPherson. The sign on his door said that he had been granted a sabbatical. Would he be going to Scotland to do research? I thought I'd heard that he and his wife were doing that. All their children were grown adults. I wonder if anyone was watching over their house while they were abroad. Someone had to be tending to a house that few would know was vacant. Oh my gosh! Jill. Jill Moreland was MacPherson's office neighbor. Jill was an unencumbered single woman. Could MacPherson have asked Jill to check his house?

Waving for my waitress, I asked for the check and for a phone book. Harriet and Seamus MacPherson lived at Twelve East Gusset Road. A look in the map pages in the phone book revealed that Gusset Road was a small rural road, probably with many trees and few homes.

On my way. In about fifteen minutes I pulled into Gusset Road, and a minute later into a long driveway marked by a number twelve sign. The driveway went past a number of pine trees, and then curved behind another row of mixed birch and pine. As I pulled up to the house, I spied Jill's Ford Mustang parked behind yet another cluster of trees. I smiled at my own cleverness.

As I had done at her office, I tapped on the door and verbally announced my presence, somewhat loudly for there was no one nearby, perhaps for a mile or more. The slightest rustle of curtains caught my eye and confirmed my belief that someone was inside the house. Indeed, Jill answered the door, but quickly rushed me inside, with a, "You're alone aren't you?"

My, "Yes, yes," was immediately followed by a bear hug and Jill's words, "I've been so scared. A few minutes ago, a dark car slowly cruised down this road, then parked briefly roadside."

"Jill, there's no one there now."

"Merc, how did you find me?"

I recounted a short version of the story, leaving out the crossword puzzle and Elle Macpherson, but somewhat consciously trying to appear a bit Sherlockian in my powers of deduction.

"But, Jill, why are you here? I thought we decided that you would keep your normal routine."

"They were at my house, Mercator. The police were at my house."

"What did they want?"

"I didn't wait to find out. I was driving home from the supermarket and was about to turn onto my street, when I spotted three police cars in front of my house. I steered slowly and straight ahead, instead of turning. I saw two officers on my porch, and this is the scariest part, they had their guns drawn. I was too scared to stop."

"But, Jill, maybe they were there only with questions for you."

"Merc, I wondered that too, but when I saw the guns drawn, it seemed that the police were there to arrest me."

"Jill, you didn't kill Munson. Maybe you should talk to them?"

"But Mercator, I look like a great suspect. I was at the scene of the crime. My handkerchief was in his blood. I have a plausible motive for killing

Munson. I have no alibi. Isn't that exactly what the police want—motive and opportunity?"

"Yes, plus fleeing from the police can be construed as evidence of guilt."

"What?" The increasing paleness of Jill's skin heightened the contrast with her crimson hair.

"By running away, you can be seen as the guilty party trying to escape."

"Oh, no. But can't I argue that I'm looking after the MacPherson house? I come here regularly to water their plants and see that everything's okay."

"Maybe, in fact, I think that we should emphasize that this is a week of vacation at the college."

"Mercator, I can't go to jail. I can't bear to go to jail."

I wasn't sure whether the expanding whiteness of her eyes came from fear or insistence, but I felt compelled to act.

"Jill, I understand. But, I don't know if this is the place to hide. If I could think to look here, then probably the police can too."

"But where? Mercator! Where?"

"I know a place, but you'll have to follow me to get there. It'll take about an hour. Can you gather up your things?"

"I hardly have anything. Give me a minute and I'll be ready."

I spent that minute wiping fingerprints off anything that I might have touched.

"Okay, I'm ready," Jill moved back into the room, a long strapped bag over her shoulder.

We climbed into our respective cars and pulled out of the driveway. The moment after we turned onto the highway, I heard the sirens. As we rounded the first bend in the road, in the rearview mirror I could see the faintest flicker of red and blue lights in the distance. Moving ahead apace but not over the speed limit, both our cars headed north. The blare of sirens remained in the distance, undoubtedly stopping when the squad cars reached Twelve East Gusset Road. I came to the mental conclusion that the police were called there by the driver of the dark car, undoubtedly that being the man in the blue Chevy outside Jill's house the previous night.

20

Hide Jill

*I*t was in the 1970s when my family had purchased a lake cabin on Chisago Lake, northeast of the Twin Cities, but not quite to the Wisconsin border. In this regard we were like many Minnesotans, for the presence of over ten thousand lakes in the state had prompted a tremendous amount of recreational use, from fishing to water skiing, and correspondingly a large share of lake property ownership. Like in neighboring Wisconsin, Minnesota's large number of lakes originated with glacial activity that carved out depressions for water to fill. Although Minnesota touted more lakes than Wisconsin, the close proximity to Wisconsin for the large population of the Twin Cities had prompted some of these Minnesotans to purchase lake property there, in fact, in higher numbers than Wisconsinites owning lake cabins in Minnesota.

In urgent need of a place to take Jill, I found that the family lake cabin came to mind. Although used mostly in the summer and early fall, the cabin was winterized and heated enough so that pipes didn't freeze and the occasional visitor was comfortable. Light a blaze in the wood-burning stove, and then the cabin would be cozy enough. I expected none of my relatives would be at the cabin just then, and likely few neighbors either. Indeed, when we arrived, there were no lights in any of the nearby cabins.

I spent a few minutes showing Jill around the place and explaining where she could go for food and supplies. So far, the police had made no announcements naming Jill as a suspect, so I figured that she could go to large grocery stores without concern. I gave her all my cash, which when added to her own wallet seemed to be sufficient for her to supply herself for a week without traceable credit card usage. Probably she could use her credit cards in metropolitan stores without trouble anyway.

Before leaving, I needed to settle a nagging concern. "Jill, I need to ask you something."

"Okay."

"Jill, there's word on campus that you're a particularly sexy professor."

"Is that good? I want to be viewed as a professional, as an excellent teacher, but not appraised solely for my physical appearance, even if students see me as attractive."

"Then why did you wear a wet t-shirt to class one day?"

"What!"

"Jill, I heard that you wore a wet t-shirt to class one day."

"Mercator," she said in a half teasing, half correcting tone, shaking her head slightly back and forth. "Mercator, it wasn't what you think."

"Then what was it?"

"When I teach my geography classes, I try to use props or other devices to help students remember what they've learned. When the lecture in Physical Geography class is on glaciers, I buy a block of ice from the grocery store and use it to model glacial features and to discuss proportional size. I have it in front of the class on the lab table for the whole class period."

"That's hardly the same as a wet t-shirt."

"That's obvious. When I lecture the same class on deserts, I try to do something offbeat to prompt the students' attention and memory. I wait until I'm two minutes late. The students are all there and have become slightly impatient and expectant. Working with this tension, I bolt into the classroom panting and exclaiming, 'Water, I need water! This desert is so dry. Water! Water!'

"I have left a small bucket hidden but easily accessible at the front of the room. I find the bucket and pretend that it's full of water. Holding the bucket in two hands, I tip it and my head back, pretending to take a quenching drink. Then as I walk about the room, I remark how satisfying the water is. At that point, I pull the old Harlem Globetrotter trick, tripping and tossing the contents of the bucket high into the air and over the students' heads. Of course, the bucket's filled with confetti, not water.

"So, Mercator, last year I decided that some of the students probably had heard of my antics with the lecture on deserts, so I decided to up the ante slightly. I enlisted the help of Professor Jim Stratford in the Biology Department. I gave him the bucket and the confetti ahead of time. The plan was that I would come into the room doing my usual routine of panting for water. Stratford then would arrive and circle the room with the bucket. I would say, 'Water! Water!' and he would move about the room with verbal offers of, 'I've got water!' Finally, I'd say, 'Give it to me,' which would prompt him to rush toward me, pretend to trip, and toss the bucket of confetti over me.

"The plan was working smoothly. The students were laughing uproariously. Stratford tripped and threw the contents of the bucket across my chest. Oh ho! Stratford's own little joke was that the bucket really was full of water. At first the students were taken aback, but then let out another roar of laughter, probably prompted by my shocked expression. Stratford impishly tiptoed out of the room, leaving me dripping wet in front of the class."

"Oh, my gosh, Jill! What'd you do?"

"I was wearing a thin cotton blouse that day. The water transformed the shirt essentially into a single layer of shrink-wrap around my bra and torso. In one of the drawers of the lab table, I found a small terry cloth towel to dry myself somewhat, and then in the classroom's closet I located a Masterton College windbreaker that I wore for the rest of the class. That's it! That is the so-called 'wet t-shirt incident.'"

"Amusing and sexy, but certainly not intended to be provocative on your part. In fact, not at all."

21

Dean André Sholé

rriving at the Administration Building Monday morning, I wondered how difficult it would be to focus on my usual tasks as alumni director at Masterton College. It had been quite a weekend, beginning and ending with Carole.

Friday night's lovemaking had been an exhilarating start to the weekend, though somewhat tempered by her absence the next morning. Finishing Sunday with a conversation with Carole also did not match my expectations. In order to quell Carole's anxiety over Jill's disappearance, I stopped at her place to indicate that I had safely found and hidden Jill. Although I thought it an unnecessary risk to tell Carole exactly where I had secreted Jill, Carole's vehement insistence on knowing the location forced the issue. I could only hope that Carole would neither say nor do something that unintentionally revealed Jill's secret location. Worse for me, Carole made no invitation for me to sleep at her place.

Walking in the main doors of the building, I stepped past admissions director Morris Townsend with a greeting of, "Good morning," that true to my usual form came out more like, ". . . morning." As I approached the flight of stairs up to my office, academic dean André Sholé stepped out of the double glass doors that opened into the suite of offices for top-level administrators, that included him and college president Marjorie Wheelwright.

"Mercator, come in here."

"Um, okay," in a tone that indicated my truthful puzzlement over why I warranted his attention this morning.

"Follow."

So I obediently trailed Sholé, a short man with a bulbous veined nose and a thick unruly mane of mixed white and gray hair. We paced past Lorraine Ullman, the receptionist for the suite. Veering left through an open area populated by empty chairs and two coffee tables covered with Masterton College pamphlets, we stepped up to his darkly stained oak door. Mounted on the wall outside the door was a wooden plaque of warm golden-brown tones, engraved with the words "André Sumner Sholé, Academic Dean." I had heard someone say that the plaque was the only warm thing at the dean's office.

Sholé entered the office first, with me lagging behind, then with practiced ease he flicked the door shut behind us.

"So where . . ." with the curt slam behind us, the door interrupted the dean's quick question, ". . . the police with Jill Moreland?"

"Wha . . . at?" Could Sholé already know that I had ensconced Jill at my cabin?

Placing his hands on his hips and leaning his head forward with eyebrows pushed together, Sholé repeated his question. "So where are the police with Jill Moreland?"

"Wha . . . at?" Again. With my eyebrows also furrowing, but head and shoulders leaning away from the dean, I queried back, "What do you mean? Do the police have Professor Moreland?"

Hands bursting forward from his hips and with all fingers separately extended in the air, Sholé tightened his facial features in hostility, so that the left eye was nearly closed. "The police have not arrested Moreland yet." Sholé then repeated, for emphasis, "Yet!"

"But, Dean Sholé, certainly Professor Jill Moreland couldn't have killed Gordon Munson!"

The dean's response, "Of course, she did." came in a staccato burst of words fired at my chest.

Stumbling backward a step, my eyes momentarily examined Sholé's office as if through a wide-angle lens. Spartanly furnished with the minimum

102

of necessary furniture, the room actually was dominated by two walls nearly covered with framed photos, documents, and artwork. My abrupt glance was strongly drawn by the largest item, a movie poster of "Dirty Harry." Clint Eastwood appeared in red and orange hues, coming out of an ink black background, gun drawn. That explained a lot.

As Sholé opened his mouth again, I braced for another blast, however, his next words suggested that his shots were blanks. "Who else would have?"

"Obviously someone did, but I cannot believe that Professor Moreland killed him."

"Grow up!" Sholé gruffly commanded. "Your youth is no excuse for such nonsense."

Though Sholé was old enough to be my father, I didn't enjoy his chastisement. Stepping back and standing tall, I looked down at the man and coldly questioned, "So why are you asking me this?"

"You're buddies with the policeman. You must know something."

"Dean Sholé, I'm hardly buddies with Detective Dafney—"

"See, that's his name, you do know him." Sholé snapped.

Pausing to make sure that he had completed his comment, I went on, "Dafney's wife is a Masterton grad and . . ."

"You were seen talking with the detective at the funeral. You've been to his office twice in the last days." Sholé's breath was coming in short bursts now.

"I found the body, so it is natural that . . ."

"I know you found the body. So what? I want to know if the police are going to arrest Moreland."

"Actually, Dafney suggested that *I* might be the killer."

This actually unfurrowed Sholé's brow, as his eyes popped open. Quickly recovering, he exclaimed, "Balderdash!"

"Of course, I didn't kill him, but with finding the body and all, the returning to the scene of the crime and such, Dafney is keeping me on the hook as a backup suspect."

"Bal-der-dash!

When I didn't respond, but merely lifted my shoulders in agreement, Sholé continued, "What about Moreland? Does he suspect her?"

"Why the obsession with Moreland?"

"Obsession?" This word ricocheted out, though his teeth remained tightly together, bared. "Moreland is the only one with a motive."

"Do you mean the tenure case?"

"Grow *up*! Of *course*, I mean the tenure case. Munson was going to see that she didn't get it. He would have slapped her down hard." Sholé paused to lick his lips, perhaps in vicarious appreciation for this anticipated but not yet consummated slapdown. "We'd have to tolerate her for one more year, but then she'd be gone." Then switching from spectator to willing enforcer, he added, "Go ahead, make my day!"

"Dirty Harry?" I questioned, nodding at Eastwood on the poster.

"Of course. His famous line, 'Go ahead, make my day.'" Munson posed right index finger cocked in front of a closed right eye.

"*Sudden Impact*."

"What?" The dean's eyes returned to glare at me. Angry red splotches were beginning to appear on his neck.

"'Go ahead, make my day' is from the movie *Sudden Impact*."

"Listen here! Moreland's the one who'll get some sudden impact."

"But I understand that Jill Moreland is one of the students' favorite teachers on campus!"

"As a teacher, maybe she's good. As a professor, no, she's gravely lacking."

"She's participated in a variety of campus activities and programs, even attending some alumni events." I tried to detail some of Jill's positive influence on students at Masterton College.

Dean André Sumner Sholé was unaffected by my assertions. "Useful, fine, sure, but of no importance in an assessment of her as a professor." The word "professor" was stated as "pro . . . fess . . . or" with pronounced and slow emphasis, as if I was the class dolt.

Allowing a trace of hostility to enter my tone, I slowly said, "Teaching and campus work don't matter?"

"A professor's standing, or value, if you like, is judged by his or, in this case, her professional scholarship. Moreland's refusal to write a doctoral dissertation makes a mockery of her academic career. Masterton College cannot tolerate such contempt for its academic standards."

Adding another measure of hostility, I countered, "Her ability to teach her students a geographic understanding of an increasingly internationalized world—"

Cutting me off, "Isn't included in the assessment equation. Now listen, I asked you here to inquire about the police and Moreland. Do they suspect her?"

"I really don't know."

"Eliasson, you talked to the policeman at his office and at the funeral. You've been asking all around campus about Moreland. Obviously, you know or want to know about Moreland's guilt. So what is it?"

I tried to replicate Sholé's glare, but doubted that I matched his intensity. "I don't think that Jill Moreland is the murderer. The police haven't named her as a suspect, as far as I know." This was technically true, though I very clearly understood that the police wanted to find Jill Moreland.

With a wave of what seemed to be a combination of disappointment and disdain, the dean dismissed me. Sholé couldn't resist getting in the final word as I was exiting, "Simply because Covington is infatuated with her, doesn't mean that he's correct about her innocence."

As I left, I wondered to myself how it was that the dean knew of my talks with the police. Did he also know of my talk with Professor Covington? Or was it common knowledge that Covington was infatuated with Jill Moreland?

As I reached the outer office door, I turned back to see the dean's door. In my mind's eye, I winked at Eastwood through the wall. *Go ahead, Clint, make my day.*

22

Professor Soren Timicin

Professor Soren Timicin, a tall, husky, bearded man, looked more like a lumberjack than a professor. Even the jeans and checked flannel shirt lent emphasis to this image. In my brief employment at Masterton College, I had learned that Timicin indeed could and would curse like a vulgar outdoorsman, but knew his scholarly discipline of chemistry better than most of his colleagues knew their respective fields.

As introduction I offered yet another rendition of my interest in the Munson case as being a product of alumni inquiries.

"I can see right through you, Mercator," he noted with a chuckle as he invited me into his office. "You're more interested in the welfare of Jill than you are worried about the reputation of the college."

"Admittedly, I am concerned for Jill . I fear her contested tenure case possibly infers that she had a motive for murder, that is, in the eyes of the police."

"Mercator, Moreland is like a knight on the academic chessboard. As a knight, she has the ability to take multiple directions in fulfilling her task, which is teaching. Still in the game of academic power, she's not the most powerful piece in play," Timicin explained metaphorically. Chess appeared to be among the chemistry professor's interests, as suggested by a poster on the office wall depicting Russian world champion Boris Spassky preparing to play Bobby Fischer for the title in 1972. On the poster the bushy-eyebrowed Soviet leader Leonid Brezhnev is asking Spassky, "But Boris, what if he doesn't play 1) P-K4?"

"But," I pondered, "if like a chess master, she has the knowledge, skills, personality, and imagination enough to be the fine teacher that I understand she is, why does it matter if she has power or not?"

"You may be more naive than she is," chortled Timicin, adding a couple profanities as if to spice up his remark before going on. "In academia power is *everything*." Here Timicin threw both arms widely open, causing me to take a step backwards. He didn't seem to notice, but unabated continued with his commentary. "I know this may counter those views you and many people share. However, at university or college, schools of research or teaching, public, private, or church setting, the primary dynamic is power."

"Ability?" I queried.

Timicin's face turned to a smirk as his head bounced from side to side, now also pointing his right index finger at me. "So-called ability may *lead* to power, but on its own, a professor's teaching ability has little value—except for students, naturally. Now it is true, of course, that students are the paying customers of the college, the true focus of the college's mission, its elemental reason for being. Nevertheless, students' wishes, ha ha, students' wishes are viewed as irrelevant dung by the power players of the faculty and administration. The Board and the administration have their own games to play."

"Maybe I am naive," I admitted, "but this makes no sense."

"The answer is mainly sociological and goes back to childhood. Let me take my own application of some of the philosophical thoughts of Robert Nozick and direct them to this situation. So, tell me, when professors were still children, were they good students?"

"I would think so," I ventured cautiously, wondering whether this might be a trick question.

"Yes, most were good students, some even great students. And how were they rewarded at that time?"

With a bit of a pause to think, I suggested, "With good grades?"

"Yes, yes, yes. I expect more from you, Mr. Alumni." Timicin grunted, cursed, and continued. "They always receive compliments and attention from teachers and parents, as well as the admiration and envy of fellow students. This support continues from elementary school through high school. Does it go on after that?"

"I would think so. It goes on long after that," I boldly proclaimed. Not seeking to look timid, I was venturing blindly ahead.

"Certainly so. As the more confident and more verbal students, they can gain the attention and interest of their professors. Good grades, scholarships, internships, and more damn good things follow."

"And graduate school?"

Timicin proceeded, "Oh, yes, the pattern is accentuated. The sense of being an elite is enhanced. Grad students get increased personal attention from their professors, probably particularly so from the Ph.D. advisor. The sense that only the finest of the fine are graduate students is exuded from every aspect of their university experience."

"This is understood to be true, but what does this have to do with power?"

"EVERYTHING!" Timicin bellowed. "From the precocious toddler to the time of being hired as a professor, the typical intellectual has received so much ass wiping accolade, primarily through school, that this brand-spanking-new professor has had no difficulty in believing that he is among the very best and brightest in the country. As such he expects continued rewards. Now though, in the adult world, the primary reward is money. And soon the professor realizes that he's average in terms of salary. This is a dismaying understanding."

"But some professors can make $100,000 a year," I countered.

Timicin responded with a gruff expletive, which he pronounced with slow satisfaction. Although this word in the vernacular can be used as most any part of speech, here I took it to mean something to the negative. My sense proved right, for he continued with a look of disgust.

"Not here at Masterton! But at some institutions, yes, you're correct. However, even that wage pales in comparison with the earnings of corporate officers. Face it, on the pecking scale of wealth and income, the college professor is valued in the middle, certainly not at the extreme top to which the professor is accustomed and not where the professor feels he deserves placement."

"And professors resent this?" I pondered.

Here Timicin made a loud reference to the excrement of male cattle before continuing his soliloquy. "Of course! Dismay and anger are the results. Sometimes this anger is in the form of conscious rage, sometimes it's subconscious fuming. Remember that in all their formative years, their context for status was the school. Within these settings these people consistently received the highest awards. Can you see that after years of being cited as THE VERY BEST, they experience a change in the criteria for judgment? And, the new judgment places professors nowhere near the top. For many this creates the format for anger."

"I had never considered professors in this light. How does the professor adjust to this new standard?"

"With the new knowledge of money being somewhat unreachable, the college professor seeks authority and power. Trying to win on the standard of wealth is like being the one-legged man in an ass-kicking contest." Timicin paused to chuckle at his own joke and catch his breath before continuing. "On one new level this is the very frequent criticism of the scholarship of others. Ostensibly this is done in the name of furthering academic understanding, but it mainly serves to boost the pride and sense of authority of the professor making the criticism."

"But how does this get linked with Jill's, um, I mean, Professor Moreland's case?" I asked.

"Through the second new level. In this case the professor adjusts for the loss of esteem from lack of wealth by increasing his or her own power on campus. This is where Professor Moreland's case arises. On the merits of her teaching performance and her contributions to the campus community, it is inconceivable that she could fail to receive tenure. Nevertheless, given her lack of a dissertation, those wielding power, the freaking power of academic authority, seize their chance to express that power too."

Realization of the implications of this theory was ebbing into my consciousness. I blurted, "Do you mean that the Personnel Committee members voted against tenure, simply because psychologically they seek a chance to exert the authority of their positions?"

"In a nut—" I presume that Timicin intended to say "nutshell" probably followed by a cuss word or two, but he was abruptly interrupted by a shattering crash of his office window. As his window shades started to chime in a cacophonous and atonal mix that could hardly be called musical, we both broke from our stunned immobility to crouch near his desk and bookcases. Jarred by our sudden movement, a two-foot tall stack of papers toppled off the desk, splashing at my feet.

Would another projectile be on its way? As the seconds so slowly ticked by, we came to a shared realization that nothing else appeared to be incoming. Timicin carefully peered past the blinds and remarked with agitation, "No one there." I searched under Timicin's desk and found a slowly rolling baseball to be the offending object. I handed the baseball to him as we both stared at the window, ruined with a large hole slightly off-center and jagged cracks emanating from the hole and winding out to the all edges. A glance at the ball showed an imprint of the words "Masterton College."

Timicin cursed again.

23

The Doctor

On one leg I was the hale and hearty thirty-two-year-old sometimes athlete, on the other a ninety-year-old arthritic. Friday's fall on the basketball court had popped a bursa sac inside my right knee, a problem that I had experienced twice over the years. There was so much water on that knee that I momentarily considered starting an irrigation service for Minnesota farmers. Any touch to the ballooned surface caused tendrils of pain to leap in multiple directions. Mentally I imagined these bolts as lightning strikes meandering across my kneecap and emanating from a single overcharged source.

For a few years I had brought my medical woes to the East Suburban Medical Clinic in the southeastern corner of the Twin Cities. Geographically in efficient proximity to my home and work, the clinic housed a number of doctors, including my personal physician, Dr. Kristine Kelly.

In consulting a physicians' referral service a few years before, I originally chose Dr. Kelly from the large pool of doctors in the metropolitan area. My selection criteria were female, thirty-something, and near my location. I realized that directly seeking a young woman might sound sexist, but I knew my needs. I could tolerate many woes and some pains, but when I was hurting, I didn't need some gruff male doctor to brush off my pain. I wanted compassion and sympathy. I figured that my odds were better with a female doctor. Maybe that was sexist, but so be it.

In the case of Kristine Kelly, I hit the jackpot. She was a skillful diagnostician and a compassionate healer. Additionally, she had a bubbly exuberant personality that almost made me glad to be ill or injured.

Today though, pain was on the agenda. She would be divining for water over the hilly landscape of my knee. Prospects were good for a gusher and prolonged pumping. The worst part was the needle, her divining rod. The painkiller would help some, but I already was visualizing an inch-wide needle attached to a foot long syringe pulling fluid and life out of me. Bravely, I reminded Dr. Kelly that I had a fear—actually, a dread-filled phobic terror—of needles. She noted this sympathetically and added that she was aware of research that demonstrated that those who tended to overfocus on needles or similar fears also seemed to be those who possessed exceptional power of concentration, which generally would be an advantageous skill to hold. I was reflecting on this positive aspect, when she struck.

"Aughh," in a guttural tone was my exceptionally concentrated response.

After what seemed an eternity, she retracted the needle.

"It's over!" I sighed with palpable relief.

Her head bobbed up and with a wry smile she quietly noted, "That was just the anesthetic, Merc."

I sank back to my supine position, as she reached for what I assumed had to be the BIG needle.

As she sank it and began to fill the syringe with the fluid and blood that sat on my kneecap, she noted professionally, "We call this pre-patellar bursitis—a problem of fluid from the irritated bursa on the knee cap. It is sometimes called 'housemaid's knee,' due to washing floors on knees, but I suspect you got this from spills on the basketball court." Observing my total disinterest in both her clinical and colloquial observations, she went on, "Many patients find conversation useful in distracting themselves from the procedure. What have you been up to lately?"

"I'm preoccupied with the, uhhh, Munson murder case at, ohhh, Masterton College, ahhh, south of the Cities." It was difficult to speak a whole sentence without some verbal acknowledgements of the pain.

"Oh, the regent who was killed by a knife from his own collection!" she said with interest as she reached for a new needle and syringe, given that the first vial with full.

"No," I moaned.

"That isn't the case?" She was puzzled, but inserted the needle anyway.

"No. I mean, yes, it is the stabbing case, but I said 'no' because I was hoping you wouldn't stab me again," I explained, with a hint of frustration.

"Ah," she offered, looking at me with those big, sympathetic brown eyes. "But there's still more in there."

Back to practicality.

"I like Jill," I paused as the double l in Jill formed a needle-like pattern in my exceptionally concentrated mind, "Moreland, the potential suspect."

"Umm, hmm," focusing on her work.

I managed to spit out a few other facts of the case, before lapsing into a painful silence, as the doctor probed and squeezed my knee. The light-headed and queasy feelings had set in.

In one moment of lucidity, I realized that as this conversational diversion wasn't nearly succeeding, I needed to attempt another approach. Why not a standard male fallback strategy—the sexual daydream? Recalling that picturing the audience naked was a noted strategy for nervous public speakers, I created my own variation of this ploy. I imagined Doctor Kelly naked. This process was not too difficult, given that she is rather attractive. Still, not wanting to stray too far from the professional realm, I managed to prevent the daydream from progressing beyond a simple image and into visions of action.

"All done," she indicated, surprisingly soon.

Starting to rise, I groaned, and then observed, "Those nipples sure are hard for me."

She gave me the oddest look, and then I realized the Freudian slip I had made, having intended to complain about the needles. Trying to cover up the error, I slipped back on the examination table and tried to mumble any statement quickly, "And thinking about blood isn't breast either."

I hoped that the subsequent two minutes of feigned semi-consciousness were enough to direct attention away from my gaffes.

In any case, after getting me to a sitting position and a cleared head, Dr. Kelly seemed to be fine.

"This case you're working on. Was the deceased struck directly in the heart? Was one of the arteries severed?"

"Oh, Doc, don't get me fainting again."

"Okay," she chuckled, "I'm curious since his company provides some of the products for the clinic."

"Doctor, you may know a patella from a prostate, but you don't know a company from a charity." I paused, and then added, "Sorry, but I'm a little testy after having my knee probed for two hours."

"It was ten minutes!" she contended, with precisely the right hint of exasperation to suggest that she liked my teasing.

"Doc Kelly, you're my favorite physician, but Munson's company was Minnesota Mission, a noted charity. It doesn't sell products."

"Merc, flattery will get you nowhere. I'm your only physician. But a charity? Mr. Franklin said that we bought products from Munson's company."

My interest was piqued. "Who is Mr. Franklin, and what does he do, besides smile on the fifty dollar bill?"

"*Bill* Franklin is the clinic's administrator, but actually he's so tight that most everyone calls him 'One Dollar Bill.'"

I pulled a crisp Washington from my wallet and handed it to her with a "Show the way."

24
Financial Aid

Although this week was the break between the Interim or "J term" and the spring semester, some students remained on campus. In particular for me, a few of my student workers stayed on so that they could put in some hours making calls to alumni. Naturally, these calls were placed in conjunction with the college's development program seeking donations.

In this realm of alumni and development money, there are a variety of strategies for maximizing donations. One approach was having students call their own hometowns. Coed Janie Everest was from Edina, a prosperous Twin Cities suburb. I assigned her to call alumni currently residing in Edina. A similar approach was based on the students' academic majors. Chemistry students call alumni who were professional chemists. My predecessor, Trentville Rebuchierre, the previous alumni director, had taken such notions so far as to have students call alums who shared a first name. Student Julie Warnfield told me that forty percent of her calls were to women named Julie. She also told me that Rebuchierre claimed that the strategy worked best for alumni named Bert, though she never could get Rebuchierre to show her confirming data. One day I overheard this Julie telling another student worker that she questioned whether Trentville Rebuchierre had ever applied the name strategy to his own calls.

My statistical analysis of the data I inherited showed that all three approaches were somewhat successful, though the "name game" strategy produced the smallest gains above random calling patterns. Furthermore, Janie Everest reported that students felt embarrassed using the name gimmick. Many student workers already felt shy, intimidated, or nervous making these calls. When I succeeded Trentville Rebuchierre and inherited his office, I discovered a copy of a dissertation written by Denton Skolx for a Ph.D. in Psychology, a dissertation entitled "Measuring the Neuropsychological Approach to the 'Name Game' Strategy of College Development Staffs: Does 'Your Name Is Bert Too!' Garner More Dollars?"

This morning's meeting with the student workers outlined the current call policies and strategies. The meeting took longer than I expected. Upper classman Frank Jeffries was a talkative fellow and easily went off on tangents. I tried politely to steer him back to business, but even so, the numerous digressions consumed minutes. As a techie, Franklin Spaeth communicated better online than in person. It took more time than I wanted in order to extract clear information from him. At least Janie Everest was concise and helpful in her comments, but she did have a number of student concerns to address. Also, several times Janie or I said, "Frank." At first both Franks always answered, but later after some confusion over this, neither would answer but would sheepishly look around for clarification.

Thus, it was later still when I got a chance to drop by treasurer Sebastien Kroon's office. He confirmed what I had learned at the clinic. While Gordon Munson was the director of the charity Minnesota Mission, he also was president of a corporation known as Minnesota Academic Supply, or MAS, which, in spite of its name, sold office supplies both to colleges and to businesses. Kroon indicated that Masterton College was a regular purchaser of a variety of products from Munson's company. Almost as an aside, he shared that he thought Munson's prices were higher than those at national office supply stores. When pressed on this point, Kroon simply expressed that the college liked to support Minnesota businesses. Upon my request, he provided me with a list of the college's annual purchases from Minnesota Academic Supply.

Stepping out of Kroon's office with this list in hand, I noticed Financial Aid director Roger Black. Waving him over, we stepped into his office.

"Roger, this Munson murder has been a hot topic. You know, I didn't realize that Munson had a business too. I only knew about the charity, scholarships, and such."

"Oh, yes, Munson had a number of irons in the fire, with Minnesota Academic Supply being his largest business venture."

"I was talking to Sebastien about the college's purchases from MAS."

"A bunch of stuff, I'm sure."

"And then the charity directed some scholarships here."

"Naturally."

"Could I see the magnitude of these scholarships? Could you give me a list of scholarship dollars each academic year from Minnesota Mission?

"Um, okay."

So, Roger Black got me a list of figures for annual scholarships granted by Minnesota Mission to Masterton students in the 1990s. Each year showed a roughly similar figure, except for academic year 1993-1994 which showed a figure of zero.

"Ouch," I commented, pointing to the year and dollar amount, "nothing in ninety-three/ninety-four."

"Yes, we were a little shocked that year."

Since I still had Kroon's expenditure sheet in my hand, I spread it out for a quick review. "There's also a zero here, but for ninety-two/ninety-three."

"Interesting coincidence, Mercator, but they don't quite match."

"No, Roger, they do match. When the college stopping buying Munson's products, then the next year Munson's charity gave our students zilch."

"You mean that Munson cut off his scholarships *because* we were no longer purchasing from his supply company?"

"Looks like, though these two documents don't exactly prove that."

"Mercator, I have a friend in Financial Aid at Augsburg College. I'll mention this to him and see what he knows."

If such a link existed between sales and scholarships, if Munson was withholding scholarship moneys except if the college purchased his office products even though they were higher in cost, it appeared to me to be unethical. Perhaps it might even be illegal. Would that be enough motive for murder?

25

Professor Monroe Wilder

Math professor Monroe Wilder's office reminded me of a cave. With only two of four fluorescent tubes working in the ceiling lights and his desk lamp partially hidden behind a stack of books, the room was dimly lit. It was difficult to see what was in the room, partly due to the limited light and partly due to the clutter. Every flat surface was the base of a different, impossible tower of books, journals, and papers. Bookshelves comprised much of the walls, but other shorter shelves had been added to the room, jutting out at acute angles from the fixed wall units. On top of these shorter shelves were more books, none matched evenly with the one below it, so that each stack was a unique stalagmite of height, width, and multiple angled edges. Only portions of the walls were visible between built-in shelves and around the various piles. At one time in a less cluttered era, Wilder had hung a movie poster, but only a portion of Jack Lemmon in drag was currently visible. Similarly, there were framed diplomas, also partially blocked from view. A clock took another square of wall, but it had stopped at 7:15. Spelunking my way through the narrow passageway left in the office, I found Wilder seated behind his desk. The only other chair was covered with four textbooks and an unwieldy pile of tests. I stood.

"Alumni director. I've heard that you've been asking questions about Jill Moreland and the Munson murder. Why? What's your angle?"

"Well, I've received a number of phone calls from alumni worried about the college getting negative publicity. But why do you say Jill Moreland?"

"It seems that you and the police seem to think that she might be guilty."

"No, no." I blurted. I would have preferred to have made a more convincing affirmation for Jill, but that's what came out.

"No? So why are you asking around then, alumni man?"

"Okay, I acknowledge I've discussed her situation. So what? Do you think she's guilty? I did hear that you opposed her case for tenure."

"Guilty? Probably. I don't know the evidence. I was at the theater myself," Wilder handed an oversized, torn ticket stub to me. Apparently he sat in Row 4 to see *Noises Off* starring Aimee Forbes at a prominent Twin Cities theater at 7:00 p.m. on the night of the murder.

"Any good?"

"I'm not much for theater, but compelling drama, you know."

"And, Professor, what about Moreland's tenure case?"

"Obviously I opposed granting her tenure, since she doesn't have a Ph.D. In fact, she arrogantly told the college that she wouldn't write a dissertation, given that she already had become a fine professor."

"Professor Wilder, I spoke to Moreland about that. She didn't seem arrogant. She simply contended that writing an esoteric tome wouldn't help her be a better teacher of undergraduate students at Masterton."

"That's crap. The Ph.D. is the gold standard of academia. Any professor without it is inherently second rate."

"So Moreland is a second-rate professor? That's not what her students say."

"Students know crap. You can't measure a professor's value in terms of student satisfaction. Not at all!"

"Students are the customers, aren't they?" I proposed.

"That like asking a child if Pop Tarts taste good. The child's parent knows that caviar and truffles are best."

"So Jill Moreland is a Pop Tart, and you're caviar?"

"She's a tart anyway," he said with a smirk. "In contrast, I have a Ph.D. from one of the top western math programs. I have published research. Here," he said, flipping a magazine out of a pile from the desk corner to my right.

Catching the *Western Journal of Mathematics*, I read aloud, "'Critiquing Zermelo's use of dynamical systems and the Poincare recurrence theorem' by Monroe Wilder. Impressive. What do your students think of it?"

Looking at me as if I had suggested eating caviar off of a Pop Tart, Wilder snorted, "Students! Are you nuts? My students can't comprehend this high-level stuff. Your question is the reason why I have this on my desk." Wilder angled a left index finger toward a framed photo standing on his desk.

Oddly, the photo seemed to be the only unobstructed image in the room. At first I thought it was one of the trendy motivational photos that in various sizes often adorn walls or stand on desks in the corporate world. However, the image displayed many light bulbs resting on a gleaming black surface. The title read "Cluelessness" with the caption "There are no stupid questions, but there are a *lot* of inquisitive idiots." Motivational or demotivational?

"Then, Professor Wilder, how does this research help your students?"

Evidently I was repeating my suggestion about caviar and Pop Tarts, for Wilder's stare only intensified. "Students benefit *directly* from their association with me. Students have a big edge when they can tell a graduate school admissions committee or prospective employers that they have studied under Monroe Wilder."

Hadn't he accused Jill Moreland of being arrogant? Apparently, she was just in training compared to his level. "So students would come to Masterton College specifically to take classes from you and other Ph.D. professors?"

"Damn right." The stare had ceased, and a self-satisfied Wilder apparently felt that I now comprehended his message.

"Professors who don't have a Ph.D., the so-called union card, don't have that drawing power; they don't convey that direct advantage?"

Beaming, Wilder ended the interview, "Now you've got it."

26

Professor Goren Eidechse

ello, Goren," I offered, choosing the familiar approach on Wednesday morning, for I had met this professor at two separate college functions. To be safe I added, "Mercator Eliasson, alumni director."

"Yes, yes," replied Goren Eidechse—associate professor of Philosophy, while peering at me with rapidly blinking eyes.

I wondered how it was that his eyes—what were they, green?—were adjusting to some new light source, but then I seemed to recall that he had been blinking the other two occasions of our limited acquaintance. Anyway, I commented invitingly, "Quite a time for the college," as I made my way past the threshold and into his office.

"What's that?" The blinking eyes continued, now with a puzzled expression added to the facial display.

"The Munson murder has been in the news. I've even received calls about it. What's your read on the situation?"

More blinking, this time coupled with licking his lips. An image was pushing its way to the forefront of my brain—a lizard? a frog? a toad? As Eidechse began to speak rapidly, I lost the image as I tried to listen.

"Philosophically, of course, I cannot justify homicide (lick). Nevertheless, Munson's own personal charm (blink) mixed with deceit covered by business avarice (lick) often engendered (lick, lick), shall we say, antagonistic engagements."

"What?" Now I was blinking, having not caught all the words, between the blinks and licks.

"In layman's terms, he had it coming."

"I trust or at least hope that those faults didn't extend to his leadership on the Board of Regents," I said, hoping that Eidechse would take the bait and talk about the murder case.

Tongue almost snapping now, the professor went on, "Munson! (blink, lick). It's strange, you know. For being so charming on the personal level, my goodness but he was tremendous with the ladies (blink), at the business level Munson raised the standard of antagonism (lick) and controversy (blink) on campus to a new height. He treated his authority (blink) as a mandate to micromanage (lick, lick) nearly every facet of college activity, similar to the way he ran his company (simultaneous blink and lick—would that be a blick?))."

"Company? Yes, I now understand that in addition to the charity, he ran a few business ventures."

(Blink, lick, bulge—now the eyes seemed to be popping outward too) "A charity, yes, but with a profitable (blink) company intertwined with it."

As I was beginning to feel a bit dizzy from these quirky mannerisms, a bell rang in the corridor. With a sudden jerk of his head, Professor Eidechse became rigid in his chair. At that instant, an image came to mind of a lizard perched on a small rock as lake water lapped on its edge. Eidechse leapt upward, snapped a folder and textbook off a shelf, as quickly as a lizard used its tongue to snap up an unsuspecting insect. He then sprang out the office door, while I imagined a lizard squirting between a gap among rocks on the shore. As this mental imagery dominated my thinking, out of nowhere the lizard shrieked as a metal arrow thudded through its body, leaving it impaled on the hard soil.

After a moment I realized that the shriek and thud seemed particularly loud and not at all a part of my brief daydream. When I looked out to the corridor through the slowly closing office door, Professor Eidechse lay face down on the floor. Blood oozed from his head. I didn't recall actually hearing a shot, but somehow Eidechse was dead.

As I stared in shock, the body stirred. I had viewed two dead men within ten days. Of course, Munson had been dead for some hours before I encountered his corpse. This happened only seconds before. Wait! Did newly dead bodies move? Like a headless chicken? A groan pulled me from my trance. Eidechse was alive and needed help.

As I stepped out of the doorway to aid him, my foot slipped. Sliding, I tried to retain my balance, eventually falling to one knee—the sore one, of course. While pain radiated throughout my knee and up into my body, I lurched to his side. Eidechse grunted an acknowledgement of my presence and tried to stand. Bracing himself on a three-foot-long wooden planter, the bloodied professor pushed toward his feet only to have the planter slide away from him. With a splat he crashed again to the floor, the point of his chin bearing the brunt of the blow. Blood spurted anew and, as I watched, floated on an oily surface. Looking down at the oil soaking into my pants on my knee, I knelt and drew an index finger across the floor. Vegetable oil—canola, safflower, not olive. Blood and oil smeared now on Eidechse's face as he tried to rise once again. Drops of blood dribbled across onto his button-down shirt, creating a post-modernistic palette of oil and red.

By now others had gathered around the wounded professor. I picked out student Bart Colson, his father Ernie was a sixty-two alum, and directed him to request assistance via the division office down the hall. Betsy Collier, a slight blonde sophomore, stood gawking along with a handsome young man whom I did not recognize. Professor Mordecai Saunders offered his help, and together we got Eidechse to a sitting position. Although he asserted that he was quite fine, even in this sitting position his speech was slurred and his eyes glazed. We kept him seated until the campus police arrived. Led by Rich Sawyer, an ex-cop now drawing a police pension while coordinating campus security as a bonus, they efficiently provided first aid. As a junior officer left with Eidechse to drive to an urgent care clinic to check for a concussion, Sawyer strode to my side.

"Mercator, are you okay?"

"Oh yes, fine—though somewhat shocked to find Professor Eidechse on the floor."

"You were the first to find him?"

"I was with him," I started and proceeded to explain the situation to him. Sawyer appeared particularly interested in any inferences I could draw regarding who could have spilled the oil on the hall floor. It hadn't been there when I entered the office, and I had to admit that I had heard nothing in the hall during my interview with Professor Eidechse and could hazard no guesses as to the professor's enemies.

Later two things struck me as curious. First, why the reptilian instinctive response to stimulus (the bell ringing) by Professor Eidechse? He was in his office doing paperwork and preparing for the spring semester. He had no classes that day, for Wednesday was part of the interim break. Apparently he fit the absentminded professor role quite accurately. Or had my inquiries made him so uncomfortable that his subconscious led him to bolt unnecessarily out of his office at the first stimulus? Second, I had to consider the possibility that the hazard had been left for me. Was someone trying to send me a message?

27

Minnesota Mission

*T*he Minnesota Mission charity headquarters were located in the Gustavson Office Building in St. Paul. Not in the downtown center of expensive rental properties, this three-story building stood next to a warehouse, near a strip mall of five stores, and adjacent to similar office buildings, warehouses, plus one light manufacturing center.

My arrival at 4:30 Wednesday afternoon neared the end of the business day. One of the hazards, yet common elements, of winter life in Minnesota is the pothole. This is so completely understood that almost every Minnesotan has heard the joke that in Minnesota there are only two seasons—winter and road repair. Snow and ice wreak havoc on even the best roads in Minnesota. Here next to the Gustavson Office Building a section of road was cordoned off, due to severe road damage. This also restricted parking so much so that I had to park around on the other side of the block, and then walk back to the front door of the Gustavson Office Building.

Noting that Minnesota Mission occupied Room 312 according to the posted sign in the building lobby, I chose to take the walk up instead of waiting for the elevator. I mentally applauded my decision to burn a few calories, though in truth my choice was largely determined by my aversion to idle waiting.

As I opened the heavy metal door that swung smoothly on oiled hinges, two voices wafted down the stairwell.

". . . academic supply orders are up. They still like our scholarships," said a low male voice.

"Yes. Gordon had been concerned about meeting production goals for both," responded a dour female voice.

The click of a door's latch was repeated seconds later, and the voices disappeared. Throughout my college years, I often climbed stairs two steps at a time. Today I was content to ascend one by one at a brisk pace. Exiting from the third-floor platform, I reached a deserted hallway. Simply following signs and arrows, in a minute I stood outside the charity's door.

Emblazoned on a polished brass placard were the black scripted words—Minnesota Mission. I simply pushed open the door and entered. The reception area of Minnesota Mission wasn't spartan, but did convey a sense of fiscal conservatism, perhaps done intentionally to give visitors an understanding that contributions to the charity were not diverted to administrative costs, but indeed were used for philanthropy.

"Hello, sir. My name is Megan. How may I help you?" The receptionist, Megan Orlov, according to the nameplate on her desk, also appeared to be a selection consciously made to give a good first impression. Twenty something and pretty enough to be included in Pete Putnam's ten percent, Megan was sedately dressed in a light gray blouse and silk blue jacket. Her blonde hair looked like it could tumble to luxuriant length, but was pulled into a tight bun. I found myself mentally wondering what she would look like at a sports bar or a backyard barbeque.

"Hello, Megan. I'm from Masterton College. I have a few questions about your scholarship program."

"Oh, well. Of course. Normally I'd refer you to Gordon Munson, but, obviously, you know, you know that, um, that he, he is dead."

Noticing that the lights were beginning to glisten more and more in her eyes, I attempted to sound apologetic. Sighing with a sympathetic, "I know," I continued, "I regret having to interrupt you."

"I'm so sorry, mister. It's still difficult to face the fact that he's gone. We're all taking it so hard. Gosh, who could have done it?"

Shaking my head in shared dismay as I looked into her disheartened face, I went on, "I know. I mean, I don't know who killed him, but I understand that it must be challenging to continue at work without the boss. I hate to trouble you, but it's important."

"Lyn's still here. Maybe she can help you."

"Lyn?"

126

"Yes, Lyn King is, or, oh dear, *was* Gordon's, um, Mr. Munson's administrative assistant. She's been here the longest now, about twenty years. You'd think that having been with him so long, she'd take his murder the hardest, but she's such a . . ." now looking furtively in both directions and leaning forward, with a fluttering of the proper gray blouse, "She's so uptight all the time, but she seems to be taking his death the best of anyone."

Megan took me down the office hallway, knocking on one of the first doors. Entering, she announced my presence and line of inquiry. As she left me with a nod, I took her place in the doorway.

Seated behind a computer monitor was the mousy woman from the cemetery. That is, Lyn W. King, according to a nameplate on the desk, was the woman I had seen at Munson's interment as well as at the reception that followed. Though she too was dressed in a conservative manner, there was no need to obscure beauty as Megan had done. Lyn King was plain. Even with well-applied makeup, she would not even be pretty. She didn't even make this effort. As she rose to shake my hand, I noticed her amorphous form, female, yet somehow almost neuter.

My college roommate, Fritz Riley, once told me that the sexiest women in *Playboy* magazine were the ones who were smiling. As I said hello to Lyn King, I knew that she would not be pretty even if she smiled. Which she didn't. "So. What is it?"

As she spoke, I recognized her dour voice as the one from the stairwell minutes earlier. King's office was somewhat dour too. A simple clock and calendar with a pale desert scene adorned the wall behind her desk. A wall of shelved files stood to my right. I noted the only bright element of the room, a movie poster of *The Seven Year Itch* with its famous portrait of Marilyn Monroe with white skirt flaring high on her legs over a street vent. On her desk stood a framed photograph, showing Gordon Munson in the foreground, his posture expressing bold confidence as his faced the camera. In the background the whirling blades of a helicopter were suspended in time by the camera. Descending out of the helicopter was President Bill Clinton.

"I'm sorry to trouble you, but I'm from Masterton College and have some questions about Minnesota Mission's scholarship program."

"Yes."

"I know this is a difficult time with Gordon Munson's murder and all."

"Yes." No shimmering eyes, no fluttering voice from Lyn King. Apparently Megan was right about managing the loss well.

"Ms. King," glancing at her unadorned ring finger, "it is Ms. King?"

"Yes." The slightest sigh of impatience breathed past her lips.

"Could you review or highlight for me the scope of Minnesota Mission's scholarship program?"

Frowning slightly as if to imply that I should know this information already, Lyn King explained that Minnesota Mission had a number of charitable avenues, or, as they liked to call them, "missions," and that college scholarship funding was one of these categories. For some time now they annually had given out dozens of scholarships, each at least worth $10,000.

"So, that's really a remarkable sum in scholarship funds?" I mentally worked on the math.

"Yes," Ms. King continued her terse theme.

"Do donors give designated funds to Minnesota Mission for these scholarships or do these funds come from the charity's general funds?"

"Yes and yes."

"How does Minnesota Mission determine the winners of these scholarships?" This was a question that she could not answer with the word "yes."

Frowning slightly she did answer. "We have an elaborate evaluation protocol used by a committee of professors at a set of colleges and universities in Minnesota. They rank the students' applications according to the protocol and then submit their findings to Gordon Munson, who made the final selections."

"Do winning students have to be attending a Minnesota college or university?"

"Yes."

"How does an individual college's purchase of products from Minnesota Academic Supply affect the probability of that college's students getting scholarships from Minnesota Mission?"

With the mention of Minnesota Academic Supply, Ms. King's facial expression changed from that of routine boredom to attentive focus.

"What?"

"It seems that Minnesota Academic Supply—"

"Let me assure you that there's no relationship between Minnesota Academic Supply and these scholarships."

"But," I clarified, "Gordon Munson owned the company and directed the charity."

"Of course, he did. Additionally, I myself have worked with him at both entities. However, there's no corporate connection between the two."

"I see. But don't colleges and universities purchase products from Minnesota Academic Supply?"

"Minnesota Academic Supply is pleased to have numerous educational institutions as customers. That's what the corporation does."

I continued to press the point. "So, wouldn't colleges that make major purchases from the company also receive major funding in scholarships from the charity?"

"There's an obvious relationship. It's common sense. The University of Minnesota has a huge population of students. This magnitude suggests that it'll also have many students apply for our scholarships. Similarly, its magnitude creates a sizeable demand for our products."

"I find it curious that when Masterton College chose another supplier, the supply of scholarships from Minnesota Mission evaporated."

"Purely coincidental, I assure you."

"And when the college returned to the higher-priced products of Minnesota Academic Supply, the supply of scholarships shot up."

"Mr. Samford." She queried sternly, "It is Mr. Samford, isn't it?"

"No, actually my name is Mercator Eliasson."

"Oh, I assumed you were the new assistant to the Financial Aid director Roger Black. You are in Financial Aid, then?"

"Well, no. I'm the alumni director."

Upon hearing this clarification, Ms. King abruptly rose from her chair. Although her attire was tidy and clean, everything fit quite loosely, serving to mask her form.

"Hmph, I don't see your interest then. It is time to close the office. If you have any more questions, please have Roger Black make the inquiries."

Unceremoniously I was shown the door.

28

Blue Chevy

I stepped out of the office building, the lock clicking behind me. Knowing that my car was parked all the way around the block, I walked briskly, my mind trying to process the information that Munson not only ran both a charity and a profitable business, but apparently with some very questionable overlap. Could the particulars of this overlap be illegal? Lyn King seemed reluctant to discuss the issue.

A harsh sound my mind identified as barking from down the street was immediately followed by a chipping of several pieces of the brick wall next to me and by a single burning pain in my right bicep. Angrily looking around, my glance took in a mostly empty street with no one on the sidewalks and only a scattering of a few parked cars, the closest being a dark vehicle across the street some yards back, now idling even in front of the office door behind me. As I stared toward the sapphire-colored car, the muzzle of a shotgun was thrust outward from the driver's window. And towards me! One step back toward the office door was all I took. Then I realized how fruitless it was to move closer to a locked door that offered no santuary and nearer the shotgun at the same time. Reverse pivoting, I ran away from the car. This maneuver, though not actually intended as a feint, caused the next blast of the shotgun to miss. I heard the percussion of shotgun pellets clattering off the brick façade, but they missed me.

With blood now oozing down my arm, I sprinted ahead. Putting the pain aside, I sought to focus on the location of my car, one block to the left. Reacting to an immediate opportunity, I spun left into an alleyway. After dashing down the alley some twenty yards, to my astonishment I came to the realization that this passage did not cut all the way across the block, instead reached only to the rear of buildings that must face the next street. My shoes scuffed on the rough pavement of the back street, as I came to an abrupt halt. Was this a complete dead end? Or in the shadows ahead was there a narrow egress branching off to the side? I sure hoped so.

Naturally, the alley was considerably darker than the avenue where pools of white light shone from street lamps, creating overlapping ellipses on both the sidewalk and the street. With Minneapolis geographically located at about forty-five degrees north latitude, the sun would be setting in mere minutes. The twilight already had turned the alley into multi-shaded grays. Disadvantageously for me, two single light bulbs provided the only additional illumination of the alley, one white bulb and the other yellow, both next to single closed doorways.

Catching my breath, my body quivered as a bolt of adrenaline pulsed through my bloodstream. The narrowness of the alley prevented me from seeing whether or not a slim passageway might fork away in the dimness ahead.

Checking my fears, I decided to return to the street, but after only two strides, I changed my mind as the dark-blue car turned into the alley. The driver of the car and I, too, realized that I might be trapped. The vehicle lurched forward. I ran farther down the passage. Almost immediately I knew I'd never reach a possible exit before the car would overtake me.

In life there are those occasional moments of inspiration, or epiphany. Sometimes these moments are profound and life changing. My own last such moment had come on the basketball court at the Ramsey Athletic Club. I took a pass in the low post, the basket behind me and to my left. With the defender pressing behind me, I simply took the ball, switched it to my left hand, and tossed it blindly over my head. I didn't even look to see the result. I knew it would be good.

This moment was much more important, for its outcome was not a basketball score, but my life. With no hesitation, I spun around and bounded directly toward the onrushing car. Though I'd never seen such a tactic and I was putting myself ever closer to death, my instincts compelled me onward.

131

The blazing headlights threw the alleyway into starker black and white. The roar of the engine competed with the pounding of my heart. As the automobile closed, I leapt. My leap was a combination of track styles from my high school training. Beginning with the high hurdles, my front foot rose above the fender to land on the front edge of the hood. Finishing with the triple jump, I pushed off the hood, landing again with one foot, but now on the linear intersection of the roof and windshield. I pushed off again in a final frenetic lean, arms and legs swinging for the last bit of length. I landed on the pavement with few inches to spare past the rear bumper. This third leap of my triple jump brought an awkward gymnastic landing—I'd surely lose points with the judges—as I banged my injured right knee on the harsh asphalt.

Still, I maintained my momentum toward the alley's outlet, lurching on, trying to ignore the pain in my arm that now competed with spider web of hurt in my knee. Glancing over my shoulder as I ran, I saw the red burn of taillights flaring with the car's brakes. Letters and numbers flashed briefly, but the sudden flash of the shotgun muzzle put my focus entirely on running. Bursting out of the alley, I spun left.

Undoubtedly slowed by the difficulty of driving fast in reverse, the car didn't appear so quickly. I had reached the next corner and turned left again, before I heard the rumble of an engine and the screech of brakes in the background. Thankfully, there were people on this street. Moving toward them, I looked back in time to see the blue Chevy hover for a moment at the intersection, then charge straight ahead, leaving me safe. I hoped that my recollection would help Detective Dafney find the shooter.

A young man was walking up to the Speed Copy Center, when I dashed around the corner. Noting my clear distress plus the bloody arm of my jacket, he offered help and ran into the store to call the police.

Officers arrived quickly to take my story. They also drove me to a convenient care clinic where my gunshot wound was treated. From there I phoned Detective Dafney, telling him to find the shooter in a car with a Utah license plate 3IH159S. Sadly, I couldn't offer a description of the gunman, for in the alley I'd been blinded by the headlights, and every other opportunity to see the driver had found me totally focused on the barrel of the shotgun.

29

Theo T. Sar

I drove back to Masterton College with my arm in a sling. Even more so now I found myself determined to solve this crime. I wanted to interview others who could tell me about Jill Moreland. Given the location of the visitor parking spaces near the science building, I chose to start with Theo T. Sar, who as the head of Information Technology (IT), had his office and lab there.

Sar greeted me with surprising exuberance, but explained this by noting that he had heard of my activity on campus and was eager to help Jill.

"She's one of the most eager computer users among the faculty. She regularly has her students doing computer projects. She even has her own web page. It's so great what she's doing with computers here. AND, she's a Mac user!"

He continued, "You have a computer in your office. Remind me. What do you have?"

"I use a Mac—"

He cut me off with, "Excellent. A man after my own heart. As head of IT here, I have to put up with the many jackass Windoze machines here, but I've managed to expand the Macintosh population. I'm trying to breed the beauties!"

"Yes, I really do prefer the Macintosh myself."

It wasn't difficult to figure out Theo's computer preferences. A four-foot-by-two-foot nylon banner lightly fluttered above a workbench. The banner featured the familiar Apple Computer logo apple, in this case colored in rainbow stripes. Underneath this banner, Sar had positioned a small flag, held by a dowel, with white, blue and red horizontal stripes.

It was hard to get in my opinion, for he quickly continued, "You look like a man of the world, Eliasson."

"With a name like Mercator, yeah, I try to be worldly."

Laughing loudly, Theo clearly thought I was hilarious. Pity my world had gotten a little too up close and personal for me to appreciate my own humor.

"You're all right," he said. "I like that. I'll tell you my secret then. Working with computers is like sex. The platform makes a difference though. Working with Macs is like a satyr having sex with virgins—it's always new and exciting, and you'd do it for free. Working with Wintel machines is like a gigolo screwing butch lesbians—you're paid to do it, but it ain't no fun!" Sar, I guess I'm his Mac friend now, laughed uproariously at his own joke, slapping my shoulder in delight.

Knowing my own preference for Macs, I allowed him his moment. Once he had settled himself, I probed onward, "I need to learn a bit about your e-mail system. One of the bits of evidence against Jill Moreland is an e-mail from Gordon Munson."

His face dropped, "Jill got an e-mail from him?"

"Yes, on the evening of his death."

"Oh, no! Then I must have given it to the police. I didn't know!"

"Theo, relax! It isn't your fault. The police would have gotten hold of it one way or another. But I need to know what was in it. Tell me about it."

"Munson did have a college e-mail account. He requested it a couple of years ago, when he became chair of the Board of Regents. He wanted to receive campus-wide e-mails and to be able to send e-mail easily to individuals on campus."

"But couldn't he do that with any commercial e-mail system—America Online or some other provider?" I asked.

"Sure, but Munson apparently wanted to save money. Our setup was free. With a modem, he could dial into our local number and then access our e-mail system pretty much any time he wanted. He was a fairly regular user of the system. The police had me check our records to find out when he'd been logged on. I found out he'd been online in the late afternoon and then again briefly after seven o'clock on the evening of his death. Police officers asked me for all e-mails that he had sent or received that day. I accessed the list and simply printed them out. I guess I was stressed out enough about having the police in here that I didn't bother to examine the names closely or to read the messages. Jill Moreland got one?"

"Yes, the police indicated that she received an e-mail about Munson's decision to vote against her in the tenure fight. The police are considering that a possible motive for murder. But, Jill told me the email *supported* her case."

Sar was dismayed at this news. I had to settle him down again about giving information to the police, even going so far as reminding him that not cooperating would have put him in legal jeopardy. Finally, he agreed to provide me with copies of these same e-mails. It turned out that there were seven in-coming e-mails as well as three messages Munson had sent out. The damning message looked like this:

To: Jill Moreland (moreland@inst.masterton.edu)
From: Gordon Munson (hgmunson@inst.masterton.edu)
Date: 24 January 1998 - 19:12
Re: Tenure

Jill,

It is with regret that I inform you that I cannot support you for tenure at Masterton College. Although I have spent considerable time evaluating your case, I have concluded that granting tenure here without the Ph.D. would be a mockery of the college's standards. I find it difficult to sit at home and send you this e-mail, but I decided that you deserve to know.

Gordon Munson

Gordon Munson
President, Board of Regents of Masterton College
President, Minnesota Mission

I read through it twice even though it seemed clear enough on the first read. Having the hard copy in my hands somehow made it more damning. I was puzzled.

"How could Jill Moreland read this as an endorsement of granting her tenure? It states the exact opposite very clearly."

"Wow, it's pretty straightforward, isn't it?"

"Why would Munson sign his name twice?" I asked Theo, showing him the document.

"Oh, that final segment is the computer signature. Users define this option and then it's included at the end of every message."

So why would he sign his name above it? He didn't do that on these other messages."

"Probably he simply forgot. People do different things. Some will sign off with a first name or an initial before the computer signature. There's even a librarian here, you know, when he sends me an email message, he signs it as "Edison" or "Tesla" or "Graham Bell" before the computer finishes it off with Charles Worthington, Reference Librarian.

"Again, I don't understand why Jill Moreland would think she got a seemingly optimistic message from Munson when she logged on at about 6:30 that evening, yet not account for this message."

Theo was puzzled too. "Could Jill have received two messages from Munson?"

"Two? I understood from Jill that she read a message around 6:30 p.m."

"This one is time stamped for 7:12 p.m."

"I don't know everything there is to know about e-mail," I said, "but I don't get how Jill could claim to have read a now-missing message at about 6:30 and then not the 7:12 message."

"I'm looking in Munson's sent mail file, but there's no record of such a message having been sent."

"What about in Jill Moreland's in-box?"

With a few adept clicks of the mouse, Sar noted no presence of that file in Moreland's account. A further check in the college's email archiving area also showed no such file.

"So, does the system show whether or not the message is new or has been read."

"As a superuser, I've opened her account."

"And so, superman?"

"Just superuser, thanks."

"Did she read the negative message?" I persisted.

After carefully scrolling along, he paused, apparently finding what he wanted. "The message was opened," he said dolefully.

"And read?"

"Of course . . . well, I can't tell if she read it, but the email was opened."

"Can you tell when it was opened?"

"Yes, it says 7:13 p.m."

Damning. Jill Moreland told me that she read a positive message at about 6:30 p.m., but there was no such message in the system. Instead a damning message opened at 7:13 p.m. provided the motivation and time frame for Jill to go to Munson's house, confront him, and then in anger kill him.

30

Morris Townsend

After my conversation with Theo T. Sar, I chose to return to the Administration Building. I knew that Admissions Director Morris Townsend would be finishing an interview with a prospective student and accompanying parents.

In fact, as I approached the administrative building, the balding Townsend was outside shaking hands with a tall, balding dad as the prospective student and mom stood nearby. With a very slight build and a unisex haircut that covered the ears but not the shirt collar, the student had one hand on the mom's coat, giving me the impression of an urge to depart. As I approached I realized that I could not tell the gender of the student. With the slim physique covered by a down jacket, a female chest wasn't apparent but could not be ruled out. The youth had no facial hair, but this was certainly true for some teenage males. When I was within five yards of the group, the family broke away, and Townsend called out, "We hope to see you here next fall, Morgan." Unfortunately, with "Morgan" being an epicene name, I still could not determine the youth's gender.

Before I could inquire, Townsend rubbed his smooth cranium and called out, "Hello, Mercator. I've got that right this time," grinning broadly at his memory for my name. Continuing on, he noted, "Brisk out here without a hat. I've got no insulation up top, as everyone can see," again running a hand over his head.

"Say, I did want a word with you, Morris."

"Sure, sure. Let's go inside. Okay?"

Although it took only a couple minutes to reach Townsend's office, I tried to focus my thoughts.

"Morris, I've been hearing a lot about the Munson murder case. Finding the body, hearing from alumni, you know."

"Oh yes! You found the corpse, didn't you? Was it grotesque?"

"Unpleasant anyway. But, one element has piqued my curiosity."

"What's that? Is it something that I can clarify for you? Is that why you're here? What's with the arm?"

I looked down at my arm in a sling and chose not to talk about that. "Ice," I said. Not a winter went by that someone didn't slip on ice and break an appendage or crack open one's head. Morris nodded sympathetically. "Perhaps you can help. I know that the murder occurred the day before the regents' meeting. And, I understand that the meeting would have included votes on tenure for three professors—Kraig Bellamy, Heath O'Brien, and of course Jill Moreland."

"That's right. But what's your point, Mercator?"

"From the point of view of admissions, I assume that there is no direct input on the tenure decision."

"Almost entirely true. In some cases a faculty member may provide a great service in recruiting prospective students. In those situations we might put in an unofficial good word with the tenure committee. But, it is generally true that any professor at Masterton is receptive to our request to speak with a prospective student visiting campus or to make a home phone call to such a student. Most would do this willingly enough."

"Sure. But might there be any situations where you would put in a negative word or recommendation?"

"I suppose if the professor somehow really put students off, or maybe repeated some sort of misconduct. Certainly a matter of sexually harassing a potential student would give us a dim view. Or, of course, a murder. But a murder would be beyond our purview anyway."

"Yes, I understand. Another question. Do you have any information about what factors are used by students in selecting a college?"

"There have been studies on this topic. In fact, reviewing some of these data prompted us to do our own studies, starting with the fall of 1996. We polled incoming freshmen."

"Fantastic! Good for you." I emphasized the word "you" though I was at the risk of sounding patronizing. "So what did you find?"

"Okay. First we gave students a long list of potential choice factors and asked them to indicate all of them that influenced their decision. Then we asked students to rank the top five factors."

"And the results, Morris?"

"Of the twenty-five items on our list, there were seventeen factors that the students cited as important to them. And, let's see, I think that the top five factors were: 1) recommendations of family, friends, and relatives who went here, 2) Masterton graduates usually get good jobs, 3) Masterton's high academic reputation, 4) the relatively modest cost of attendance, and 5) personal attention or friendliness."

"Very interesting. Still, I'm wondering. Was 'percentage of faculty with a Ph.D.' on the list?"

"I believe it was. We tried to put any reasonable factor on the list. Quality of campus food service, campus safety, geographic location, and so on."

"Geographic location, you say? Would that be in terms of site or situation?"

"What do you mean, Mercator? What's the difference?"

"Geographically, the 'site' of a location refers to the characteristics of that place. For Masterton College, that might mean the elements of the small town, the college town. The 'situation' of a location refers to the proximity of that place relative to other significant locations. For the college here, that primarily might be its closeness to the Twin Cities."

"That's interesting, but we said 'location' on our survey."

"Okay, Morris, what about the percentage of Ph.D. faculty? How did that factor score among students?"

Townsend opened a desk drawer and pulled out a folder, then started paging through it. "Not very highly, it seems. About three percent of students checked it off the long list and none of the students cited it as among the top five reasons for attending Masterton College."

"So then it would be fair to say that if Jill Moreland got tenure without a Ph.D., then the admissions office would have no problem with that decision."

"Like I say, Mercator, we try not to get involved with that. But the Ph.D. percentage might be correlated with the academic reputation of the college."

"Correlated? I suppose there could be some relationship. However, if the number one factor for prospective students is the set of recommendations from family, friends, and relatives, then it seems that former or current students' positive impressions of Professor Moreland would be more influential than her lack of a Ph.D."

"Presumably so, I guess. But certainly you know that Ph.D. faculty disparage those lesser faculty who haven't taken the same experience of the dissertation journey through Hades."

31

A Meal with Carole

Friday was a busy day at the office. While I wanted to work on the murder case all the time, I was faced with two significant constraints. One problem was my lack of experience or authority in the detective field. I couldn't demand that others answer my questions. I couldn't accusatorially say, "Prove to me where you were at the time of the murder." Additionally, I didn't really know how to proceed as an amateur detective. My experience was limited to watching detective shows on TV and to reading murder mysteries. But, I wanted Carole back, so I did my best.

The other significant issue was my real job. I had to perform my duties as the alumni director of Masterton College. Many of these were mundane, yet essential, though hardly worth a detailed description. The planning of major alumni events did not require work on a fixed schedule. My time had some flexibility, but I'd found it crucial to maintain focus on these plans. Neglect would create a mountain of work at the last minute.

So, Friday was a busy day at the office. Handling simple requests from various alumni took up some of my time. Planning for the spring alumni reunions took much of my afternoon. Still the situation with Jill and Carole, the murder, and the attack on me stayed in the back of my mind the whole time. Carole wanted an update on the situation. I was thrilled that she accepted my email offer of a dinner date in St. Paul as my suggested setting for that update.

For this dinner I chose an Indian restaurant, the Taj Table, where Carole and I had enjoyed several meals as a happily married couple. Upon my arrival, I spotted Carole walking around the corner a few yards from the restaurant. Greeting her with a peck on the cheek and a friendly hand on the shoulder, I held the door open for her to enter first. She was dressed casually, but even so, my eyes wandered appreciatively over the blue jeans that smoothly covered her hips and the lavender cotton blouse that tapered neatly to her waist.

Little had changed at the restaurant since our last meal here about a year ago. Typical South Asian artwork and decorations adorned the walls, while white tablecloths abounded. We took a table for two, but I chose to sit to Carole's right instead of across from her. This kept my right hand free for eating, while putting me closer to Carole. We ordered our usual entrees—tandoori chicken for Carole and lamb pasanda for me. I asked for "mild" given that my Minnesota upbringing had not left my palate accustomed to highly spiced foods. I loved the flavors, but didn't wish for a flaming mouthful. Plenty of water, plus a mango lassi drink for Carole, with rice and the Indian bread "naan" rounded out the meal.

Carole was shocked to learn of my brush with death in a dark St. Paul alley. Perhaps I exaggerated the danger and my athletic escape, but I did like the way she grabbed my left hand and held on tight. "You could have died!"

Really, it was true, after all. When this shock wore off some, Carole wanted to know what leads I had uncovered. Sadly, she let go of my hand during these comments. I reviewed Detective Dafney's suspicions about me and about Jill, but actually Carole knew these already, though I did add something with my revelation about providing Dafney with the remaining MJE handkerchiefs. I explained that I thought that this ploy could delay Dafney in suspecting Jill. Events and people at the funeral, burial, and reception provided some elements of suspicious behavior. For instance, why was actress Aimee Forbes there? Carole didn't think the actress could be the actual murderer.

"Mercator, I saw her play 'Mother Courage' and it's obvious that she couldn't be a killer."

I failed to comprehend the relevance of her acting ability to her capability as a murderer, but I also failed to understand the advantage of arguing the point with Carole. Instead, I explained my discovery of a possible link between Munson's charity's scholarships and Munson's company's products, along with my brief conversation with Lyn King at the charity office. Carole found this interesting but was unsure of the relevance, as was I. However, this point did allow me again to mention my heroic brush with death and my dramatic escape.

I described my various campus conversations. Professor Philip Covington was convinced of Jill's innocence, but had no proof, and furthermore seemed to be smitten by Jill. In contrast, Dean André Sholé was convinced of Jill's guilt and appeared to relish the possibility of her punishment. Soren Timicin, when not cursing, clearly favored Jill, but mainly spoke of reasons why power-hungry faculty might seek to exert their power against her. Math professor Monroe Wilder strongly opposed tenure for Jill and seemed to infer her guilt. Goren Eidechse had given me further confirmation about Munson running both a company and a charity, but hadn't actually commented about Jill's innocence or guilt, before going splat in the corridor. Jill's use of Macintosh computers granted her Theo Sar's affection, but even so he had produced evidence that helped damn Jill. Admissions director Morris Townsend's data suggested that Jill's lack of a Ph.D. didn't hurt the college's recruiting, but his final words gave an assurance that some Ph.D. faculty would condemn Jill.

We left the restaurant satisfied by the delectable food, but filled with mixed emotions about progress in the murder case. And, of course, Jill was still in hiding. Walking down the sidewalk together with Carole, I learned that the path to her car would take us past my car first. Stopping to open my trunk, I extracted my gym bag and basketball.

"Carole, I'm going over to the athletic club for a light workout and a shootaround."

"After that big meal?"

"Oh, I've done it before. I've got an iron-clad stomach." I bragged, patting my gut twice. I don't have six-pack abs, but not much belly fat either.

Looking to demonstrate my abilities, I took to bouncing the basketball down the cold sidewalk. This worked fine for several bounces until the ball landed on an upturned corner of cement and bounded quickly away from me. "I've got it!" I called back to Carole. Grinning widely, I scooped up the ball with one hand. Still enjoying my boyish spirit, I resumed dribbling the ball. Working in a few variations and some clever ballhandling, I moved ahead of Carole by some ten feet.

"Okay, Mercator. I get it. Your basketball prowess. A thousand points for you." She even used her hands to mime the process of marking points for me on an imaginary scoreboard.

Giving a quick feint toward Carole, I flipped the ball toward her in a slow lazy arc, playfully calling, "Your turn!"

"Psst!" At first I thought that Carole was hissing at me in rebuke for my pass toward her; however, I watched the basketball spin and then land with a bounceless plop on the sidewalk, as tears in the ball's orange cover allowed air to spit out, leaving a deflated mound of rubber and leather on the cement.

Only a moment later Carole joined the ball, collapsing to the ground.

"Carole! Carole! Are you okay? What happened?" Since I had covered the distance between us in a bound, I was unnecessarily shouting at her, as a surge of adrenaline similarly bounded through my bloodstream. As I kneeled over her and she looked up at me with widening eyes, I watched as several red stains dotted her lavender blouse and spread outward.

"Mercator! Help me." Her right hand reached out as if asking for assistance rising. I grabbed her hand but resisted any efforts by her to stand.

Speaking words of reassurance to her, I looked frantically around. Two bystanders were approaching with looks of concern. I called out to them, "Can you help us? My wife's been injured."

"What happened?" inquired a forty-something businesswoman.

"I don't know. Can you call 911 at the restaurant?" I asked, pointing back up the street.

As the woman nodded her assent and trotted away, a young man dashed up to expand our group. "Is she okay? Was she shot?"

"Shot?" Not knowing for sure, I paused long enough to allow him to speak again.

"Mister, this sort of bleeding reminds me of rabbits that we used to kill with shotguns on our farm."

At the word "shotguns" my skin from the waist upwards felt a surging burn not from the Indian food, but from anger and recognition. "Shotgun! Did you see anything?"

"I was way at the other end of this long block, mister, but I heard a bang that didn't seem like a city noise, you know. I looked around and I saw a car spin fast down that short street there."

All of us but Carole turned to look where he pointed. We were near the end of a double-length block, not bisected by a street, whereas on the other side were two standard length blocks, with a center street cutting away from us.

"Gosh mister, it really whipped down that street. And then I when I saw your lady fall, I ran on down here to you."

"What car? Did you get a good look at it?"

"I didn't really, I mean, nothing like the license plate or anything, but it was a dark blue Chevy." He did know that the license plate was not from Minnesota, but from his location at the far corner of the block he wasn't sure of the state of origin.

In mere moments, it seemed the street was full of emergency vehicles and St. Paul police cars. Red and blue lights strobed up and down the block. Very quickly, Carole was bundled onto a gurney and slid into an ambulance, and I climbed in with her to hold her hand.

It seemed that Carole's physique was stronger than those of the rabbits on the lad's farm. Thank goodness. The boy was Sam Stinson from the village of Lynd, Minnesota. After a tense hour at Fairview Hospital, Carole's wounds were deemed painful but not life threatening. The doctors and nurses successfully removed seven pellets from her torso. None had caused severe damage, but one had creased her left lung, which was aggravating Carole's breathing a bit. When we had a good chuckle over her concern that one repaired wound might leave a small scar on her left breast, I relaxed in the understanding that everything would turn out okay. I was immensely relieved. With her out of the woods and tucked into the hospital for the night, I was quickly taken over by the cops, who, of course, had questions.

I spent time with police officers giving them my story, buttressed by additional testimony from young Sam Stinson and from the woman who called 911.

32

Hospital

ospitals were not my favorite places. People died there. The smell was unpleasant, harshly sterile and medicinal. Visitors were scared for their loved ones and nervous about what to say to patients in pain.

Walking to the hospital in St. Paul the next morning, I felt my usual discomfort. The uniquely hospital smells greeted me as I walked in the front door. Already knowing Carole's room number, I bypassed the information desk and headed toward the elevators. The hallway wasn't crowded, but did have a mix of patients, nurses, and visitors. A frail woman, probably in her eighth decade, rested in a wheelchair pushed by a bulky woman, perhaps her daughter, though there was little familial similarity. Separately, three children, a teenager and two younger siblings, moved energetically with their father, each child holding a ribbon attached to Mylar balloons celebrating the birth of a child, apparently their newest sibling, for one balloon read, "It's a boy!"

I entered the elevator and rode up two floors with a young woman dressed all in black, with black fingernails, and pierced in at least three body locations. *Goth?* I wondered to myself. I wasn't entirely sure of the criteria for "Gothness." Loud music was leaking from her earphones. With some surprise, I realized that I liked the rhythm and tune. She looked somber to me, but perhaps that was solely the effect of being in the hospital. I doubt that I looked particularly cheerful either, and I knew I wasn't the only person on the planet who disliked the atmosphere of hospitals.

Breaking the norms of elevator etiquette that required silent and vapid forward stares, I inquired, "What's that music you're listening to?"

"*To which* I'm listening, you mean?" The possible Goth was correcting my grammar.

With a chuckle I acknowledged the error of ending a sentence with a preposition, "Yeah, to which."

"It's the "Dead Winter Dead" album by the group Savatage."

"I like the song, but I've never heard of the group."

"They formed a new band called the Trans-Siberian Orchestra."

"I know of the Trans-Siberian Railway that runs thousands of miles in Russia, from Moscow to Vladivostok. Are the musicians Russian? They can't play on the train, can they?"

"No." She gave me a questioning look, but then she smiled. "The Trans-Siberian Orchestra released a CD with Christmas carols played in a rock opera style. Do you like symphonic metal?"

"I don't really know."

At that point the elevator bell chimed, indicating that we had reached the third floor. The young woman prepared to exit. "Try it some time. Bye."

Two chatting young doctors in green hospital scrubs replaced her in the elevator. They were discussing an outbreak of Hepatitis A that had put two patients in the hospital, with another dozen in outpatient treatment. Apparently the health department had traced the source of the outbreak to an unsanitary worker in a local restaurant.

I was happy to exit on the fifth floor, where I turned left and proceeded down the hall to room 522, where Carole was in bed, her torso angled up at a forty-degree angle. She was happy to see me, thankful to have companionship, and willing to have me hold her hand. I was enjoying the moment of quietude when Detective Dafney walked into the room.

"Hello! Am I interrupting anything?" he inquired.

"No, no," I reassured him, "providing a bit of comfort for my wife."

"Hello, Detective Dafney. Did you get a report from the St. Paul police?" asked Carole.

"Yes, I did, but I wanted to talk with you personally."

"Okay, Detective. What can we tell you?" I offered.

This led to a review of the circumstances of the shooting. We each recounted our respective perceptions and recollections of the incident, but really didn't have much to add to the written report Dafney already had received. Of course, the account given by the young man, Sam Stinson, held more information than either Carole or I could provide. The detective was courteous and inquisitive, but since neither of us had seen anything of the shooting, other than Carole and my basketball on the ground, it seemed that we had little to offer. Dafney did try to elicit responses to questions like, "As you walked from the restaurant before the shooting, did you see anything unusual?"

I was tempted to say that the unusual thing was that Carole was with me, but I didn't want to be contentious. Dafney seemed to be quite interested to know if we had noticed any car following us on the roads and streets to the restaurant. Carole didn't really think so, for she had been at the Rosedale Mall before coming to the restaurant, unless someone tailed her there first. For my part, as I started out for the Twin Cities, I'd noticed that my gas tank warning light was glowing. Therefore, I had stopped for gas at Slim's Gas and Go, a convenience store on the edge of town. When I drove away and onto the highway, there hadn't been a car in either direction as far as I could see.

So Dafney thanked us for our time, as we thanked him for his efforts. With one hand on the door, the detective offered one apparently last question, "Did anyone know that you were going to be eating at the Taj Table?"

"What? I didn't tell anyone. Did you, Mercator?" inquired Carole.

"No. We set our plans by emailing each other."

"Well then," posited the detective, "if you didn't tell anyone about your dinner date and if no one followed you, how did the shooter locate you at the restaurant?"

For that we had no answer. Was someone reading our email?

33

Ace in the Hole

On the campus of Masterton College, almost every Saturday night was movie night. Although students certainly could drive to the Twin Cities or to Hastings to go to a movie theater, Masterton itself did not have one. Video rental store—yes. Movie theater—no. At least partly for that reason, movie night on campus regularly drew a large crowd.

Major feature films were quite popular, but big audiences also turned out for artsy films or indies. A committee of the student government selected the films, while seeking to provide a balance between popularity, artistry, theme, and cost.

I completed a late Saturday afternoon visit with Carole in the hospital. Carole insisted that I not spend the whole day lingering in the hospital with her. In truth, I was relieved by her insistence. There was only so much care and concern that I could express in the sterile atmosphere of her room. I was running out of things to say, topics to discuss. I left her with a kiss and a squeeze of her hand.

However, while away from the hospital I felt drawn back to it. I desperately needed Carole to be healed. Of course, the doctors told us that there should be no problem. They cautiously wanted to make sure her lung injury did not cause complications. Even so, I found it difficult to maintain mental focus. Additionally, I didn't know what work I could do on the murder case on a Saturday night. In the end I decided to go to the campus movie, hoping this would hold my attention.

I arrived about fifteen minutes early with the intention of getting a favorable seat. Some fifty students already had arrived by then and I could see a few other students walking toward the building. I mentally congratulated myself for my timeliness and grabbed an aisle seat in a middle row of the auditorium. In theaters and airplanes I prefered an aisle seat. The down side of this choice was that I had to rise to allow anyone to enter or leave the row for a bathroom visit or a snack purchase. Still, I felt this was more than balanced by the advantage of extra leg room that the aisle provided for my long frame.

In this case, my early arrival turned out to be unnecessary. I had forgotten that the spring semester would not start until Monday, so the majority of students were still off campus. Perhaps that's why an older film was chosen. I saw a few community members in the audience, prompting me to recall seeing a few flyers about the movie posted in downtown Masterton. Anyway, many student faces were familiar.

Ahead of me and three seats over was sophomore Thad Bostick. He was with his blonde girlfriend. Her name escaped me, though I recognized her as a freshman and thought that her name might be Gail. Though she clearly had gained a few pounds during the first semester, the so-called "freshman ten," I felt it improved her looks. She had been a bit skinny upon her initial arrival on campus. I made this silent observation about her appearance, while noting that they were having an argument. Thad was trying to calm her down. Not cooperating, the blonde coed was saying phrases like, "That was so crass of you" and "Why not admit it, and we'll go on." I heard Thad say, "Why do we need to start this again?" and "Because that's not what happened."

Thad seemed relieved when the lights dimmed and the movie started. Near the halfway mark of the film, he managed to put his arm around her shoulders without objection. Given my own romantic woes, I hoped that they could work it out, without Thad needing to solve a murder or Gail getting shot.

The film *Ace in the Hole* was good, even above average for a film released in 1951 and thus lacking all the high-tech elements available to contemporary filmmakers. Kirk Douglas was persuasive as the savvy and unscrupulous reporter who endangered a trapped miner, in order to lengthen the news story that was his and his alone. Though the film lost money at the time of its release nearly fifty years before, I thought its foreshadowing of the current news focus on catastrophes, crime, and anything negative was striking. For me personally *Ace in the Hole* served the purpose of distracting me from Carole, Jill, and murder.

Almost. As I was leaving the theater, a few feet ahead of me were two coeds—Margaret Maywood and Rebecca Browning. They were discussing their spring class schedules. I heard Rebecca say, "I'm really happy I got into another Geography class. I love Professor Moreland. She was so inventive and inspirational in the other Geography class that I took."

Margaret agreed, "She gave the hardest final exam ever, though. Oh my God!" Grabbing Rebecca's forearm, she continued, "But when it was over, I realized that I'd loved it. I mean, she had so got me to study and understand the material that I felt a lot of satisfaction in doing a great job on the test. I got an 'A.' It was awesome."

34

Jill at the Cabin

The previous Sunday I had escorted Jill Moreland to my family's lake cabin. In the days between then and now, I was aware that the police did want her for questioning and that the college community was very curious about her whereabouts. I was thankful no one had directly asked me if I knew where she was. Overhearing comments like, "I wonder where Jill Moreland is," I was able to put a puzzled look on my face, matching the appearance of others nearby. Since the police had not issued a warrant for Jill's arrest, technically I didn't think I was harboring a fugitive.

However, with the spring semester starting the next day, I needed to talk with Jill. It was one thing to be away for the break between J-term and the spring semester, but it was a different thing to be absent from teaching her classes. The former could be considered vacation, but the latter would be seen as avoiding the police or flight from justice.

The difficulty was that I'd told Jill to turn off her cell phone, thus avoiding the probability that police could trace her through phone calls. Even calling me from a pay phone, if she could find one, might be traced. We parted a week ago with the understanding that I would return to the cabin when possible, so that we could determine what to do next. Jill did have her laptop computer with her, so she could prepare her syllabi for the spring semester. Additionally, we thought that she might carefully be out in public, given the lack so far of an arrest warrant or all points bulletin in her name.

I had hoped to go to Jill earlier, but with the activity of the week, the attack on me, and then with Carole's gunshot injury on Friday, this Sunday morning was my first opportunity. Leaving at 10:00 a.m., I drove through the streets of Masterton. If the police were at all suspicious of me and wanted to follow along, the scarcity of traffic in Masterton made a secret tail difficult. Indeed, no one was behind me as I passed the city limits heading north.

As I drove, a variety of thoughts coursed through my mind. Frequently images of Carole in a hospital bed interrupted my attempts to ponder the Munson case. Even so, I managed to reflect on the various views of Jill Moreland that had been presented to me. Dean André Sholé and Professor Monroe Wilder offered starkly condemning views of Professor Moreland, while professors Covington and Timicin portrayed Jill in very favorable terms. The IT man, Theo T. Sar, and many students were very fond of the geography professor. These were only samples of campus sentiment, which undoubtedly held many permutations between the two extremes of the Jill Moreland spectrum.

As much as I liked Jill and so wanted to recover Carole's favor, I clearly could understand the police's interest in her. Jill had a tremendous investment in Gordon Munson's decision. His affirmative vote for her tenure would secure her a position for a lifetime of teaching at Masterton College. His negative vote would cast her adrift in the academic world, sharply decreasing her chances of finding similar employment. As a woman she would benefit somewhat from equal-opportunity hiring practices and her lack of a family would give her geographic flexibility in finding a new post, but a failed tenure case would work against her in a job search. While some had characterized her stance against the dissertation as arrogant, to me her acceptance of a huge risk for the sake of a principle seemed particularly courageous.

The case itself held a number of complexities. For one thing, the email evidence was confusing. Jill had told me that she received a positive email from Munson, but the college computer system had no evidence of this email. If it once existed, it had been erased from Munson's sent files, from Moreland's in-box, and from the college's archives. Essentially in its place was an email from Munson saying that he would vote against Jill Moreland's tenure. Jill never mentioned this unfortunate email; however, her account showed the file received and opened, thereby giving her a motive for the murder. The police could assert that Jill read the email, went to the house, and killed Munson.

Additionally, there were the bloody footprints that I knew to be Jill's. Identification of the footprints could prove difficult for the police, for a variety of women could have been at his house, from ex-wife Helen Contini Munson to administrative assistant Lyn King. Of course, as a wealthy divorced man, Munson could as easily have had female visitors.

While the footprints may be leading the police to suspect a woman in the case, my knowledge that these footprints came from Jill Moreland and my trust that Jill did not kill Munson gave me no edge in determining the gender of the killer. I had to work on the assumption that the killer, male or female, left no tracks.

And too, the handkerchief found in the blood was a problem. It was Jill Moreland's hankie and it was Munson's blood soaked through it, nearly making it invisible next to the body. Though the unique history of Jill's handkerchiefs made it difficult for the police to establish her as owner, they might yet make that connection. My ruse of having Jill mail me her remaining stock of these monogrammed hankies might delay the police reaching the correct conclusion. And yet, it still was puzzling how the handkerchief got in the blood at the crime scene, for Jill could not recall taking it out when she found the body. Even more strange, Jill had accounted for five of this set's handkerchiefs, while the sixth and last had been missing for years. I suppose that the trauma of discovering Munson's freshly murdered body could have prompted her unconsciously to bring the hankie to her face and then to drop it unwittingly so that it happened to land next to the body. However, how could that be the sixth hankie?

I tried to puzzle through all of these elements as I drove the hour to my family's lake cabin. Though the snow and ice made winter visits to the cabin somewhat uncommon, the winter landscape was lovely. The smooth white expanse was bright even considering that I was wearing sunglasses. Of course, the cabin was used mainly during the summer in Minnesota. The summer yielded obvious advantages in the weather, while also providing pictureque scenery.

Indeed, my favorite view of the lake is a summer scene. In the morning before the sun is high in the sky, sometimes the water is nearly still. While we never get large waves as on Lake Superior, the slightest motion of the water is essential for this scene. Each unique yet small movement of the water creates a corresponding unique set of reflections of the sunlight striking the water at an acute angle. If frozen for a millisecond, there are vast multitudes of individually singular rays of reflecting light. Since this suspension of time doesn't occur, the lake's surface instead is in constant motion, and yet is never exactly the same as any previous moment. Thus, the shimmering light is the result of an infinite number of possibilities and even over the shortest period of time displays billions of discrete lights in a twinkling mosaic beyond the beauty of diamonds or any sparkling gem.

Today, a mid-winter day provided no such summer viewpoints, though I was graced by an unexpected vista that, like the glistening water of a still summer morning, would burn a permanent memory into my brain. Having no safe means to call Jill in advance of my arrival, I simply drove north with the expectation that a morning visit the day before the new semester would find Jill in the cabin reviewing her course plans.

Wanting to make a discreet entry to avoid any chance of a neighbor's observation, I slipped my key into the lock and quickly stepped through the doorway. My call of, "Jill," overlapped by a hissing sound that ceased along with my voice. For a few moments I stood frozen beside the door. Jill's laptop computer rested along with a set of strewn papers on the dinner table. Bits of clothing were strewn here and there, and a red bath towel had been tossed over a chair. The light above the table mixed with sunlight coming through the picture window. Maybe it was that the winter sun came in more, but the room looked markedly different from my memories. I stood there, entranced, looking around. Now it seems odd to me, but at these several moments it felt natural to stand there silent.

As I was about to break my soundless trance to call out a second announcement of my presence, Jill Moreland stepped into the light. Like the summer scene, light glistened like jewels off the multitude of droplets of water that provided the sole cover for her lustrous body. When she turned to face me, thus discovering my presence, there was a momentary pause, before we simultaneously called out each other's name. In that pause my mental camera captured her image at the apex of womanhood, a body in full majesty, beyond the appeal of simple youth and in a fullness that had yet to glimpse the decline of aging.

Abruptly the spell was broken. She grabbed the nearby towel and adeptly wrapped herself in it. My face reddened. I felt a rush of warmth, partly due to embarrassment and partly to the visual stimulation. Bursting with an apology, I sought to explain how the last spray of the shower must have muffled my entering call. Reassuring me that it would be okay, Jill excused herself to go to the bedroom to dress. I watched her exit, her crimson hair crinkled in wetness, resting on damp shoulders while occasional drips fell onto the towel.

In a few minutes she returned, dressed simply in jeans and a University of Minnesota sweatshirt. I again sought to apologize, but she stopped me.

"Mercator, let's forget about it. I was purely an accident of bad timing."

I knew that I could not forget, could not delete that image of her, but I nodded my agreement, and then nodded even more when she spoke, "Though . . . let's not mention this to Carole."

35

Car Door

*P*arking my car that Monday afternoon two blocks from the state capitol building, I hopped out. I needed to get the official documentation registering Minnesota Mission as a charity. I wanted more information about the role of the charity.

A horn honked somewhere behind me. Were I a Californian instead of a Midwesterner, had I been in the Big Apple instead of in the Twin Cities, I might have disregarded this interruption, but here in Minnesota most drivers were too polite or too tolerant to beep their horns without a decent bit of provocation. So when a horn honked, we looked. I looked. In the distance a dark-blue Chevy was attempting to double park and had caused a string of cars to queue up behind it. I might have disregarded this curiosity, but the shot that had hit Carole and that which had struck my arm both had been blasted from a similar car. Those incidents had caused the permanent mental linking of blue Chevy and the presence of evil.

I ran. But not away. A knight in pursuit of the fire-breathing dragon. Captain Ahab after Moby Dick. Picard and the Borg. Whatever the metaphor, I was compelled to run toward the blue Chevy. With the two-lane street effectively narrowed by parked cars on both sides, and with traffic approaching and cars stacked behind, the Chevy had few options. Indeed the car lurched once, then stopped as the driver realized the predicament that was created by stopping when I parked. Better that the driver simply had first driven past me, quite possibly passing unnoticed.

158

What I was doing was not entirely clear, for I needed to dodge pedestrians and to look past parked vehicles. I was desperate to get a look at the driver, to begin to understand the threat that was aimed at me. I couldn't identify the driver yet, still too distant, but if I could just get a little closer. I ran full out.

However, Olga and Hans Olson were oblivious to my quest. A kindly pair of octogenarians from Mahnomen, they were in St. Paul to visit their grandchildren and pay a tourist visit to the handsome domed capitol. As Olga looked to Hans to inquire about the series of honking car horns, she flung open the passenger door. And struck my knee. The bad one. Pain blossomed on the kneecap, but radiated outward in a multitude of directions, as nerves reported the door's unexpected and abrupt compression of the swollen sac of fluid. I went down hard. On the pavement in agony, I did not notice the blue Chevy's departure.

36

Secret Collection

I returned to campus with a sore knee and only a slightly better understanding of the business of charities. Though I was not yet ready to make a public accusation or refer Minnesota Mission to the attorney general for investigation, my general inquiries revealed that the use of a quid pro quo, such as the practice of dispensing charitable funds only to organizations that also made purchases, was decidedly illegal.

I stopped at my office after picking up my campus mail. Among the notices of lectures coming up, reminders to get parking tabs, and such, I found a note written in a cramped thin script. It simply stated, "Meet me at the Munson house at 8:00 p.m. tonight." It was signed, "Jill."

With Jill back from hiding, it seemed unlikely but not impossible that she had written the note. Someone wanted me out at the Munson house. Jill? Calls to her office and home phone went unanswered.

In hindsight, this might have been a good time to bring Detective Dafney into the loop. That would have been a good plan. Had I thought of it. Instead, I thought of something else. I decided to review the scene of the crime ahead of the requested meeting. Since I was unsure of the note writer's identity, it seemed prudent to be there before the appointed hour, in order to scout out the setting and perhaps catch this person off guard. Even so, I was about two thirds of the way there, when second thoughts strongly began to present themselves. Undoubtedly, the house still would have yellow crime tape surrounding it. I was unsure how much the police suspected me for the murder, but certainly I was on their list. Spotted again at the scene, I could draw further police suspicion.

Damn! Logic directed me to turn back. Desire, that heartfelt desire to have Carole back, decreed that I go forward. It was a battle for maybe a minute. Then I continued on, simply promising a cautious approach as a sop to throw to the logical side of my brain.

Arriving in Munson's neighborhood, I chose not to drive into the cul de sac where the house stood. Instead I drove along side streets where my map preparation had shown that an alleyway connecting Louis Avenue and Rook Avenue must run close to the farthest reaches of Munson's backyard.

The half circle of Old Stone Moor Drive naturally created a semi-circle of homes and yards. Munson's home was the original house in the neighborhood. For years it stood alone, a large wealthy estate originally built for a wealthy Minnesota businessman who had made his fortune in shady dealings. Upon his death, his heirs sold the property—the house and its surrounding acreage. In the subsequent years developers created an unusual enclave around the original house. The arc of new houses stood along the half circle of the drive. The respective backyards extended up to the handsome man-high cedar fence ringing the complex, corresponding geographically and geometrically to the half circle of the drive. The result of this design was that the alleyway behind the homes on Old Stone Moor Drive essentially was an abutting tangent to the half circle created by the fence. It reminded me of high school geometry problems.

I quietly steered my car down the alleyway. I could see that the Munson estate at the center of Old Stone Moor Drive had its back fence almost at the alleyway. Some of the properties had many square feet of area behind the arc of fencing and had tool sheds, piles of cordwood, and other storage behind the fence, but the Munson property barely had enough room for a modest tool shed pressed fully up to the fence. Each property had its own gates in the fencing, connecting these various sized alley arcs to the respective backyards. Driving through the alley, I observed that one owner had placed a shed immediately adjacent to the alley, leaving a modest gap between the shed and the fence. By carefully driving into the gap, two lots down from the Munson house, I was able to conceal most of my car from view. My strategy was not very original, for I could see the very tip of the bumper of another car parked similarly three more lots down the alley.

Quietly edging my car door closed, I stepped over to the fence. My black jeans and dark jacket helped me blend into the darkness. My hands, comfortable in deerskin gloves with black silk undergloves for extra warmth, guided me along the fence line. Munson's neighbor to the left had lights blazing throughout the house, but the home on the right was dark. Reaching Munson's gate, I tugged on the handle. It groaned slightly, but held in place, clearly bolted from the inside. Although pleased about having found a good spot for my car, I now began to worry about getting into the yard. As I walked to the next gate, I mentally started to evaluate my chances of going over the fence. Although not a low fence, the six-foot barrier potentially was scalable. I might be able to do it. Alternatively I could go back and stand on my car, using it as a platform to swing over the fence. However, that choice would land me in a well-lit area, distinctly increasing my chances of being seen. I figured these neighbors might be a bit skittish having had someone in their midst murdered. They might have an itchy 911 finger. I thought that any advantage of surprise demanded my arriving unseen and from the back of the Munson house.

The next gate was ever so slightly ajar. At my gentle touch the gate silently swung open another three feet. As I started to step through, I noticed an irregular circle of mud in front of me. By a quick lengthening of my stride, I stretched over the mud to land my foot on grass. A shoe print from athletic footwear showed that an earlier visitor had a shorter stride and had hit the mud. Inside the high fence, each of the individual yards was separated by low scalloped fences that delineated the property boundaries, but did not obstruct views of the development.

Munson's house remained dark, as did the one neighboring home. In that yard I lingered only briefly before continuing. I decided to walk casually, as if I belonged there, instead of skulking suspiciously ahead. Approaching the rear of both houses, I was startled to see movement in Munson's house. Sometimes my eyes sensed a zephyr of motion that I couldn't prove occurred, so I paused and watched attentively for confirmation of that movement. This time I saw brief flickers of light, perhaps from a small handheld flashlight. Someone was inside the house, but in the darkness both inside and outside the house, I couldn't identify the person, in fact could not even discern the person's gender.

Who? It could be a well-wisher who discreetly wanted to give me confidential information in a private setting. But why the Munson house? Unless, perhaps the confidential information was specifically *in* the Munson house.

162

Who? This person could be the murderer, perhaps being given over to me by my anonymous tipster who somehow knew the murderer's home invasion plans for the evening.

Who? This person could be the murderer, luring me into a trap.

If I found a supporter here, that would be a good thing. However, if the murderer was lurking in the house, this would be a risky entrance. Still, what if I caught the murderer red-handed! A rush of tactile sensation stroked me, as I imagined an exuberant Carole giving me a sensuous hug of thanks for proving Jill innocent. Braced by this very pleasing sensation, I resumed my silent quest. Reaching the back door I found that the knob turned freely. Did the murderer, or whoever was in the house, have a key?

The rear entrance opened into a mudroom. With the police tape still on the house, Munson's things had not been removed by relatives. I found a hooded jacket, a woolen coat, and a windbreaker hung on hooks. A couple pairs of athletic shoes sat on the tile floor. In Minnesota we regularly call them "tennis shoes," in New England often they call them "sneakers." My father would have called that a bit of cultural geography.

Stuffing my deerskin gloves in the pockets of my purple and black down jacket, I treaded cautiously into the adjacent kitchen. I had been accustomed to a bit of diffuse light outside and some of these rays filtered in through the kitchen windows. A few dirty dishes remained on the counter, several more in the sink. Now, though, I became cognizant of another light source. A faint glow was coming from the next room. Not the motions of a flashlight in the hands of a murderer, the light emanating from that room was indistinct but clearly generated from a fixed source.

As I entered the next room, even in this minimal lighting, I immediately recognized the setting. This was where I found the body. The display cases on the walls still tidily held their contents, though the handsome chess set on a table remained disturbed, with several pieces missing. Quickly I counted nine pieces absent from the board, but could only see eight on the floor.

It was a bit eerie to be in the dark in this room of death. Additionally jarring though was the discovery that the light source was behind one of the display cases. Not that the collection wall was backlit. No, with my heart racing, I realized that one of these floor-to-ceiling cabinets had swung several feet open, hinged at the corner. A secret room.

This was my moment. Either my unknown helper would be in the secret space behind the display or it would be the murderer. Taking a deep breath I prepared to enter this concealed area, ready for cooperation, but braced for confrontation. With righteous conviction I edged through the gap between wall and hinged cabinetry. I leaped into the secret room, arm out-stretched and accusatory finger pointing. At no one! The room was empty. Not exactly empty, rather that no one else was in the room. Instead, I found what appeared to be another collection.

Struck with curiosity, I stepped farther into the room, puzzled by what I saw. Organized into individual displays, like the knives in the outer room, here there was an odd assortment of items. Near me, two brassieres hung from hooks. In scattered locations there were panties of various colors and patterns from white to pink to black to polka dot. Next to each lay a small white card. As I reached to touch a red satin bra, I heard a scrape behind me. Turning toward the sound, I pivoted in time to see the wall close. Instantly the lights were extin-guished. In this secret collection room, now in complete darkness, I dashed to the closed wall and pushed. Then I pushed harder. In both attempts the wall refused to budge. I was trapped in complete darkness in Munson's secret room!

I tried to say calm. I was reassured by two considerations. First, it seemed logical that there would be a mechanism to open the door some-where inside the secret room—a button, switch, or lever that would release me. Second, I had my blue light.

Though I often thought of it in comparison to "The Blue Light" tale of the Brothers Grimm, mine was newer technology. In the Grimms' story, an old soldier was commissioned by a witch to retrieve her blue light from an abandoned dry well. Indeed, he found the blue light at the bottom. As the witch pulled him up, he refused to hand it over until he was on solid ground. Angered, the witch released the rope and deposited him and the blue light at the bottom of the well. Drained of all hope, the old soldier decided to have one last smoke. However, when he touched the blue light to his pipe, a small magical man appeared to do the soldier's bidding. Ordered to find a way out, the little man led the soldier through a secret passageway to safety. Alas, my blue light would produce no such little man. Almost wafer thin and shaped in a flat parallelogram, the gadget produced a narrowly concentrated beam of blue light when activated.

Pulling the device out of my pocket, I turned it on and shone the blue beam around the room. A quick survey failed to reveal any obvious buttons or switches to open the door. Of course, a secret room might have a secret button.

Instead of finding the way to open the door, the blue light gave me additional glimpses of this collection. What was this? Again I swung the blue beam across items in the collection. Women's lingerie, underwear. Two small bottles of perfume—Tabu and Quartz. Earrings. A thin silver necklace. An autographed photo of well-known Twin Cities actress Aimee Forbes. What kind of collection was this? My subconscious was trying to point out that I should be striving to find an escape; however, by now this mysterious room captivated me.

When I edged quite close to individual displays, I again observed that a small card accompanied each item. With the red satin bra, the card read:

#203—Angela Sanders
November 11, 1992
Fort Worth, Texas

With a pair of inexpensive triangular earrings, there was this card:

#212—Ashley ??
February 27, 1994
Madison, Wisconsin

On impulse I picked up the bottle of Tabu, rolling it along my left palm and fingers. Removing the stopper I held the opened bottle under my nose as the seductive, exotic scent wafted upward. As the arousing aroma ticked my olfactory sense, my memory transported me to a scene from my years as a college student. I recognized this Tabu scent as belonging to only one woman. Though sales of Tabu undoubtedly numbered in the many thousands, from my perspective that fragrance only touched Beth's body. On that day, standing in Munson's secret collection room, the scent of Beth delivered me back to an evening in her dorm room, both of us stretched out lengthwise on her bed, watching a state tournament hockey match on TV. Soon we stopped paying attention to the game. Eventually, our smooching was interrupted by Beth's roommate, Shauna's, return. She asked about the score. When I said, not too convincingly, "Three to two," Shauna gave Beth a sharply questioning look. Though sometimes I reflect with wonder over that evening, Beth and I never did go all the way, but remained friends.

It was quite apparent that Munson did go all the way with many women. Indeed, this was his trophy room of his conquests! That had to be it. This was a collection of memorabilia from his sexual partners. Part of my male mind said, "Wow!" A different part said, "Really now! How self-possessed and audacious!"

I looked back to the signed publicity photo. With it a card read:

#200—Aimee Forbes

October 1, 1992

Minneapolis, Minnesota

Aimee Forbes had been at Munson's funeral. She may have been the woman in black who put flowers on his casket, after the mourners had left the gravesite. What was Aimee Forbes' interest in Munson some five plus years after they had sex? Each of the cards apparently chronicled a single sexual episode, though perhaps the actress had more than the one encounter with Munson. Could Aimee Forbes have been more involved with Gordon Munson than just a one-night stand? Might there have been a longer relationship? On and off? And what was the actress' final act with Munson? Did he break off the relationship only to cause her to kill him?

I moved to the far left, where the collection seemed to begin. With a pair of simple white panties was the card:

#1—Susan Hudson

July 17, 1954

St. Cloud, Minnesota

A bit farther over:

#9—Helen Contini

April 10, 1960

Hastings, Minnesota

Even with Munson's wife there was only a single mention, though undoubtedly they were sexually active throughout their marriage. Browsing along, I noticed a gap of several years, which I took to be his early married years. Quite evidently though, he cheated on his wife a number of times before eventually divorcing her.

Munson's murder had been a crime of passion or at least of anger without premeditation. The evidence suggested and the police contended that the killer acted on impulse, grabbing an immediately available weapon to kill him. I couldn't imagine that Susan Hudson of 1954 was the killer. Logically it seemed more likely that a woman from a more recent entanglement could be a suspect.

Moving to the other end of the displays, I found this card, next to a golden colored thong:

#251—Barbara Stevens

January 4, 1998

St. Paul, Minnesota

Immediately next to that was a mostly empty spot of the display case. Only a sliver of a card remained under a corner of metal, apparently where it abruptly had been torn away. The fragment had only bits of its notation intact.

#250—M

Janu

W

Adjacent to it was #249, a Margaret Henshaw, on December 14, 1997, also in St. Paul. Mystery woman "M" had slept with Munson on January 1st, 2nd or 3rd. Whether this had anything to do with the murder, I didn't know; however, the card fragment and the apparently missing bit of sexual memorabilia felt suspicious.

Giving the room a glancing review, I realized that there were not 251 individual displays. I estimated seventy-five or so instead. Did Munson have something from all 251? Or from a select group? It was then that I saw the file cabinet in the corner.

In the drab-tan two-drawer cabinet, the lower drawer was mostly filled with tagged items. I found a pair of pantyhose from #127 Barbara Palacio and a hair tie from #223 Bobby Jo Allison. The top file drawer was filled with numbered files. In numerical order they ended with #249— Margaret Henshaw. What about #250 and #251? Had they been taken or had Munson not recently updated his files?

As I looked further, the latter possibility seemed the more likely, for I found a master list. It started with Susan Hudson in 1954. Further down the list was Munson's ex-wife Helen Contini in 1960.

I skimmed down the list. Ann Smith in 1966. Frances Anderson in 1973. What! Marjorie Wheelwright in 1982! Wheelwright had not become president of Masterton College until 1989. In 1982 she had been a dean at the University of Minnesota. So she and Munson had had an affair. What an odd coincidence! Or was it? The more I delved into this murder, the less I believed in coincidences. Could Marjorie Wheelwright be the murderer? Had she sent me on that fateful day to Munson's house, knowing that I would find the body?

Still pondering that idea, I resumed my perusal of the list. Suddenly, I was forced to remember how an ocean wave once had pummeled me, knocking all my breath from my lungs, as I tumbled helplessly in the surf. Now abruptly gasping for breath in Munson's secret room, I actually thought that I could smell the ocean. I re-read the notation—#175—Jill Moreland. In February of 1992, Jill Moreland had made love with Munson.

That must have been about the time she was hired. Could Munson have intervened on her behalf? Worse, could she have slept with Munson in order to assure herself of getting the job? Or was this a coincidence? How would this information affect the police's attitude toward Jill? Could the police argue that Munson had demanded sex in return for the job, as a rejoinder to sex for the original hire?

While all these questions ricocheted inside my head, I scanned the list for any other familiar names. At first I noted only two. Stephanie Grant, assistant professor of English, was #207 in 1995. Sarah O'Toole, whom I knew to be a dentist in Hastings, was #240 in 1997. Well, well, #245 was Megan Orlov, the charity's receptionist. Oddly, I felt a sense of relief in not finding Roxy Gannon's name on the list. Of course my greatest relief was that my Carole's name was not on the list either.

I decided to take the list and Jill's item also. Not knowing what Munson had taken from Jill, I started rummaging through the clutter of memorabilia. A white tag with #183 and the name Veronica Garrett on it was attached to a red thong with a safety pin. #93, Angela Zackley, rubber band, tube of lipstick. #17, Harriet Kitston, paper clip, four-by-five photo. Where was #175, Jill Moreland? Aha! Digging some more, I found it. Moving aside several other items, I grabbed the tag #175, Jill Moreland. Attached to it was a safety pin that snagged one tiny white thread. That memorialized Jill Moreland? I spent a few more minutes look-

ing through the drawer, but could not find any detached items. Except for Jill
Moreland's memorabilia, everything matched.

I still had to get out of this locked room, taking with me evidence
against Jill—the list, the file, and the tag. Using the blue light I again scanned
the walls. There had to be a button or a switch somewhere. First, I carefully
examined the hinged wall, but there was nothing apparent there. I expanded
my search to the adjacent walls, yet again nothing. Quite possibly the activat-
ing mechanism was hidden, though it made more sense that the button to get
into the room would be disguised. I tried the far wall too—still nothing. Finally,
I turned back to the file cabinet. In the top drawer, I found a remote control
device with five unmarked buttons on it. Facing the hinged wall I pushed the
top left button and waited. Nothing happened. I depressed the top right button
and immediately was rewarded with a hydraulic whirring sound, but the wall
didn't move. Instead, now I heard police sirens. Turning around toward this
sound, I discovered that a passageway had opened on the rear wall.

Where did this passageway lead? Were the police already in the
house or now on their way? What would happen if Detective Dafney found
me in the secret room? Already the detective was suspicious about me. I did-
n't think the police could pin the murder on me, but certainly being appre-
hended in Munson's house wouldn't help. I could be viewed as an accessory
to the murder if Jill was arrested.

Whirr. The doorway closed. I hadn't pushed any other button, but
the door closed, apparently on a timing mechanism. Silence. No longer could
I hear the sirens. The room kept sounds from entering, but would it keep the
police from hearing me, if I made noise inside the room? Could the police
already be in the house?

Three brisk strides took me to the back wall. I pushed the button again
and the concealed doorway opened once more. I was through in a moment.
Several stone steps led down to a narrow passageway. Apparently I was at the
basement level, but not in the basement. I continued to hold the blue light in
my black silk gloves, shining it ahead of me. With only a couple inches of clear-
ance above my head, I brushed one side of the concrete wall with my shoulder,
leaving a slight damp spot on my purple and black jacket. The rough surfaced
concrete failed to catch the blue beam smoothly, dispersing it into a flickering

glow. Behind me I recognized the whirring noise as the sound of the hydraulics sealing the doorway behind me. The damp air caught in my throat as I advanced toward an unknown exit. Though it seemed longer, this tunnel bored through only about one hundred feet before reaching a door at the other end. This door was held in place by a powerful spring lock. This meant that my choice to leave the below ground corridor would be irrevocable. Like the door into the tunnel, this door too would close behind me. Still, I had to proceed. With a synchronized twist of the lock and push against the wall, I propelled the door open. To my ears the *creak* that sang out from the apparently rarely used door was startlingly loud, but I hoped that in reality it wasn't loud enough to bring the police running. The door opened into a rectangular earthen space and then snapped shut, essentially vanishing. Designed to fit perfectly into the dark soil, the door was all but undetectable. No doorknob or handle or lock. From this side there was no way to know of the hidden corridor and probably no way to access it.

Above my head a rope dangled from a trapdoor. Handily, a small stepstool stood in the corner. Taking the stepstool and placing it under the trapdoor, I rose up and pushed the trapdoor open. Pulling myself up, I found a number of tools hanging in a small enclosure. I was in the shed behind Munson's house. While in the tunnel I could hear sirens faintly, but could not determine their direction or location. Now in the shed I knew the sirens clearly were coming from the front of the house. With the evidence still in my pocket, I tiptoed the ten yards to my car. Due to a fortunate incline and with a slight push off, I was able to glide my car, unstarted and in neutral, down the alley. Before reaching the intersection of the alley and Rook Avenue, I noted that the other car parked along the alley also was gone. I started the engine and drove off. No police followed. I would have to ask Jill Moreland why she was in Munson's collection.

37

Jill Arrested

As I arrived on campus Tuesday morning, nearly to the front door of the administration building, I noticed two police cars pulling into the adjacent parking lot. The familiar Norm Dafney twisted out of the driver's seat of the lead car. Thinking that his intent might be to interview me, I paused with one hand on the door. Had Dafney learned of my adventure in Munson's house the previous evening? If so, would he be able to find the items that I had taken from the secret collection?

My self-centered focus was broken when I observed Dafney turning away from the administration building and walking authoritatively in the other direction. Obviously, now my concern shifted to Jill Moreland's welfare. Dafney headed toward the York Social Science Building. Choosing a brisk walk that I hoped would not alarm Dafney or give away my intentions prematurely, I set out to intercept him.

"Detective! Good morning!" I called out when I'd nearly caught up to him and the officer accompanying him, my left hand cupping my mouth to magnify and project my greeting.

The detective didn't seem pleased to see me. "Mercator, I'm busy."

"Blustery this morning, don't you think?" Indeed the wind chill must have been below zero.

"Not looking for chitchat now, Mercator." The detective wasn't offering even remote encouragement.

I ignored this. "So how's the case going, Detective?"

"I'm working on it. In fact, I could do my job better if you would go on over to your office and do your job."

"Oh, I see. Sorry, I thought that you were here to see me."

Now he did pause and turn to me. "Do I seem to be walking toward your office, Mer-Ca-Tor?" The policeman had a tendency to pronounce my name in three spat syllables when he was frustrated.

"Oh, I guess not, but it's over this way. Follow me."

He let out a hiss and turned back the way he'd been going. "I'm not here to talk with you. I have other business."

"Really? Is it the Munson case?"

"Mer-Ca-Tor, I don't need to discuss police business with you."

"But detective, the least I can do is direct you where you need to go."

"We're already here," Dafney asserted, as we reached the doors of the York Social Science Center.

"Here? But what . . ." Dafney and the silent cop with him simply moved through the double set of doors and headed to the main office.

I trailed behind them and heard Dafney say to Elsie Norris. "Would Professor Moreland be in her office or in class now?"

Elsie said, "Excuse me," and I said, "Moreland?" alarmed, our words overlapping.

Dafney glared at me, then turned back to Elsie. "Answer the question," he demanded.

Elsie Norris consulted a chart of teaching assignments. "She's been in class since eight o'clock in Room 124. It's a Tuesday/Thursday class that lets out at 9:25."

We all looked at the office clock that beamed 9:18 in bright red digits. Elsie continued, "But why do you want to see her? She didn't kill Munson."

Dafney raised an eyebrow to meet Elsie's angry glare. "There's evidence otherwise."

"What! What evidence?" Again Elsie and I were speaking simultaneously, though in this case our words were identical.

Dafney and his colleague didn't reply, but instead turned to exit the office.

Elsie, though, wanted a response. "Wait! She couldn't have. No!"

Her interjections failed to deter the policemen who stubbornly kept going. Elsie's glare now turned to me. "Do something, Mercator, do something."

Though I didn't know how I could stop Dafney, I again followed him out the door.

"Detective, don't you think that it would be best to wait until Professor Moreland's class ends. You don't want to create a scene in the classroom and get all the students upset. The class is almost over anyway."

Dafney's unhappiness with this suggestion was transparent, but he grunted an acknowledgement that my logic had some merit. "We'll wait in the hall for her."

"But, Detective, that's hardly any better. In fact, if several classes get out at the same time, there'll be even more students present in the hallway than in the classroom."

"We aren't letting her get away."

"Of course." I paused while an idea came into my head. "Detective, I'll offer to escort Jill Moreland directly to you. I give you my word of honor that I won't let her get away. Then we can avoid a scene. Okay? How about it?"

Again logic superceded Dafney's own frustrations. "All right, Mercator, but listen and listen good. If you don't bring her directly out to my squad car, I'll arrest you instead. Faster than you can say the word 'geography,' you'll be in handcuffs and under arrest for obstruction of justice. You got it?"

Dafney's angry glare was of a much greater magnitude than Elsie's look. Mildly I acknowledged him. "Yes, detective, I've got it. I'll bring her to you but could we not go directly to the squad car? I mean, that's the same issue again."

Dafney looked about ready to barge straight into Jill's classroom and make his arrest.

"There's a small open lounge around the corner there," I said. "Why don't you go wait there until I bring her to you. There's coffee."

Thus I stood outside Room 124, waiting for class to end. Soon it did, and a cascade of people poured out the door. I eased my way into the room, edging through the outgoing students. Two students stood next to Jill Moreland, seeking information or something. I didn't wait to find out.

"Hey, guys. I'm sorry, but Professor Moreland needs to go. She'll have to help you later."

Jill looked affronted. "Mercator, what do you mean? These are my students, not yours."

One of the students attempted to be polite, trying to excuse himself, but Jill was insistent. "Mercator, surely this can wait."

"Jill. Jill. Okay, come over here." I said, waving my left hand toward the corner of the room.

"What? Oh, okay. Students, you wait right there. Mercator, what's going on?"

Positioning us so what we said could neither be heard nor seen by the students, I said, "Jill, the police are here. They intended to break into your classroom. I persuaded them to wait, but only by my promise that I'd bring you directly to them after class. They're waiting down the hall in the lounge."

I'm certain that the students couldn't hear my words, but Jill's face change from a rosy hue of irritation to a pale white of fear while her eyes widened, and the students apparently could see something was up. They muttered excuses and bustled out the door.

Now alone with Jill, I stepped away from her, while she asked me what the policemen's intent was. I really didn't know as they hadn't volunteered any useful information. I only knew that I must deliver Jill to the officers.

I completed my mission, escorting Jill in as casual a way as I could to the lounge, but when I sought to linger in order to participate in the conversation, Dafney's colleague physically took me by the arm and marched me out the door. Over my shoulder I heard Jill agree to take Detective Dafney to her office.

It was forty-five minutes later, forty-five minutes of glancing out my window to check on the police car in the parking lot, when I saw Jill Moreland being directed into the back of the police cruiser. I learned later that my assumption of her arrest was correct. Damn. Carole would not be pleased.

38

Aimee Forbes

Sometimes, often even, life is about connections. In the alumni business I found this to be true. Emily Weber, a Masterton graduate of 1964, was the executive secretary to Owen Wells, the agent for actress Aimee Forbes. It was through this connection I was able to secure a brief time window during which the actress would take my call. I made this request the previous Thursday in order to get the call Tuesday morning. Even so, I didn't get the actress' actual phone number; instead, the call was routed to my office through her agent.

"Ms Forbes, thank you for taking my call."

"You're quite welcome, but really, call me 'Aimee.' I don't stand on much formality."

"Okay, Aimee. Thank you. But call me 'Mercator' then."

"So, Mercator, what can I do for you?"

"As the alumni director at Masterton College, I've received quite a bit of attention, quite a few inquiries regarding the murder of our regent Gordon Munson."

"Ah, yes, poor Gordon. So, it appears that you've heard that I knew him."

"You were acquainted with Munson, then?

On the phone there was no chance to read body language or facial expression. Even so, I could imagine a slight twist in body and face as she replied. There was a definite squirm in her tone. "We were . . . friends. Yes, friends."

Of course, she didn't know that I had seen her autographed photo— "To Gordon, with all my love, Aimee"—in Munson's collection. I said, "I saw you at his funeral. I also presume that was you who surreptitiously left flowers at the grave."

"Surreptitiously?" She laughed lightly. "Really? I'd say 'discreetly.' My intention was simply not to draw attention to myself, though the flowers need not be a secret."

"Okay, I understand. The whole thing certainly has been uncharted water for us too. It's quite a shock for the campus community."

"Yes, I'm sure. What kills me is that he should have been at the theater that night."

"What's that?" I didn't know anything about theater plans for Munson.

"Yes, I gave Gordon four tickets to my show for that very evening, the very evening that he, oh damn him, that . . . that he was killed."

"I had no idea. He should have been at the theater?"

"Yes. It may be that only the family knows this."

"Why is that, Aimee?"

With Aimee Forbes being an accomplished actress, it was difficult for me to discern the difference between an emotion-laden tone and dramatized inflections, but it certainly seemed that her mention of the four tickets was husky and tinged with grief, while the next words proceeded at a faster, more excitable pace, "When the lights went up at the end of the show, I looked to see Gordon. Instead I saw his son, Nathan, and his mother, that is Gordon's ex-wife, Helen, and then two empty seats."

"So, apparently Gordon gave his tickets to family members."

"Two of them, anyway. Probably to his son, who then chose his mother."

"Yes, he may have given two to other people who then didn't attend, or maybe he kept two himself but also obviously didn't attend."

"It's kind of strange that Gordon and I were friends." Another light laugh, but this one seemed a little uncomfortable.

Not really, I thought. Gordon Munson apparently could be at least a certain kind of friend to any attractive woman. "Oh, how so?"

"It's odd, but Gordon didn't really like plays or going to the theater, and of course that's my career. I thought maybe the free tickets and my role in the play would get him to come. Honestly, I think Gordon didn't enjoy watching others being the centers of attention, even on stage. He so loved being the life of the party himself or the personal charmer of any attractive woman."

"Yes, I've heard that he was a ladies' man. Odd though, that he didn't like the theater."

"I suppose I should have told him that the play was hysterically funny, but I thought if he attended and was surprised to laugh so much, then he might be willing to reconsider his taste for live theater."

"Aimee, it was a valiant try. I wish that Munson had used the tickets. He might be alive today. I appreciate that you took the time to speak with me. Thank you."

"You're welcome, Mercator. Oh, the play's last weekend is coming up." For a moment I thought perhaps she was going to offer me free tickets, but she simply said, "You ought to come out and see it. The play is called *Noises Off*."

"I'll think about it. Good-bye." Then as the play's name set off images in my memory, I shouted into the receiver, "Wait! Wait! I thought—" but I heard the click of the disconnect at her end before I could say, "someone told me that *Noises Off* was a serious drama."

That person had been Monroe Wilder who had a waved a ticket for the evening of the murder, a ticket to *Noises Off* for Row 4, exactly the type of excellent seat that Aimee Forbes would have given to Gordon Munson. Did Wilder have Munson's ticket? Had Wilder, by going to the theater, thus in an indirect way caused Munson's death?

39

Lyn King

My earlier conversation with Financial Aid director Roger Black had given me a start on the issue of a charity's legalities. Based on analysis started by his academic counterparts and then confirmed by him for Masterton College, Black showed me that a pattern of probable illegal behavior did exist for Minnesota Mission. With this information I returned to the charity's offices. Given the life-threatening experiences of my last visit there, I parked and then cautiously viewed the streets outside the office building. In fact, during the whole drive to St. Paul, I frequently checked my rear view mirror for signs of the blue Chevy.

Having spotted nothing of note, I prepared to open my car door, when I saw pretty receptionist Megan Orlov stepping out of the front entrance to the building. Given the time, 12:05 p.m., I assumed that she was leaving on her lunch break. Remaining motionless, I allowed Ms. Orlov to walk past my car, clearly oblivious to my presence. When she reached a distance of twenty yards down the sidewalk, I quickly slipped out of the car. Fifteen strides took me to the double glass doors of the entrance.

Inside I chose the stairway as I had in my previous visit, quickly reaching the third floor entrance and then the door to Minnesota Mission. As expected, the front desk was unguarded. I offered an intentionally quiet, "Hello?" before stepping down the corridor toward Lyn King's office. A plush maroon carpet led down the hallway, as mahogany paneling gave a dark, to me a pretentious, tone to the walls. Several office doors were open ahead of me. From one of these emanated a harsh, though somewhat muted, grinding sound. Given my hope of catching Ms. King off guard, I tiptoed down the carpeted hallway. Drawing even with the first office on the left, I peered inside only to find the office empty—though the level of clutter said it obviously had regular use.

The low gnashing sound persisted farther down the hall. Examining and passing the next two offices, both empty, I clearly heard the growling noise coming from the next office on the right. Silently moving forward, I discovered that the room's entrance positioned nearly the entire room past it, meaning that I could look through the open doorway and see most of the room, labeled on the outside wall as the office workroom.

Indeed, the room held several shelves loaded with reams of computer paper, boxes of toner cartridges, and containers of various other office supplies. On another wall there was a countertop and sink, with the requisite coffee maker and several mugs, in addition to tea bags, a jar of granulated sugar, small plastic tubs of coffee creamer, a partially closed box of doughnuts, a large decanter nearly full of some kind of golden-colored spirits, and an open purse. A bit incongruous now in February, Christmas decorations and candles remained in a corner of the counter. Two of the candles actually were lit. In the center of the room, Lyn King, her back to me, stood beside a table, feeding papers into a shredder.

"Destroying the evidence?" I queried.

Ms. King gave a great start, arms flying wildly. Her agitated swings crashed into the tabletop shredder, sending it careening toward the floor. She simultaneously looked to identify me and to catch the falling shredder. In the second task she failed, but dislodged the shredding mechanism from the basket that caught the strips of paper, sending the shredder clanging onto the thin carpet of the workroom. Freed of this mechanism, the nearly full basket disgorged much of its contents, leaving irregular piles of paper bits across the floor.

"How did you get in here?" she challenged in a shocked, strident tone.

"I think Megan must be on her lunch break. There was no one at the front desk." I shrugged, while recognizing this didn't really justify my coming down the hall. At the same time I shut the door behind me, to avoid another surprise interruption, if anyone else might be somewhere in the office suite.

"You have no reason to be here." While her tone was more subdued now, her hands on hips and overall body language still expressed her dissatisfaction at my presence.

I remained undeterred in my mission. Picking up a page from the stack of papers to be shredded, I read aloud, "Scholarship summary 1994. Augsburg College—3 scholarships, $300,000 office supplies." Scanning the page, I quickly noted the spreadsheet entries of academic institution, scholarships, and office supply purchases. "Ms. King, you told me there was no relationship between purchases from Minnesota Academic Supply and scholarships granted by Minnesota Mission."

Distress wrinkled her otherwise plain features, as she struggled to find a response. Choosing to disregard my assertion, she stammered, "You have no right to be here! I must ask you to leave."

I leafed through more sheets. "But this is evidence that should be public knowledge."

A shrill panic had returned to her voice, "This is evidence of nothing! Nothing!"

"Oh, I must differ. I suspect that these pages, at least those not shredded, demonstrate a direct correlation between office supply purchases and scholarships. Probably this is illegal. If not, then certainly this'll cause considerable public embarrassment for Minnesota Mission."

Ms. King's cheeks now flushed red, perhaps from anger or fear or embarrassment or most likely from a combination of each. My presence at the door effectively trapped her in the room, increasing her tension.

Reaching for the remaining large pile of papers on the table, I righteously announced, "As a public citizen, I'm going to confiscate these documents."

As I gathered up these papers, King skittered to the countertop, frantically pulling at her purse. Numerous small items scattered across the counter and floor. The clatter of their falling caused me to glance downward, noting a tube of lipstick, a packet of tissues, and a plastic barrette. Before completing my survey, I looked up to find Lyn King pointing a small gleaming handgun at me.

"The other day I bought this gun for my safety. It looks like a timely purchase." Stress still rippled in her voice, though a layer of control now was present too. "Put the papers back on the table." Her voice twittered a bit, but still this was a command.

"The papers prove it, don't they?"

"Put the papers down." A command, but still shaky.

I reviewed my options. I could make a dash for the exit, but a sprint with a two-foot pile of papers in my arms would be unwieldy. Would I even get the door open? Could I run down the hallway? Probably such a dash would end with a bullet in my back. Would Lyn King be a good shot? She said that she had very recently acquired the weapon. Had she any training?

"Really, Lyn, you could hurt someone with that thing."

"Listen, Morley, I . . ."

My frustrated shout interrupted her, "My name is Mercator!"

"I have a gun!" Her outraged yell seemingly indicated that she didn't feel that I was taking her seriously enough.

I didn't care. "Talk to me first about the papers. They prove it, don't they?"

"Damn it!" And with this exclamation, King slammed her gun hand down on the tabletop. The subsequent explosive discharge sent a bullet streaming a few feet to my right and into the wall, while also jarring King's balance. Taking advantage of her stumble, I stepped forward and hurtled my two-foot high stack of documents directly at her.

Had Lyn King been a professional criminal or a trained marksman, doubtless she would have fired another shot through the cloud of papers and into my chest. Or she wouldn't have taken the first wild shot at all. However, in this case she used both arms to shield herself from the tossed papers. My bull rush immediately trailed the flight of documents. Knocking her backwards, I forced both of her arms upward, then pinned her wrist and the gun against the wall above and behind her. The gun fired again, this time the bullet shattered a compact fluorescent light bulb in a recessed ceiling fixture. A few sparks floated down to the floor. Although the gun's second discharge startled us both, my pressure continued unrelenting. Even though she struggled, my substantial advantage in both size and strength quickly overcame her defenses, and I wrestled the gun away from her.

Gaining my composure, I explained, "Roger Black at Masterton College and his Financial Aid colleagues across Minnesota will be interested in these figures. Already Black and the Financial Aid director at Augsburg College have identified correlations between purchases and scholarships. So who is responsible for this link?"

King's briefly held senses of outrage and command had vanished. Following the angle of her slumped shoulders and downcast eyes, I saw two shreds of paper on the carpet smolder from descending sparks, then extinguish in tiny swirls of smoke. King answered almost in a whisper, "Gordon Munson."

"Perhaps you're trying to shift blame away from yourself. Aren't you truly responsible for this?"

A small fire was fanned in King's suddenly upturned eyes, "Now you also want to shift the guilt to me?"

"Who else tried to blame you? Munson?"

The fire's glow drowned in the tears filling her eyes. Though she had pulled a gun on me and I found her unappealing, I realized that I had a small measure of sympathy for her.

My tone reflected this new emotion, "Lyn, someone blamed you?"

Helplessly she answered in a wee voice, "That day Gordon got a call from Frank Jeffers at Moorhead State. He claimed we were manipulating the scholarships. Moorhead had switched suppliers, and Gordon had shut them out of scholarships."

"So there is a link. How was it done?"

"Gordon had the final word on the scholarships. The committee submitted its ranked list, which Gordon then adjusted based on the institutions' purchases. We never released the whole list, but let the colleges publicize their own separate lists. I don't know if the committee ever compiled the separate scholarship lists to compare to their overall recommendations."

"What did Jeffers want?"

Still talking to the floor, head turned down, she simply said, "The end. He wanted to end all this."

"And Munson wouldn't go for that?"

"Gordon was very upset. He claimed that he had the right to distribute the scholarships any way he wanted. He said it was his charity, no one else's. But then . . . then," here she looked up at me with eyes wet pools now overflowing, "then he wanted me to take the blame. He wanted me to say that I had adjusted the lists before giving them to him."

"And you hadn't?"

"Are you kidding? Gordon was right in saying that he considered Minnesota Mission his own charity. Anything, and I mean anything important, was his sole prerogative. I never could have done something like that."

"So Munson wanted you to be the scapegoat?"

Her "yes" was a plaintive plea for understanding. "He told me that evening that he needed me to say I changed the scholarship list. If I did that, he said he'd see to it that it turned out okay for me. I told him 'no,' but he insisted. I told him I didn't understand how he could ask me this after, I mean, after . . ."

"After all your years of working for him?" I prematurely completed the sentence for her.

Her subsequent pause made me think for a moment that she had been about to say something else, but she only confirmed my answer, "Well, yes."

As I adjusted by position, my left foot bumped something loose and small on the floor. I glanced at it, again seeing the scattered contents of her purse on the carpet. Then I spied something else. Puzzled I reached down and picked up one item, leaving keys, a ballpoint pen, and small packages of Advil, dental floss, and Tic-Tac on the floor.

"Why do you have this?"

She had no response but only looked at me with eyes seemingly stuck in an expectant stare.

Brandishing it in my extended right hand, I declared, "This white king is from Munson's chess set. That it is in your possession is rather damning."

In a voice now lacking both conviction and emotion, she blandly replied, "That piece could come from anywhere. It means nothing."

"Gordon Munson has an eclectic set of possessions. I'm sure his chess set is unusual in some way, easily identifiable. This is from his set. You only could have taken this at or after his murder."

Wide-eyed but now speechless, she allowed me to continue. "Munson wouldn't have had an incomplete set on display. You couldn't have taken this before his death. Really there are only three possibilities. One, you murdered Munson and took this chess piece at that time. Or, two, sometime between the murder and my discovery of the body, you were in the house and took the piece. Or, three, Monday you crossed the police line and took this king.

"Possibility number two is absurd. Certainly, if you were in the house in the hours right after the murder, you would have reported the murder to the police. You didn't do so. Therefore, I can eliminate this alternative."

"Yes." Meekly and almost hypnotically, Lyn King nodded.

"And why would you have taken this chess piece out of the house earlier this week? Unless you had slain Munson, what motive would you have to take evidence from the house? And why the king? Why not a pawn or a queen or a knight?"

Her breath coming in short puffs, she had no response, but continued to stare at me, unable to break the spell of my analysis.

"Aha. Your name's King. Are you this piece? Does this king represent you?"

Without moving her lips, a soft, "Yes," escaped.

"You are the king. But why?" Understanding dawned within me. Although my conclusions didn't match with Munson's apparent preference for attractive women, I felt confident in my analysis.

Nodding ever so slightly as if in agreement with my unspoken realization, she let me continue.

"Is it the collection? You're in the collection, aren't you? But I didn't see your name." Now I paused momentarily puzzled, but once again her silence acted as acquiescence to my continued evaluation. "Woman number 250, her name plate had been torn away and there was no trinket or memorabilia with it. Only a torn paper with the number 250 and some letters for January and an 'M' for the woman's name and a 'W' for the location. The 'W' could be for Whitmore. Are you 'M'? Your name is Lyn. Is that your full name? What is your given name?"

"Marilyn," she said, then sighed. "It's Marilyn."

"Marilyn." I repeated with full understanding. "'M' for Marilyn. Fill in the blanks for me. What happened?"

"Gordon called me on New Year's Day, asking me to come to his house to pick up some papers. When I arrived, he was in a downright jovial mood. He'd already had a good bit to drink and offered me one—a Scotch, I think. Usually he is, I mean *was*, businesslike with me, so I felt flattered by his sociable approach. My one drink turned into a few drinks and then he started touching me—my shoulder, my hair, my cheek. I was taken aback at first." She looked at me as if asking for permission to continue.

I gave it to her. "Go ahead, Lyn."

"I've never had much luck with men. I was married once when I was really young, but it didn't work out. I've been alone for years and years. I really admired Gordon. So when he, when he began to flirt with me, it seemed so unfamiliar, but the Scotch made me feel so warm, and then he kissed me. And so I kissed back. And then his hands were under my shirt. And I let him. Soon we were upstairs in his bedroom."

Now searchingly she looked at me, trying to gauge my approval or disapproval. "It's okay, Lyn. I understand."

"Afterwards I left him asleep in bed and went home. For the next couple of weeks he was slightly friendlier to me, but I understood that we needed to maintain a businesslike relationship at work. Still, occasionally he would put his hand on my shoulder or smile when we passed in the hallway. At least I thought he was being more friendly."

Curiously, I began to feel my role changing from investigator to confessor as I listened to Lyn King's account. She evidently found it cathartic to share her private knowledge with a stranger.

She continued, "So when Gordon called me on Saturday evening, asking me back to his place, I anticipated that he wanted to make love again. I agreed to come out to his house. I even put on perfume for him. I hadn't opened the perfume bottle since my cousin Theresa's wedding nine years ago."

"And did he want to have sex?"

"No." A forlorn look now dominated her face. "No. He called me to the house to tell me that he needed me to take the blame for the scholarship scandal when it become public. I was shocked."

"And you objected?"

"Yes, first I told him that I wouldn't do it, that I wouldn't take the blame for something I hadn't done. But he persisted. He told me that I had to do it, that he needed to maintain his public image. Then I questioned how he could ask me to do this considering that we had made love."

"And what did he say?"

Now finally her tone changed. In a croaking voice laced with angry dismay, she explained, "He laughed. He laughed at me, like my whole line of conversation was preposterous. Then he told me that he had been drunk and that he hadn't meant to do it, for he didn't find me attractive. 'Sorry about that,' he said. I started crying and stammering that I thought he liked me and that the sex had meant something to me and how could he do this to me."

"It didn't mean anything to him?"

A long lamenting wail of confirmation was her answer.

"And then what, Lyn?"

"And then the phone rang and he stepped into the next room, leaving me. I was alone with my horrified feelings. I must have staggered back to the wall for support. Next thing I realized was that my elbow had struck one of the built-in cabinets. I noticed that one of the cabinets, essentially part of the whole wall, was slightly ajar, creating a narrow opening to a room behind it. I think that Gordon must have thought that he had closed it when I arrived, but it hadn't quite shut properly. I peeked into the secret room. It took me a moment to realize what it was, but then I saw my name and the king piece by it. It was his secret collection of conquests."

"I know. I saw it Monday."

"You did?" She paused, but pursued her story again. "I took the chess piece and I ripped my name from the display. When Gordon was done with

186

the phone call, he asked me if I had decided to take the blame. I demanded to know the meaning of the collection room. He laughed at me. I told him that I'd taken the king and my nametag away. He laughed again and told me that he regretted having sex with me. He said, 'I had been saving number 250 for someone really pretty and special.'"

"I backed away from him and bumped into the glass shelves with knives. The magnetic catch popped and the glass door opened a bit. I saw the chess set on the table in front of me and swung my hand at it, knocking some pieces to the floor. One pawn skittered part way across the room. Gordon said, 'You pathetic bitch!' and walked away from me to pick up the piece.

"And then my self-control snapped," she continued, "A wave of searing anger flashed through me. The knives were right next to me and I simply grabbed one. When Gordon bent over, I jammed the knife into his back. He dropped the chess piece and fell straight to the floor. I . . . I'd killed . . . him. And then I went away. When I got to my car, I discovered that the king piece was still clutched in my left hand."

For a few moments we paused, gazing at each other. I broke the silence. "Lyn, I'm so sorry. I empathize with you, but we still have to go to the police. I'll go with you. It'll be okay." I said these words, but realized that in truth they were empty consolations. I couldn't truly empathize with her, a murderer and a woman scorned. Still she would face prosecution for her act.

Abruptly her eyes changed from forlorn to frantic. "No."

"Lyn, a innocent woman has been arrested for Munson's murder."

"NO!" And she stepped toward the counter top. Grabbing one burning candle she threw it into the pile of shredded paper. A flash of orange flame burst from the debris.

"Lyn!" I shouted. "Lyn, what are you doing?"

But she wasn't done. Picking up the decanter she threw it hard toward the door where it shattered against the metal doorframe. The golden liquid sprayed wildly all over the door before most of it splashed downward saturating the carpet near the door. A strong odor of alcohol permeated the air. She threw the other flaming candle at the door, where with a whoosh of sound a wall of fire burst from the alcohol that had dripped down the door and pooled on the carpet. Though much of the alcohol quickly burned off, its high temperature flame ignited the carpet. An acrid black smoke rose in front of the closed door, then continued across the room, where thin gray smoke rose from the strips of paper flashing into ash.

I shoved the gun and chess piece into my pockets and raced for the door. I reached for the doorknob. Though the metal knob was still hot from the burn of the alcohol there, I succeeded in turning it.

Flinging the door open, I swung my arm toward the front exit of the office suite, signaling Lyn to follow me. Seeing her step forward, I burst through the doorway, taking two quick strides into the hallway. When I turned back, I saw Lyn's arm raised. A flicker of metal zipped from her hand. I lunged backward, sending my shoulders and head out of the way of the pewter letter opener that caught in the mahogany paneling behind me, quivering in the wood like an arrow shaft. My next look at Lyn King found her shutting the door, closing herself inside.

I looked down into the shocked face of Megan Orlov, who was just returning with a bagged lunch in hand. She shouted, "Why'd she close the door? The room's on fire."

I leapt back to the door, stunned to find that Lyn had locked the door from within. Megan, now looking at the letter opener, shouted, "What's going on here?" Her register had risen even higher.

"Lyn confessed that she killed Gordon Munson."

Megan's eyes and mouth went wide.

"Then she started a fire when I told her that we needed to go to the police. Now she's locked herself in."

"She killed Gordon?"

I shouted back, "Right now we have to get her out of there! Do you have a key?"

She nodded dumbly, then ran to her desk. Even from the hallway I could hear her frustrated cries in search of the key. In the meantime, I tried shouldering the door, but to no effect. Quickly Megan did return, thrusting the key into the lock. The knob turned but the door failed to move. Panicked, she turned to me in dismay.

188

"Megan, she must have moved the table in front of the door. Call 911. I'll get Lyn." Given that this simple metal table was not massive oaken furniture, I was able to force the door open and table back. As I did so, the onrushing air produced a whoosh of flame. Beyond the flames Lyn King cowering in the far corner. I leapt through the fire and reached down to pick her up. Though her death wish may have been considerable only moments earlier, now in the presence of increasing and potentially toxic smoke and fire, her objection to my rescue consisted only of a few feeble arm motions that I easily overcame. When we were about to exit the room, its smoke detector belatedly rang once and then remained silent, its batteries apparently dead. At the same time one of three ceiling sprinklers opened, but only produced a trickle of water, far from sufficient enough to gain ground on the flames.

Running into the reception area, I spotted a couch and stretched Lyn across it. Both of us were coughing badly, Lyn mixing gasps for fresh air in between forceful rasping coughs. Between my own hacks, I asked Megan for a fire extinguisher.

Horrified awareness enlivened her face. "We keep it in the work room, under the sink."

I sighed heavily. Closing my eyes and bowing my head downward, I could only say, "Damn." With considerable reluctance I went back down the corridor. Taking as deep a breath as I could hold, I once again burst through the doorway. Amid the flames and black smoke, I located the Class ABC extinguisher canister, pulled the pin, pointed, and fired. Like the room's built-in fire defenses, this also failed to work entirely properly. Instead of producing a steady blast of dry chemical spray, the extinguisher spat and stopped, spat and stopped. This malfunction kept me amidst the flames seconds longer than I should have been and only extinguished about half of the flames.

After the fire extinguisher sprayed its last, I plunged out of the smoldering room, stumbling haltingly back to the front door. Coughing furiously from inhaling the noxious black smoke, I watched as the walls started to spin and spin and spin. I noted that a policeman rushed through the entrance, but the white ceiling seemed to turn into the wintry evening sky—starless, black, and void. As I fell, the gun quietly dropped from my pocket onto the lush burgundy carpet.

40

Peter P.P. Putnam

Thursday was spent in a bit of a fog. The medication for my mildly damaged lungs made me groggy. In addition, the acclaim I received both for solving the murder and for fighting a fire at the same time was a heady mixture. Even Detective Dafney offered a gruff, "Good job," though he did rail on me about acting on my own without notifying the police who were trained in dealing with crime. He also pointed out that I could have been killed nine ways to Sunday after I told him all the stuff I had done on my own. All that was absolutely true, of course, but he didn't have to impress my wife, and I did.

With Lyn King's confession, Jill Moreland had been released from jail on Wednesday night. In contrast, I had lodgings in the hospital, while I received treatment from a pulmonary specialist. Upon my release Thursday afternoon, Jill and Carole stopped in for a visit at my apartment. Jill wrapped her arms around me in an exuberant bear hug. Her thanks even included a firm kiss right on the lips, without appearing at all self-conscious. Carole's hug was less exuberant, but more tender. Her kiss was a long-lasting wet smacker. I relished it. Even more, Thursday evening Carole thanked me in bed, though with both of us having had recent injuries, particularly our injured lungs, we were panting more than usual. And, when I awoke on Friday morning, she was still there. Risking life and limb was totally worth it.

Back on campus Friday, my body battled the contrasting weariness of medicated lungs and the continuing joy of success—saving Jill and regaining Carole. Nevertheless, I still had a job, so I returned to check on accumulated paperwork in my office. I walked among the leafless deciduous trees clustered near the administration building. On other sides of Vinstrom's Veldt a scattering of evergreens lent some natural color to the winter landscape.

Given that I had arrived at 11:50 a.m., many students were out on the campus grounds, coming from various directions to the campus cafeteria. I said hello to several of these students—Karen Witter, her mother, Janice, was class of 1975, and Bruce Baker, whose father was class of 1972. Stepping on, I noticed two coeds nodding their heads toward someone approaching, and then coquettishly giggling behind cupped hands.

Looking up, I caught a flash of powder-blue pants. "Pete Putnam. Hello." Though sometimes I found Pete to have annoying personality traits, today he wasn't a bother. In fact, with the elation of identifying Gordon Munson's killer, freeing Jill Moreland from jail, and receiving Carole's exuberant thanks, I felt entirely magnanimous. Today it would take more than Pete Putnam to disturb me. Even the continuing pain of my bullet-pierced arm, my inflamed knee, and my singed lungs seemed virtually unnoticeable next to my emotional high.

"Hi, Mercator! Say, would you sign my Pi Day petition?"

"Your what? What kind of pies do you want to bake?"

"No, no. Not pie. Pi."

"You know, Pete, my favorite pie is coconut cream. Could you make that?"

"Mercator, I'm not talking about baking. I want to have a day on campus, designated as Pi Day, in honor of the mathematical number pi. You know, three point one four one five nine two six five three five eight nine seven nine—"

"Hold on, Pete." I halted him with a gentle tug on the arm of his red jacket. "Now I understand. Pi. Math. Three point one four."

Frowning with slightly outturned lips, Pete countered, "Not really three point one four. That's simplistic. Pi is so much more. It's really three point one four one five nine two six five three five eight nine—"

"Pete, okay, I understand, but come on." Peering at him with one squinting eye, I added, "Pete, how many digits of pi do you know?"

"I've memorized the first one thousand digits, but, hey, some math geeks have memorized many more than that."

"Okay, okay. I do know that pi is the ratio of the circumference of a circle to the diameter, and I realize that pi is an transcendental number that has no end, but don't you think that citing pi to be three point one four is okay for convenience sake? Sort of like calling you Pete instead of Peter Putnam."

He was working himself up into a huff. It was kind of fun baiting him into sputtering. I'd never had so much fun with Pete before. I'd completely underestimated his value. "Actually, my full name is Peter Perry Prescott Putnam."

"Peter P.P. Putnam!" I tried, but couldn't prevent myself from chuckling.

"Anyway, would you sign?"

"So when do you want this Pi Day to be?"

"Duh! March 14, of course. Three fourteen."

I laughed as hard as my poor lungs could stand. "Sorry, I guess that was obvious. All right, Pete what do you need?"

"I want the college to declare March 14 this year to be Pi Day on campus. The Math Department's going to do some things in celebration. If the college would make it Pi Day, I think other parts of the campus might do things too."

"Maybe the cafeteria would make coconut cream pie. I could go for that. All right Pete, where do I sign?"

Pete flipped over the clipboard that he was carrying to reveal his petition. So far, he had seven signatures, three at least being fellow math majors. The petition read:

Pi Day
3/14
In honor of pi, the most important mathematical constant, we the undersigned request that Masterton College name March 14, 1998, as Pi Day. 3.141592 . . .

I signed my name on line eight. I was about to hand the clipboard back to him, when I found myself staring at the number 3.141592. Suddenly the day's thirty-five-degree cold seemed to penetrate my down jacket like two icy claws until it reached into my chest and squeezed my damaged lungs. As I gasped, the cold penetrated down my torso and limbs so that my whole body shivered. In alarm, I pulled the clipboard back to me and ripped loose one of the back pages of paper, flipping the sheet over so that I could write on it.

"Mercator. . . hey, what are you doing?"

"Wait, Pete, just wait." The near scream of my words convinced him to take a step back and let me proceed.

I re-wrote the numbers in large print:

3141592

and then underneath those numbers wrote:

3IH159S

I knew in that moment that in the darkness of the alleyway the other night, I had gotten the Blue Chevy's license plate number wrong. Pushing the clipboard into Pete's chest, I took off at a run for my office, as pain tore through my knee, arm, and lungs.

41

License

How could I not have remembered the car that nearly killed me outside the offices of Minnesota Mission? True, the medication, the accolades, Jill's release, Carole's lovemaking—all that had been very distracting. Now, however, a huge problem had surfaced. While Lyn King had confessed to the murder of Gordon Munson, it was evident that she couldn't have driven the car that nearly trampled me in a dark alley. That day after I had left her in the office building and walked directly outside, the car, shotgun, and driver already were waiting. And, if that were so, then it was impossible that the shotgun blast that had hit Carole was fired by Lyn.

"Detective Dafney, please." I frantically told the receptionist, hoping the detective might be at police headquarters.

"Who's calling, please?"

"This is Mercator Eliasson. Listen this is really important. Is the detective in?"

"Please hold."

It was only a few seconds before Dafney was on the line.

"Hello, Mercator, you barely caught me. My wife and I are leaving for Wisconsin in thirty minutes."

"Detective Dafney, the car that tried to kill me. It couldn't have been Lyn King. Wait, I mean, she *couldn't* have been the driver."

"What, did you only realize that now?"

"Yes, but wait, you knew that already?"

"Mercator, this is my job. You amateurs get lucky now and then, but we professionals keep grinding out results. When Lyn King confessed to the Munson slaying, I also interrogated her about the attempt on your life and in regard to the shooting of your wife."

Now nearly shouting into the phone, I exclaimed, "What! Did she shoot Carole?"

"No, she's says that she knows nothing about either incident. I'm inclined to believe her. She was forthright in explaining the murder. She put up no resistance to our questioning, but she seemed totally shocked that your wife had been shot."

"Then who did it?"

"Mercator, we are working on that. Lyn King says that no one knew that she was the killer and that she acted alone. It's really perplexing. The cases would seem to be related, but we can't find a connection. It's unfortunate that the license plate number that you gave us didn't turn out."

"Wait!" Now I was shouting again. "Wait! That's why I called. I realized that I made a mistake. It's a bit of a long story, but I feel sure that the license plate is three one four one five nine two."

"Give me that again—three one four."

"Yes, three one four. Then one five nine two."

"It sounds like a phone number."

"No, it's pi."

"Pie?"

"Detective, run it through the computer! Please!"

"Okay, okay. Hold on."

Dafney put the phone down, but I could hear the clicking of computer keys in the background.

"Are you sure about this, Mercator?"

"I think so, why?"

"That license plate used to belong to a Gregory Allan Shumpert of Salt Lake City, Utah. It says that the car was sold for demolition and scrap. Sorry, Mercator, but I think you might be wrong about the license still."

Dafney couldn't see me throw my head back or press my eyes shut, but could hear the exasperated breath that escaped my lips.

"Look, Mercator, a lot of these sorts of identifications or eye witness testimonies turn out to be inaccurate because people are under great stress or the conditions are dark or just far from optimal."

"But I was *so* sure. *So* sure." I really couldn't believe that I had it wrong. Dafney and I shared a few additional comments and I closed off. A couple minutes later, I realized that I hadn't asked Dafney about the vegetable oil on the hall floor and Professor Eidechse or the baseball and Professor Timicin, but even if these minor assaults were related, I failed to see how Lyn King could have been involved. Certainly she wouldn't have been able to throw a baseball through Timicin's window. Damn.

I had come to my office to do paperwork, and there was a stack of it awaiting my attention. I sat, determined to reduce the pile, but my mind was filled with racing thoughts. If truth lay where my thoughts were headed, danger still lurked in the form of the driver of the blue Chevy, and the case was far from solved.

42

Another Student

After an hour or so of paperwork and not really accomplishing much at all, my energy began to wane. My lungs were not processing as much oxygen as usual, so fatigue set in more quickly. After tidying up a bit, I left my office, and slowly made my way out of the administration building, heading toward my car. A few students were outside, but with the lunch over, most were in class, back in their dorms or studying in the library.

Sophomore Thad Bostick was crossing campus and passed not far ahead of me. "Hi, Thad," I called.

"Oh, hi, Mr. Eliasson."

I didn't really know Thad well, but he sometimes came to the college gym for noon basketball games. "Thad, where did I see you recently?"

"I think you were at that movie last Saturday. It was okay, I guess. My theater prof was all geeked up about it, wanted all of us to go. My buddy's journalism professor told him to see the film too; but of course my buddy Glen wasn't back from break yet. Tomorrow they're showing *Air Force One*. Sure, I saw it when it came out, but I'll go again."

"At the movie. That was it." The student activities office people always posted a flyer in the administration building. Sometimes I was interested enough to go. Now I remembered sitting behind Thad at the movie and overhearing his frustration with his girlfriend. I thought about mentioning it and decided this was another small opportunity to get to know current students.

"Thad, I was sitting almost right behind you. Yeah, I remember now. I couldn't help but overhear your dispute with your girlfriend. Have things worked out?"

"Oh, gosh, she only just seems to have forgiven me! You see, there was this one day when she left this phone message at eight o'clock, and I sent her an email an hour later to say that I couldn't attend a dinner with her family the next day. She had given this long description of the event in her voice mail. But, she says that my email was time stamped as 7:13 p.m., so she thinks that I rejected the dinner even before she had described it in her phone message."

"Oh, oh! I can see that this would be trouble."

"Unfortunately, my email only said that I couldn't go. I should have said more, since I did hear her message first, but I sent a short email. Just couldn't go. So she thinks that I listened to her voice mail afterwards."

"So, how long for this to blow over completely?"

"Wow, it's been nearly three weeks now. It was that day that the regent got murdered."

"Really!" Tilting my head to one side, I peered at him, eyes tightened. "That same night?"

"Oh, yes, that next day I was trying to distract her by talking about the murder, but she was so mad at me."

"And your email was off, I mean, not time synched correctly?"

"Yep. So anyway," Thad started to move on his way, "are you going to see *Air Force One?*"

"Oh, I doubt it. Though it can be a fun evening on campus at the movies. The last one was okay, I thought. *Ace in the Hole.*"

Thad nodded politely, though his words came slowly and with no rise in the timbre or volume of his voice. "I guess so. In the discussion afterwards, they said that *Ace in the Hole* was like the guy's sleeper film, though he is better known for movies like *Some Like It Hot.*"

Though these last words were thrown over his shoulder, I then matched his strides to stay with him. "Wait a minute. Who was the producer?"

Puzzled either by the question or my continued presence, Thad's face twisted into a frown. "Heck, I don't remember. I was talking about the director, not the producer. I guess he was kind of famous, though he must be dead now. I don't know, maybe he's like the Spike Lee of his time."

I was now staring so fixedly at Thad that he took a step back, almost in apprehension. "You okay?"

"Yeah. Sorry about your email. Okay. Bye."

Though I didn't run this time, I did pace quickly back to my office. I could tell from my rising sense of uneasiness that my body was producing adrenaline, but my conscious mind didn't know exactly why.

It was strange that Thad Bostick's complaint about email time stamps stemmed from the night of the murder. I decided to call Theo Sar about this. I tried calling his campus lab.

"This is Sar."

"Oh, Theo, you're here."

With a chuckle, "Let me check. Yes, I'm here."

Not really in the mood for his humor, I identified myself. "Sorry, Theo, this is Mercator. I've got an odd question."

"That's how I like them! Go ahead."

"I was talking to a student who thinks, well, it's a long story, but he thinks that one of the emails he sent was time stamped incorrectly. It got him in trouble with his girlfriend."

"Sure. It's possible. Could be something with the system. Don't know of anything that's been going on, though. Is he in his email system now?"

"No, that's the thing. This happened on the night of the murder."

"Oh ho! But Mercator, isn't that all settled? You caught the murderer yourself."

"Yes, Lyn King did it, but some things are bugging me. For instance, she couldn't have shot me."

"You were shot? What! Are you all right?"

"Yes, but that's a long story too, Theo. I can tell you all about it, but first help me with this. Could the email system have been malfunctioning on the night of Munson's murder?"

"Nope. I would have a report on that."

"Damn," I said, scratching my head to release some of this energy that was brimming inside me. "You have nothing. Really?"

199

"Nope. Sorry, I'd like to help you, Mercator."

"Okay, then, thanks anyway." As I started to put the receiver down, one more question came to mind. I felt a bit like the TV detective Columbo, who often had one more question just he was about to leave and the person he had been interviewing had just begun to relax. "Wait, Theo, wait," but he'd hung up. I hit the redial button.

"This is Sar."

"Theo, I one more question."

"Mercator? What's going on?" Apparently catching the zealous hope in my tone, he sounded concerned. "Are you all right?"

"But, Theo, could anyone have changed the time on an email message?"

"Changed . . . the . . . time? Hmm. I don't think so. Not on an individual email."

"Okay, well . . ."

"But," he interjected with a tone that suggested that an idea was blooming, "It might."

"Theo, what might? What might?"

"I know that it's possible to reset the system clock."

"But wouldn't you have noticed that?"

"Not if that person then corrected the clock."

"Can you see if that happened?"

"Sure. Hold on."

I pondered while Theo made his review. If the time had been altered as Thad Bostick's email suggested, then it could be that Gordon Munson's email also had been altered.

After a couple minutes, he was back. "This is strange. That night Munson was killed, someone did alter the system clock and then changed it back seven minutes later."

"And that would account for Thad Bostick's email? He said that his email was logged at 7:13 p.m."

"Yes, the clock was wrong by two hours. That is, when it said 7:13 p.m., really it was 9:13 p.m. It was off by two hours for seven minutes starting at what really was 9:07 p.m."

"So that's it." Thad Bostick was right. The email from Gordon Munson that said it was sent at 7:13 p.m., actually was sent at 9:13 p.m. Jill Moreland told me that Munson was dead when she arrived at his house a bit before 8:00 p.m. Thus, Munson didn't send that damning email. He was already dead.

"Theo, who changed the clock? Can you tell?"

"Sort of."

"What do you mean 'sort of'? Can you tell or not?"

"Mercator, the system says that I . . . that I changed the clock."

"What? Theo, did you change the clock?"

"Of course not. But that's what the system says."

"So, someone else changed the clock but did so in a way that points to you."

"Yes, Mercator, that's it."

"Who would have the capability to do that?"

"On campus there are three so-called superusers—me and my two colleagues in IT—Mike Pfingston and Darryl Morton, but neither of them would have done something like this in my name."

"But if they didn't, then who could have? Who could have changed the time system, changed it back and made it look like you did it?"

"Someone must have hacked the system. A computer science or math geek, someone with enough skills to infiltrate the system and then cover his tracks."

"Could the same person have accessed individual user accounts to add or delete emails?"

"I suppose so. Hackers sometimes do odd things for strange reasons, but why would anyone bother to alter the clock for seven minutes?"

"Someone who wanted Jill Moreland to be convicted of murder."

I thanked him and hung up. Next I dialed police headquarters again to talk with Detective Dafney. Unfortunately, he had left the building, undoubtedly for his trip.

There were several computer science professors on campus, not to mention a number of math professors or scholars in other disciplines who might have the skill to hack the college's computer system. Of course, the system break-in may have been done by a student or outside hacker solely for kicks. Quite literally, the person didn't even have to be in the state, or the country. Then I checked myself. I didn't need to go there. With Sar's statement, I could prove that someone had messed with the clock and I could contend that someone had also tampered with email files, but I couldn't prove who actually did it.

Pondering this, I again put on my coat and left the office. About to leave the main floor entryway into the cold weather, I noticed the posted flyer on the bulletin board. On one emerald-colored sheet of paper, I saw the Student Activities Board's promotion for this week's movie. There was an image from the film and a brief set of comments about the movie and its reputation. As student Thad Bostick had said, this week's film would be *Air Force One*, the popular action thriller.

Whoever had posted the flyer simply stapled the new copy over the previous movie announcement. In fact, the edges of several different colored flyers were visible behind the current promotional page. Lifting up the green page, I found a red sheet giving information about last week's *Ace in the Hole*, which was cited as the board's "classic film" contribution. The blurb stated, "Kirk Douglas stars as washed up reporter Charles Tatum, who stumbles upon and then manipulates a news story to his advantage. Director Billy Wilder's film foreshadows current issues in today's media."

Without being sure why, I ripped the page from the bulletin board, popping out one of the staples, sending the green flyer floating to the floor and the remaining movie flyers fluttering, only one corner remaining pinned to the board. Billy Wilder. Monroe Wilder. Wilder. There are other famous people named Wilder. Pioneer woman Laura Ingalls Wilder. Actor Gene Wilder. Writer Thornton Wilder. Did any of this have to do with Monroe Wilder?

I didn't particularly like Monroe Wilder. Was I using that dislike to turn a coincidence into a conclusion? Could Monroe Wilder be the shooter? His outspoken opposition to Jill Moreland's proposed tenure was clear, but would that translate into violent action as a response to my inquiries about the murder?

The shooter drove a blue Chevy with a Utah license plate that might bear the number pi. The pi thing might appeal to Wilder, the math professor, but I'd seen him drive to campus in a silver Oldsmobile with Minnesota plates.

Further, Wilder said he'd been at the theater the evening of the murder—"compelling drama" he had called it. Then I remembered that Aimee Forbes had described the play as a comedy, something "hysterically funny." My uneasiness sent me back toward my office for the third time, but this time I veered toward Human Resources. I doubted that director Hugh Dierckx would approve of my browsing in personnel files, but, Hugh wasn't looking. No one was.

Monroe Wilder was born in Bozeman, Montana. He got his undergraduate degree at Boise State University in Idaho and earned a master's degree and a Ph.D. in mathematics at the University of Utah.

Carrying the file in hand, I hustled back to my office. The blue Chevy definitely had a Utah license plate. Dafney told me that the license belonged to a demolished car. What was that owner's name? I had written the name down, absentmindedly when Dafney gave me the news. Gregory Shumpert. With the help of directory assistance, I got the phone number for the University of Utah.

"Hello, this is the University of Utah. My name is Leah. How may I assist you?

"Hi, I'm the alumni director from Masterton College in Minnesota. Who is the alumni director at your university?"

"That would be Catherine Clancy."

"Yes, I remember now. I met her once at a national conference. Cat Clancy. Please connect me."

Only a few seconds later I heard, "This is Catherine Clancy."

"Cat Clancy, this is Mercator Eliasson at Masterton College in Minnesota. You and I met at the Dallas meetings."

"How are you, Mercator? I certainly do remember you. I mean, how many times do you meet someone named 'Mercator?'"

"True enough. Say, can you look in your records to see if you have an alum named Gregory Shumpert?"

"I can check for you, Mercator, but I already know that we have a faculty emeritus by that name."

"Faculty emeritus, really? That might do. In what department did Gregory Shumpert teach?"

"Mathematics."

When Cat Clancy then verified that Shumpert was a math professor at the University of Utah during the years of Monroe Wilder's graduate studies there, it became certain that Wilder knew Shumpert. Could Wilder have taken Shumpert's license plate when the car was set for demolition? Maybe.

After the call, I stood up intending to return Wilder's personnel folder to the file cabinet, but instead I inadvertently dragged the newspaper off my desk. As it fluttered toward the floor, I made an awkward grab for it, but only succeeded in knocking it farther from the desk. Landing with the bottom half of the front page facing up, the newspaper displayed a single column article headed "EMPLOYEE HELD IN REGENT'S MURDER." Recovering the paper, I started to read.

> In mid-January the campus of Masterton College as well as its eponymous community was shocked by the murder of H. Gordon Munson, head of its Board of Regents. Yesterday evening St. Paul police officers in coordination with Masterton police detective Norman Dafney arrested Munson's administrative assistant for this crime of passion, a bloody killing from a knife in the back. Authorities apprehended Munson's assistant at the headquarters of Minnesota Mission where fire fighters also were called to an office fire last night. Dafney told reporters that Minnesota Mission employee Marilyn Wilder King had confessed to the murder.

Although the article continued, I abruptly stopped. Carefully I re-read the last sentence to be sure—Marilyn *Wilder* King. Lyn King had mentioned a short-lived marriage of her youth, but I had not known her maiden name was Wilder. Were Monroe Wilder and Lyn King brother and sister? Marilyn Wilder and Monroe Wilder. Marilyn. Monroe.

A quick call to theater professor Virginia Loop confirmed that Billy Wilder directed Marilyn Monroe as she starred in two huge hits—*The Seven Year Itch*, the poster of which was displayed in Lyn King's office, and *Some Like It Hot* in which Jack Lemmon and Tony Curtis spent some of the film in drag.

The circumstantial evidence was suggestive. I called Wilder's office. No answer. The spring class schedule in his file indicated that he didn't have a Friday class. Must be at his house. Could I put the shotgun in Monroe Wilder's hands?

43

Along the Mississippi

I knew that Wilder, a loner, chose neither to live in Masterton nor in nearby Hastings, but resided on rural property some miles from campus. Perhaps he liked the aesthetic elements of natural surroundings, but more probably he preferred the isolation and concomitant opportunities to lose himself without distraction in problems of dynamical systems theory, his obtuse specialty. As I drove, I recalled that a student had mentioned to me that sometimes Wilder missed a day or two of class, only to be found at home having lost track of the days. With Detective Dafney out of the office, I felt I needed to confront Wilder on my own.

From the address I figured the property probably approached the embankments of the Mississippi River. Turning off the county road I slid down a gravel road to the east. The gravel was mixed with snow and spots of ice, so my passage was slow. Still, my angry conviction that Wilder was entangled in the murder made me press on, probably faster than I should have traversed the poor road.

Two miles from the paved county road I approached a fork. I grabbed for my map and applied the brake. Hitting one of the numerous icy patches, the wheels locked, then released wildly upon the gravel. I wrenched at the steering wheel, but the car shimmied and landed with a lurch in a snow bank, directly in between the two roads of the fork. Muttering under my breath at the Toyota, I flung open the door and jumped out of the car to check for damage. Fortunately, none was apparent. Unfortunately, three of the wheels were sitting in about two feet of snow. Perhaps I'd need to follow Carole's brother's lead and buy a Saab. His classic Saab 900 with Finnish snow tires would not have ended up in this snow bank.

I placed myself back in the driver's seat and attempted to back out of the predicament. The wheels spun and the car stubbornly refused to budge. I got out again and popped the trunk where I had a shovel, standard equipment for winter in Minnesota. In fact my trunk contained the shovel, a box of kitty litter (for traction), a blanket, matches and candles, a supply of candy bars (Zagnut and Nut Goodie), and an unread mystery novel. If I couldn't dig myself out of trouble, and if the weather was too harsh to walk for assistance, then I had all the accouterments to bunker down in the front seat trying to be warm, fed, and entertained while I waited for rescue.

Perhaps a call for police assistance would have been useful, since I did suspect that Monroe Wilder was linked to the death of Gordon Munson. Unfortunately, I lacked proof. I told myself that Dafney wouldn't respond without some motivation that I flat didn't have. And, I was mad, a condition made much worse by being stuck in the snow. I didn't have a cell phone, so where was I going to call for help anyway—Wilder's house? Being deep into the snow bank might have been a metaphor for my involvement in the case. I was in deep and could use assistance. I knew it but my ire was overriding pretty much all common sense I might have.

So, I put my angry energy into scooping snow away from the wheels and reviewing what I knew about Wilder. He was on record as being adamantly opposed to granting tenure to Jill Moreland. Was this sufficient motivation to attempt to frame her for the murder? Not really. Not all by itself. As a math geek who very likely possessing exceptional computer skills, he could possess the ability to break into the college's e-mail system in order to send an altered message to Moreland that ostensibly was from Munson. Sadly, I didn't know this for sure. Now it seemed that Munson was dead at the time that the message was sent. Had Wilder sent the message? Had he had anything to do with Munson's death. I mean, yeah, sure Lyn had stabbed him, and it clearly had been a crime of passion, but why had Wilder or anyone changed the time around that? How had he even known Munson was dead in order to mess with the whole thing? Whatever the reason, why would he have taken a huge risk? Why would he ensnare the innocent Moreland?

After quite a few minutes of dedicated shoveling interspersed with gasping as my lungs objected seriously to this kind of hard work, I managed to extricate the car. I had expended a great deal of physical energy but only increased my mental agitation. None of this was making any sense.

After two miles of careful driving, I came around a bend and found myself approaching a small home. I stopped the car where some scrubby trees gave me a little concealment from the house. Lacking all adornments the place fit my image of Munson's need for getting away from everything in order to think deeply about math. I could imagine stacks of books, a computer setup, a bit of furniture, and little else inside. It turned out that I never got inside to look. As the car quietly idled about one hundred yards from the house, Wilder exited from a side door. Oblivious of me, he strode toward a stack of wood piled in what seemed to be random heaps. Now about fifty feet from the house, he grabbed an axe and prepared to chop some of the larger blocks of wood.

Leaving my car quietly and gently nudging the door shut, I cautiously, although not really stealthily, walked toward Wilder. Still, he didn't sense my approach and I was in no mood for amenities.

When he was in the downswing of the ax, I shouted, "Wilder!"

Quite off guard, he lurched, and turned to see me, while still continuing the swing of the ax. A cry of surprise was followed by a grunt as he missed the wood entirely, burying the blade in a pile of snow and ice.

He stared, clearly shocked to see me. "What are you doing here?" he shouted while regaining his balance.

"I know about you and the e-mail," I asserted. I could claim that I did anyway.

"What e-mail?" he countered, as could be expected.

"I know that you sent the e-mail to Jill Moreland, the e-mail that supposedly came from Gordon Munson."

He screwed up his face. "Again, I say what e-mail?"

"Jill Moreland received an e-mail from the account of Gordon Munson. The e-mail said that Munson would vote against her case for tenure and would see that the board as a whole would do the same. The police used this e-mail as evidence that Moreland had motive to kill Munson. The trouble is that *you* sent the e-mail. Munson was already dead."

"Listen Merlin . . ."

"The name's Mercator."

"Whatever your name is, I'm getting tired of you. I don't know anything about any e-mail. I couldn't send the e-mail from some other account anyway. That's crazy. So get lost." Wilder turned back to his wood and picked up the ax.

"She confessed, you know."

Wilder froze, the ax held above his shoulder. In obvious shock he blurted, "Moreland confessed?"

He didn't know. Dafney told me that Lyn King had not wanted to make any phone calls, not even to an attorney. If she hadn't called Monroe Wilder and if he had been caught up in his work at home, oblivious to any news reports, then he wouldn't be aware that the murder was solved. Well, not entirely solved.

With definite emphasis on each word, I made it clear, "H. Gordon Munson was stabbed by your sister. She confessed to the crime Thursday night."

His eyes widened, but he maintained his composure, "My *sister*?"

"Yes, your sister Lyn—that is, Marilyn Wilder King. Due to fiscal irregularities with the charity's allocations of scholarship funds, probably criminal activities that Munson initiated, Munson wanted to have your sister take the blame. Apparently, there were additional personal motivations, but she admitted to police yesterday that she stabbed her boss with his Gurkha knife. There is no question of the validity of the confession."

"Why would Lyn confess? She was clear."

Aha! The first hint that my speculation was at least partially true. "You were clear too, but now I know of your complicity. It's called accessory to murder, and it's a crime."

I had not seen the shotgun that stood behind the tree to the right of Wilder's chopping pile. I'd seen the ax, of course, and made sure I was too far from him for him to put that into use. I hadn't thought of the shotgun. Now it was pointing at me. The look of bewilderment that Wilder had feigned in response to my initial accusations had been replaced by a frenzied grin.

"I underestimated you, Mercer. The last alumni director we had was a moron." He laughed, mouth wide and teeth bared, in a way that actually scared me more than the shotgun.

Perhaps I should have bolted, but my mind was a jumble of different possibilities. The car was a hundred yards away. I might be able to beat Wilder, but would I beat shotgun fire? Oddly, in my anger I hadn't considered Wilder this dangerous as I drove out to confront him. Was I thinking that he simply would collapse into a sobbing pile when I laid out the truth? I'd be the strong hero, and he the whining coward. But now the maniacal way he laughed convinced me that he'd shoot me dead without much thought or provocation.

Should I lunge forward at him? I was several paces back. Perhaps if the barrel of the shotgun would edge away from the direct line to my chest, but now it was aimed dead on. In going for the shotgun, Wilder had dropped his ax into the snow on his right. Could I grab this as a weapon without getting shot in the process? I doubted it. Would it be more difficult for the right-handed Wilder to swing the shotgun to his right and away from his body or to his left and across his body? To the right seemed more difficult, but I didn't know. For a moment I regretted my lack of deer hunting experience.

"Surprised to see me armed, Alumni Man? Hunting is very mathematical, you know. It's all angles and geometry."

"Is that all life is to you, Wilder? Forms of mathematics?"

"I wouldn't expect you, Mr. B.A., to understand the precision that math brings to life."

"Lyn, that is, Marilyn is your sister. What's the deal with your names—Marilyn Monroe?"

"My parents were eccentric. My mom was convinced that my dad was Billy Wilder's third cousin. My dad was hot in lust with Marilyn Monroe.

So they combined the two oddities to give us our names. In middle school kids made fun of us. I'd tell them to get lost, but Lyn was embarrassed."

"So you protected your sister from a murder charge because your love for her is greater than your concern for justice?"

"I correct myself. You are a moron." He laughed that same maniacal cackle again. I saw the barrel of the shotgun rise a foot during the laugh before settling back into its place, aimed straight at me. Again I wondered whether I should have acted, but I remained rooted in the snow.

"You understand nothing, Mark."

I almost corrected his misnaming me, this the third time.

"I didn't send the fake e-mail to protect Lyn," he said, seemingly needing to explain himself. "I drove to Munson's house that night."

As Wilder said the word "drove," I glanced over at his garage, a two-car garage, where a silver Oldsmobile and a familiar blue Chevy were parked. THE blue Chevy.

"You shot my wife!" As I braced to rush Wilder, he raised to shotgun into full aiming position. I stopped.

"I tried to warn you, to stop you from asking around about the murder. Damn it, I did warn you! Why wouldn't you just stop? I slicked the hallway outside Eidechse's office with the canola oil Professor Bosson keeps in her workroom for a physics demonstration about friction, but Goren left first and took the damn fall. Should have been you. I even threw that baseball into Timicin's window. I hoped it would hit you or the broken glass would. Damn it! Couldn't you have just let it alone?"

Furious, I could only stand there, my lungs battling the damage and the adrenaline rush, thereby letting Wilder continue.

"I approached the Munson house, I saw her through the window. I saw her kill Munson. I managed it so that she didn't see me when she left. Then I went inside. Munson was dead. I also discovered that the secret opening to his conquest collection. Pervert! I also saw Moreland approach the house, and I hid in the collection room."

"No, you couldn't have," I said. "There's no way back into the house from that room after the door closes."

He sadly shook his head at me. To him I was even more of a moron. "I didn't take any chances getting locked inside, you idiot. I slipped a credit card between the latch and the jamb. I heard Moreland arrive and then leave in a panic. Curiosity got the best of me in the room, and I looked around. I found a monogrammed handkerchief from Jill Moreland's tryst with Munson. His souvenir. I dropped it into the blood. Later I hacked into the college's computer system to make it look like Munson had sent a negative email to her. I took Munson's theater ticket, in case I needed an alibi. But you got it all wrong. I didn't do all that to protect Lyn, though in murdering Munson, she did me a favor."

"A favor?"

"Yes. Munson was going to vote for granting tenure to Moreland. By eliminating his vote and his influence, Lyn did me and the school a favor."

"I disagree with your appraisal of the college's best interests, but why did you take all these risks?"

He stared at me, as if I had suggested that two plus two could possibly equal five. "I framed Moreland in order to save the college. Even with Munson's death, it was possible that your geography professor might receive tenure. That would be a death blow to my quest to move the college toward becoming one of the elite private schools in the country."

"Excuse me? Your quest?" Now I was really feeling like I'd stepped unwittingly into a *Twilight Zone* episode. Nothing was as it had seemed and I'd totally lost the sense of it.

His scorn seemed to be increasing geometically by the minute. "Yes, my quest. I don't deserve to be stuck at some podunk little college in the middle of academia. You think that Masterton can't be a St. Olaf or a Carleton here in Minnesota? You think that Masterton can't be a Middlebury or an Amherst College on a national scale? It can, damn it. With people like me, with people with credentials and publications like I have, Masterton could be recognized countrywide. Then my work on dynamical systems theory would get its due acclaim."

His pomposity was growing ever more irritating. "I still don't see how this relates to framing Jill Moreland for murder. Surely, her great teaching

211

skill and popularity on campus would only assist you in advancing the college to the national scene."

I had underestimated his scorn, for before going on, he colorfully referred to me in terms of size and excrement.

"Jill Moreland doesn't have a Ph.D.," he half shouted, not even attempting to control his derision. "Worse yet, that redheaded freak publicly declined to complete her dissertation. The preposterous pattern of tenuring those who *promise*," here he paused to snort derisively as if such a promise in exchange for tenure was inherently meaningless and in some cases duplicitous, "to complete the dissertation in the future would reach its ultimate extreme in Jill Moreland. Her teaching skill is irrelevant to the stature of the college. Tenuring her without a Ph.D. would cast an indelible stain of inferiority on the college. I couldn't allow that to happen."

His vehemence was quite genuine. Interjecting, I sought to affirm his ideas by stating, "So, you framed Jill Moreland for murder, for otherwise you feared you'd be stranded at a podunk school where your true stature would remain unrecognized."

Perhaps he was startled that I finally seemed to understand. Maybe it was simply his anger at being confronted. Or, it could have been that some physical release of his rage was necessary. Shrieking "Yes" he raised both arms in visual acclamation, the shotgun held only in his right hand.

I catapulted at him, seizing the moment when the shotgun was raised skyward in his gesturing. With a contorted look that I can only relate as a mixture of horror that he had allowed me this chance and disgust for me as a rival, he swung the gun back downward into both hands and fired. The cough of the gun barked loudly into my ears as I crashed into his right shoulder.

In retrospect, I like to think that my desperate lunge toward Wilder was directed by a remarkable and instantaneous mental calculation that targeted his right shoulder. Had he held a handgun, a bullet likely would have pelted through my chest, as powder burns from the point blank shot would have singed my shirt. In reality even in the moment or two that I plunged toward him, he only could swing the shotgun down and across his body to grasp it in both hands. Halting the momentum of the weapon leftwards and beginning to swing it back to his right provided the fractional moment that enabled my body to swing past the arc of the gun. As the shotgun discharged, its barrel hit against my ribs. As the shot flew past me toward snow and trees, I thudded into his right shoulder, my right hand clawing for his face.

A painful grunt passed his lips as the collision sent both of us onto the snow drift. My years of playing sports quickly sent me to my feet. Grabbing the discharged shotgun, I stood over Wilder. Assuming the shotgun useless now that it had been fired, I broke it open and hurled it far to the side.

"You're pathetic," I shouted at him. "The police will be delighted to add this attempted murder to the accessory-after-the-fact charge."

I reached down and tried to jerk him to his feet. His slick down jacket slipped from my grasp, and he staggered back, but he did gain an upright position. I made a second grab for him, but he stepped back, turned and began to run. Since I was between him and his house, he headed away from me toward the trees and the river.

Over dry ground I think I easily would have caught him, but across the snow-covered field the footing was less secure and my pace distinctly slower. A slip at the start of my pursuit placed him about fifteen feet ahead of me. Both of us slid on ice and struggled through the deeper snow drifts. This dash continued another fifty yards through a bit of woods. The cluster of trees was not thick enough to seriously impair our progress, but a fallen branch completely covered by snow snapped under my right foot as I pivoted to swing around another tree. With an "oomph" I plopped face down in the snow, my momentum plowing out a large snow divot around me. As I looked up to note Wilder's position, I saw that my brief falling cry had caused him to slow and look over his shoulder. A glimmer of hope seemed to flash in his eyes. Not wanting to let him escape, I struggled to rush to my feet, only to fall back on my belly. A second attempt to rise was successful, but a quick glance showed no sign of Wilder.

At this point—how many opportunities had I missed now?—I should have sought police assistance. I should have returned to my car, left, and let the authorities have at Wilder. That would have been the smart thing to do. I mean, now I knew what had happened, that Wilder was, in fact, involved both in the framing of Jill and in shooting me and my wife. Did I follow this prudent route? No. My personal outrage at Wilder for what he'd done boiled within me. I couldn't see Wilder even though he was hardly camouflaged in a red plaid shirt and a down jacket, but I could follow his footprints in the snow. I ran ahead.

As I neared the cliffs where the Mississippi River cut across the landscape, the snow under the trees thinned and rocks protruded through the surrounding whiteness. Here I had to slow my pursuit, partly so as not to dash off the edge of the cliff, but also because Wilder's footprints had disappeared where wind had blown the rocks clear. I thought maybe he had stepped or jumped from rock to rock. If I had been any kind of hunter or tracker, I'm sure I would have seen where he passed, but I wasn't, and I had no idea where he'd gone. A couple feet from the edge I was forced to stop, my poor lungs burning, breaths coming in short rasping gasps.

I had ignored any sense of personal danger so far. I mean, Wilder could have attacked me in the woods, hidden behind a tree and jumped me. Or he could have turned in the field to try to overpower me. I hadn't given either possibility a moment's thought. But confronted with the icy cliffs, my acrophobia was beginning to have an effect. Heights scared me. Hesitantly, I stepped a foot or two closer the edge, looking from side to side for a glimpse of Wilder. The math professor was here somewhere, but I couldn't spot him.

While I faced the river, to my left a chickadee abruptly fluttered up from a low tree branch. As I turned to see what had startled it, I caught the rapid, blurred motion of Wilder swinging a heavy tree branch at me. The bird's inadvertent warning had given me enough time to avoid a blow to the head. Instead Wilder's club caught my arm as it followed through. The blow tipped me off balance and I fell to one knee. Had this been my bad knee, I probably would have perished right there, not being able to react quickly enough to thwart Wilder's next parry.

However, not stunned by pulsing patellar pain, I was able to rise quickly, my back now perilously close to the cliff's edge. I was in time to see

214

Wilder prepare for a second blow, his face a contorted grimace of determination. Leaning back slightly, I forced him to attempt a long stride forward as he swung the thick branch, baseball bat style at me. As he aimed for my head as if for a high fastball, the moment, although in reality very brief, slowed. As the branch swung, I began a dive to my left, that is, to Monroe Wilder's right. The result for Wilder was that of a baseball player looking for that high fastball, but getting a curve that swept down and away. Many a ballplayer has looked foolish on this type of swing, but the consequences for Wilder were more serious. The lengthened stride over snowy, icy ground combined with the awkward swing of the heavy and unevenly weighted branch caused him to lurch toward the edge of the cliff. Trying to recover his footing Wilder clung to the heavy branch too long, and the momentum of the swing slowly propelled him over. As he realized his error, I saw his expression change. The hatred vanished, and shock and terror took over. He looked at me. His body hung suspended in the air, and he looked at me. Even in the face of his death, he glared that overpowering hatred again. Then he fell out of sight.

For a long moment, I did nothing. Then time resumed at its regular pace, and I yelled to him. I actually told him I was coming. I still wonder if I could have saved him, had I not been momentarily frozen by the narrowness of the branch's missed arc and by my own acrophobia. Instead of a rescue, I was left with two clear images of Wilder. The first was his look of horror-filled comprehension that came at that moment when he realized he was past the edge and past any chance of safety. The second image, more horrific, came after I very carefully turned my body so that my head peeked over the edge, the rest of my body prone clinging to solid ground. I watched the end of Wilder's plummet and viewed the moment when his body struck the rocky edge of the river. I wished I could have closed my eyes, but I watched, my eyes fixed open by the shocking sight.

Wilder's head smashed. Oh God, this was horrible. His head smashed directly onto a large boulder. This boulder worn smooth by the water's erosion, yet massive and, oh, so strong, cracked Wilder's head as simply as a sidewalk would have cracked a dropped egg. And too, like the gooey yolk and glyph of an egg, the gory mass of Wilder's skull oozed. The rest of his body, arms and legs no longer flailing, landed bluntly on the adjacent soft ice, ice that quickly turned red. Then with a crackling crash, his body fell through the ice, the momentum pulling his broken head along into the water. Being on the outside edge of the river, the current below the ice was brisk. Wilder, or more truly Wilder's corpse, for he was dead the instant that his head hit the boulder, sank below the ice and headed downstream. How far he went, I did not then know, for that was the last that I saw of Monroe Wilder.

Though I had discovered Munson's corpse and had mistakenly believed that Professor Eidechse had died in his hallway tumble, I had never observed the actual moment of violent death firsthand. Certainly television and movies had presented deaths, even violent ends, but I knew these were staged, imaginary for the entertainment of the viewer and the completion of the plot. Even my grandparents, who had passed quietly in their beds, had not died before my eyes. This death, a shocking violent death, made even more chilling because it could have been my own, unbalanced my sensibilities. For what seemed like a long time, I stayed at the edge, bile lingering in my throat.

Abruptly I found myself, gloved hands warm but spirit chilled, walking through the woods back toward Wilder's house, but having no recollection of standing or moving away from the precipice. Walking next to the woodpile, I absentmindedly picked up the shotgun and propped it up against a set of logs. I went back to the car and cleared the windshield of a layer of new-fallen snow. I looked up. For the first time I noticed that the sky had become cloudy, with many large snowflakes floating down, being pushed crosswise by an increasingly brisk wind.

I left. I navigated the gravel road and cruised directly onto the highway without stopping, practically without paying attention. I saw no cars—at least I don't remember any—until I reached the edge of Masterton. Even now I have only a fractured portion of memory of what I did that evening. I know, though, that I did not call the police.

44

The Aftermath

he next morning I awoke to find six inches of new snow on the ground. I contemplated contacting the police and informing them that I had sort of killed Monroe Wilder. Not really, of course, for Wilder had perished accidentally while striving to kill me. But what evidence did I have of the actual facts? The snowfall had covered and effectively obliterated any footprints or tire tracks. The body was gone, headed for St. Louis, New Orleans, and the Gulf of Mexico. Wilder's shotgun had been fired, but how could I compel the police to comprehend that Wilder had fired at me, and not to jump to the conclusion that I had killed him with his own weapon. My knowledge of forensic science is low. Would the police be able to find blood and tissue on the boulder at the river's edge? Even with snow and water present? Even if the police did uncover this evidence, would they conclude that Wilder accidentally went over the edge? Or would they think that I had pushed, shot or thrown him off the cliff?

Furthermore, I considered the other implications of reporting Wilder's peril. Wilder had tried to frame Jill Moreland for the murder of Gordon Munson. Wilder's sister actually had killed Munson in a fit of anger, prompted apparently by a mix of sex and scandal. Yet Wilder had admitted that his interest in the case lay not in the protection of his sister, for whom he showed a void of affection. Instead Wilder had sought to find Jill Moreland guilty of a capital crime, in order that his vision of academic purity would not be breached. Quite evidently Wilder deemed himself worthy of a much better post than Masterton College. However, being that the coveted teaching spots at the country's elite schools were out of his reach, the elevation of the whole of Masterton College to loftier standards became his goal. Viewing Ph.D. degrees and research publications as the essence of the claim to academic heights, Wilder could not tolerate Moreland's assertion that teaching with skill and knowledge and contributing to student life on campus meant more than paper degrees and obscure research. Rather than risk Moreland gaining tenure and the consequential staining of Ph.D. purity, Wilder had sought to have her convicted of murder. In order to maintain this frame-up and to hinder my investigation, he had shot Carole and me and had caused several minor injuries that befell me and others, such as Professor Eidechse.

Certainly my mind was clearer that morning than it had been when I had vacated the scene of Wilder's death. Even so I could not compel myself to contact the police. Perhaps I could demonstrate to them that this reclusive math professor had masterminded the false case against Jill Moreland; however, it seemed equally likely that the actual evidence would be inadequate to reach that conclusion. I had final statements that showed his culpability, yet it had reached my ears only. I had no idea what evidence the police might find in his house.

Finally, I decided that any dispute over Wilder's actions and his disappearance would not benefit Masterton College or Jill Moreland. I kept mum. It was four days before anyone notified the police about Monroe Wilder's disappearance. Students going to class and finding him not in attendance simply left, chalking it up to his well-known propensity for losing track of time. Faculty members did the same. Lyn King expressed no surprise that her brother had showed a lack of interest in her incarceration, nor did she inquire about her brother's whereabouts. I later heard from Elsie Norris that a dentist had called the science division office at the college, irate that Wilder for the fourth time in the last two months had missed his dental appointment. The dentist could not reach Wilder at the office or at home and demanded to know where he was. With a touch of trepidation, Elsie reported to me that when the science division secretary Shirley Harbridge had informed this dentist that the college could not find their eccentric math professor, the dentist had stated with gritted teeth, "I'll drill Wilder for this. Right in the bicuspid." Personally I doubted that the police took this as a serious threat against Wilder's life, even though Elsie was concerned.

The dentist's call prompted Shirley Harbridge to drive by Wilder's rural property that night. Her discovery that the gravel road into the property still carried a pristine blanket of snow gave her the impetus to call Marvin Cogpens, the chairman of the Math Department. Cogpens and his seventeen-year-old son, Bill, drove their pickup truck out to the property. With the plow attachment Bill used to clear driveways in Hastings for spending money, the two plowed the gravel road up to the garage door. Upon having no one answer their knocks and then learning that the door was unlocked, the pair entered but found no one inside the house. When retelling the tale on campus, Professor Cogpens indicated that their discovery of Wilder's wallet was what prompted them to call Detective Dafney.

Dafney sent a car out. Of course, deputies found the property vacant, for by then Monroe Wilder was some unknown distance downstream carried by the vagaries of the current of the icy Mississippi River.

Further reports carried in the local newspaper, and once also in the *St. Paul Pioneer Press*, indicated that the house showed clear signs of occupancy—the heat was on, food was in the refrigerator, lights were on. Wilder's wallet indeed lay on the kitchen counter, though it held only three dollars. Wilder's keys were missing. Evidence suggested that Wilder had been present recently.

However, given the undisturbed snow cover from the Friday storm and especially overnight into Saturday, and given that he had been in classes on Thursday, law enforcement officials contended that the professor's disappearance began either late Friday or during the day Saturday. Officers had been greatly hindered in their investigation by the snow that obscured any footprints, tire tracks, or other possible evidence outdoors. Furthermore, the Cogpens' plow and presence certainly had disrupted the scene. The discovery of the shotgun outside did spark speculation that Wilder had been shot, but the lack of a body dampened the fervor of those considering this possibility. Furthermore, law enforcement officers could not establish when the weapon had been fired, simply that it had been fired recently. Inferences could logically be suggested that the weapon's discharge was related to the man's disappearance, but conclusive proof was lacking. Although the investigation remained open, no members of the college or community were inquisitive enough to press the police for a solution.

45

Mall of America

ast the deserted shops of the Mall of America, I dashed anxiously across the tiled floors. My three pursuers had caught me by surprise in front of the Brookstone store. I had been enthralled by some of the gadgetry (an electronic bridge game, in particular) in the window display and was unaware of their approach. A slight reflected movement in the glass and the low snarl warned me in the nick of time of their presence behind me. With fists clenched they were forming a half circle around me, when I gave a head fake, elbowed the nearest one in the gut, and bolted away. At 220 pounds, I was not a swift runner. Nevertheless, I easily seemed to jump out ahead of them. Smugly I attributed this to frequent exercise gained on the basketball court. Also, genetics had blessed me with long legs on a six-foot-three frame.

Thus, as I skimmed past the Gap and rounded a corner on the third level, I was able to look back. My potential assailants were nowhere to be seen. Now I was puzzled that I could establish such a lead on them. In fact, the entire situation was rather strange. My mind had difficulty focusing on the appearance of these pursuers. One image called to mind Hank Searcy, the juvenile delinquent terror of high school days. Another mental snapshot revealed a Nausicaan, one of the tall fang-toothed beast-men of a Star Trek: The Next Generation episode. The third character was vague, an ugly blur. Also odd, the shops here at the Mall of America remained open but unoccupied. I looked over the railing expecting to see thousands of customers milling below, but was vaguely puzzled to view a vacant and quiet expanse of carnival rides.

Unfortunately, I had only a moment to dwell on these curious circumstances, for a piercing scream accosted my senses. As I swiveled back to face the

Gap, the Nausicaan charged as if to crush me against the iron railing. Instinctively, I ducked my shoulder. His impact knocked us back to the railing, but my dropped shoulder tossed him over the side. Horrified, I looked over as he plummeted down to the amusement park, which runs through the center of the lowest level of the Mall of America. With great force he crashed into a railroad car in a kiddie ride. Crushed by the impact, the car lay in pieces of twisted metal and splintered wood. My attacker stood up and glared at me.

Astonished to see that he was not seriously injured, I stared at him as he walked past a ticket booth toward the nearest escalator. Now I was really unnerved. This guy must be some kind of superman. Were his two foul henchmen the same? I didn't want to find out. Running wildly I searched for exits or safety. As I sprinted around a corner, I was met by Hank Searcy. I quickly pivoted back, but unfortunately, my reversal was abruptly blocked by the two others—the third pursuer and the Nausicaan who remarkably had survived the fall. In slow motion I looked around to check my options. A weapon anywhere? To my chagrin I found that I was positioned in front of Victoria's Secret. What was I going to do? Skewer them with an underwire bra? Brandish a crimson camisole? Ole!

Out of nowhere a stunning redheaded appeared at the store's entrance. Wearing a lacy black bra, panties, garter belt, and stockings, she smiled seductively at me as she came to my side. She extended her arm and handed me a phaser. A Star Trek phaser? Okay. Quickly I set the phaser to "obliterate" and vaporized my challengers.

The shrill flare of the phaser continued until I realized that my alarm clock was shrieking at me. I sat upright in bed. No muscle-bound assailants in sight. "Thank goodness," I mumbled, with a sigh as I banged off the alarm. After the dream about Roxy Gannon, I changed the alarm setting to ring, no longer having the alarm turn on the radio. Now I changed it back to the music setting that I preferred.

I glanced next to me in bed. I pulled up the covers and with a wisp of a smile peered underneath. There was no gorgeous auburn-haired woman. I smiled more deeply as I gazed at Carole's naked back.

The dream was becoming a familiar one. There were variations to be sure, but it had been a common feature of my nights ever since I investigated the Masterton College case. Although I'd never bedded the redhead, I had killed a man, sort of, a man whom some might call a monster.

Epilogue

It was a number of weeks afterwards, but it didn't seem that much later when commencement ceremonies were held. Little had been accomplished for Jill Moreland in the meantime. Although she had returned to her teaching, nothing had been settled about her tenure status. The regular March meeting of the Board of Regents had been inconclusive. The regents were struggling to adjust to the loss of Gordon Munson and were ill prepared to handle any issue of substance. They tabled a motion to grant Jill tenure. Although a vote on this issue was expected at the July meeting and although by the college by-laws, without tenure Jill contractually was entitled to a final year at Masterton College, by this time her anxiety over this tenuous position had increased. In order to protect itself legally, the college had extended to her a contract for a terminal year of teaching.

The commencement ceremony was held in the college's athletic arena. Although the basketball hoops had been retracted, several still were easily visible. Nevertheless, the college made a successful effort to create a celebratory environment in this forum. Festive banners hung from walls and ceilings. An elaborately arrayed stage stood at the north end of the arena. When the time came, graduating seniors filled most of the chairs on the floor and parents, grandparents, friends, and other spectators jammed the bleachers and seats that flanked the floor. I counted myself as one in the "other" category. I was here because, after this ceremony, these students would be alumni and thus would fall under my jurisdiction. I also was in attendance out of curiosity about the circumstances of Jill Moreland's life. While I was aware of a certain emotional connection with Jill, here I simply wondered how the general population might respond to a public appearance by Jill.

Actually though, she was only one of many professors who paraded into the arena in their academic regalia, robes embellished by a rainbow of different sashes and stripes. I understood that some of the colors signified fields of study, while other colors referenced the universities where a degree had been awarded. Truly it was a striking procession. I have to say, though, that it could be a much more impressive moment without those goofy caps. The mortarboards, like blackened mushrooms with a strand of grass hanging over one side, might be traditional, but they were as attractive as goatskin toupees. Jill Moreland's red hair easily could be spotted under her mortarboard, and I saw members of the audience pointing and whispering to each other during the procession. I assumed at the time that they were pointing at Jill and remarking about her notoriety. An unbiased view might suggest that parents were seeking to identify their children's favorite professors or pointing out colorful attire.

In any case, the procession completed and the ceremony began. Members of the Board of Regents sat in the front row with faculty and some administrators mixed in behind them. Along with the registrar, the commencement speaker, and a couple of functionaries, President Wheelwright and Dean Sholé sat on the raised platform facing the audience. Beginning to fear a boring afternoon, I actually started to wonder if I could rationalize leaving early. I very rarely left events in progress. The program started and my attention refocused to the activity on the stage. Various rituals were completed, a few brief words were spoken, and the commencement speaker was introduced. This introduction proved to be the most tedious moment of the afternoon. André Sholé, the dean of the college, took a full ten minutes to present the speaker to the audience. More than once the speaker started to rise from his seat, only to drop back into the cushion as Sholé droned on. More than once members of the audience near me yawned helplessly as they waited for the speaker. After this beginning, the keynote address hardly could be worse. Not surprisingly, among the events of the day, his name is a lost memory for me.

According to the printed program, following the speech came the defining moments that all were waiting for—the one-by-one calling of graduating seniors to pass across the stage and receive their diplomas. André Sholé strode to the microphone as Marjorie Wheelwright took up her position ready to extend her hand to each of the graduates. Registrar Stella Horton stood alongside a table stacked with diploma cases. Sholé began, "Will this year's graduating class please rise in preparation for the receiving of their diplomas?"

None of the students rose. A few moved idly within the seats, but no one stood. Sholé's expression of anticipation changed to one of puzzlement. He tapped on the microphone and repeated himself using exactly the same phrase and intonation. His voice rang clearly all across the arena, but every student remained seated.

Now clearly befuddled, Sholé glanced over to his colleagues on the dais for support. Marjorie Wheelwright came over to the microphone to join him. A buzz of confusion mixed with a murmur of apprehension spread through the audience. Frankly I had begun to doze off before this, but now my attention was fully directed at this spectacle.

Wheelwright appealed to the students, "Normally, we have the students stand to be recognized before proceeding across the stage for the taking of diplomas. Could you please stand so that we may acknowledge your accomplishments?"

Nothing happened. That is, nothing happened among the students, who calmly remained in their seats. Considerable activity was occurring elsewhere, for faculty were gawking back at the students, parents were talking rapidly to each other, and Wheelwright and Sholé were looking more bewildered than ever.

After a brief conference between president, dean, and registrar, Sholé returned to the microphone while Wheelwright and the registrar went back to their stations. Sholé stated that they had practiced all this, putting a petulant emphasis on the word "practiced." Nevertheless, they would skip the standing phase and go directly to the calling of names and passing out of diplomas.

"Paul Alan Abelman," Sholé intoned. No one rose. No student left his seat. Paul may have been an able man, but he did not approach the stage.

"Andrea Dorothy Agrathan, magna cum laude," he continued, citing her level of accomplishment based on grade point average.

No Andrea appeared.

"Nicholas John Allen, magna cum laude." No one.

"John William Anderson," Sholé was persistent.

John didn't rise, but a middle aged woman from about the sixth row on the east wing stood and loudly instructed, "Johnny, get up there and get your damn diploma!" The audience chuckled loudly, but we couldn't tell whether or not Johnny was amused, for he didn't leave his seat.

"Tamara Beth Arrigoni, cum laude."

"Gerald Michael Bache, summa cum laude."

"Sarah T. Bentsen."

"Mark U. Berton."

"Theresa Alice Borman."

"James Manley Brass, cum laude."

"Ford Mason Burger, cum laude."

A young man rose and began walking forward. The hubbub of the crowd increased furiously. Who was the young man? Was he the aforementioned Ford Burger? Why would he rise when none of the other students had? As he approached the platform, he abruptly veered to the left along the first row on the floor. Stopping in front on one of these seats, he bent over to speak with a man there. I recognized the gentleman as one of the regents, dressed in a suit, not in an academic robe.   After a few moments the gentleman rose and joined the student in walking up the steps to the platform. Immediately they were halted by Sholé and Wheelwright, who undoubtedly wanted to know what was happening. After this consultation, which appeared to be somewhat intense from a distance, the student approached the microphone, although all the others on the stage appeared nervous and unsure of what was to come.

"Ladies and gentlemen, my name is Ford Burger and I am president of the student body. My fellow students have authorized me to speak on their behalf and, as you can see, we are united and steadfast in our position. I have asked Harold Milligan, the acting chair of the Board of Regents, to join me on the stage, for what I have to say will require consideration of the board.

"This has been a year of stunning events in our community and at Masterton College. While we the students recognize the challenges of addressing complicated times, we feel that a grave injustice has been done and that if it is not properly repaired, then the quality and reputation of the college may be harmed irreparably. In particular we insist that excellence of service to the college must be the mainstay of evaluation of employment and that outstanding professors must be retained by the college. Therefore, we, this year's graduating class, note that the college has treated Professor Jill Moreland shabbily, both before and now after her innocence in the murder of Gordon Munson has been established. Therefore, we demand that the Board of Regents here and now officially grant Jill Moreland tenure, and we refuse to participate further in today's ceremony until this action is taken."

Bedlam! Sholé threw up his hands and spun around in a tight circle. Wheelwright took a few hesitant steps toward the podium, but halted unsure of what to do. Most of the members of the Board of Regents had bounded to their feet and started to talk among themselves. The audience was in complete disarray. Grandparents sat with mouths agape. Parents were pulling at each other. Faculty members were stirring, many trying to find Jill Moreland. A few succeeded and appeared to strive to discover her opinion of all this. At the same time the student body remained serene. As if in the eye of a hurricane, the field of seated students was calm, amidst the fury that waved and roared about them.

I looked back to the stage and observed Sholé bulling his way to the podium. Storm clouds were forming for him. Faculty and students were fully aware of Sholé's volatile temper. I had only observed this once myself, but had heard a number of accounts of blow-ups. Someone had cast the nickname "Dean Olé" to compare him to an enraged bull in a duel with a matador. Others had long recognized a preliminary sign of trouble as red splotches would appear on his throat and neck. From a distance I couldn't verify it, but I felt confident that these red spots were present.

While the students were calm, Sholé indeed looked ready to blow. He secured the microphone and tried to address the crowd. After several efforts at, "May I have your attention?" and, "Ladies and gentlemen," Sholé did manage to quiet the audience.

Barely controlling himself, he attempted politeness, "Students, while your sympathy for Professor Moreland is laudable, we cannot go outside of established protocols to fulfill your non-standard request."

Ford Burger, a few feet away from Sholé, smiled contentedly and did not move. The sea of students seated below the simpering dean sought no immediate redress, but continued to sit calmly.

"We'll proceed," Sholé suggested. He quickly paced over to the table of diplomas and snatched one from the top of a pile. The violence of his grab decreased the stability of the stack and sent a dozen or so cascading to the floor. Sholé didn't notice. Nostrils flaring and grey-white hair flying wildly as if blown by the gale force winds of his anger, he strode over to Ford Burger and extended the diploma to him. Burger's hands remained at his side. Sholé dropped the diploma at the feet of the student and returned to the podium.

"Kathleen Anita Caldwell."

"Martin John Chesterfield."

Sholé's pace increased, names spat rapid fire.

"Monica Mary Dolan, magna cum laude."

"Luther Jurgen Dovre, summa cum laude."

By now the audience was resuming its agitation, for still the students placidly remained seated. It appeared that the will of the students would not be broken easily.

"You must come forward to receive your diploma," Sholé would not be broken either, although his personal storm was surging. Now even from yards away, I could see the redness of his face and neck.

"Robert Todd Easterling, cum laude."

"Theresa P. Eggermont."

"Benjamin Q. Entenza."

"Sarah Jane Estenson."

Now though, activity had begun behind Sholé. Regent Milligan approached student Burger and began a whispered conversation. President Wheelwright was conferring with Stella Horton.

"Seth Q. Everett."

"Bart Michael Fink."

"Mark John Frenks, summa cum laude."

The students were still unmoved, but the audience's patience was wearing thin. Heckling was starting to swell.

"Let the students have their way," came a voice from the higher rows of the west side.

"Get on with it," ventured an angry male voice from way in the back. An irate father, I suspected.

Sholé, like the bull in the arena, was undeterred and relentless. "Francine Joy Galato. Beverly Jean Geneva. John Warren Grain, cum laude. Sandy W. Green. Valerie Anne Haugen."

Sholé actually overshot. Sandy Green was standing. The crowd hushed. As she walked forward to the stage, Sholé smirked, his storm beginning to pass. Even in this momentary pause, his hair appeared restored to its only somewhat unkempt status. With all eyes intently on her, Sandy Green walked across the stage. After coming up the stairs and passing Sholé, she abruptly swerved and walked directly to the second podium, the one that the speaker had used.

"I am Sandy Green. I am the vice president of the student body. I have come up to the stage to indicate that I am the last student who will ascend these steps today unless Professor Moreland is granted tenure. Also, I wish to inform you that the news media has been alerted."

Kaboom! Sholé was apoplectic and bolted to the other podium, clearly intent on washing Sandy Green and her message away from the microphone. She, however, was already done. Without further comment she walked to stand next to Ford Burger. Discreetly they knocked fists at their sides.

Sholé had thought that Sandy Green was his breakthrough in getting students to give in. It now appeared that she would be the point to break the resistance of the regents. In fact, the regents now were huddled in deep conference.

Sholé though was oblivious to this. "We will not give in to terrorism!" he roared. From the gasps, mumbles, and outright curses from the audience, it was clear that the people rapidly were tiring of Dean Olé. Perhaps many realized that the students were not practicing terrorism, but instead were using honorable methods of civil disobedience. Others simply were weary of the Dean's overbearing style. In any case, verbal suggestions mixed with slurs were being hurled at him by the audience.

Finally Marjorie Wheelwright came to the podium, displacing Sholé, "Ladies and gentlemen, if you will excuse us. I think you understand our interest in conferring for a few minutes."

"We're not waiting all day," bellowed a tall bearded man from the side opposite me.

The comment prompted a flurry of vocal directives from the crowd. Soon these overlapped so much they were difficult to distinguish.

Wheelwright again used the microphone, "Please. I understand your interests, but if you'll kindly give us a few moments to hear ourselves think."

The crowd stirred anew, but then Ford Burger raised his hands and, like a quarterback at a goal line situation, urged the crowd to be quiet. His non-verbal but obvious suggestion worked. Quickly, the noise dwindled to the buzz of many whispers, quiet enough for Wheelwright to conduct her impromptu huddle. I found myself wondering who was in control here. It was apparent André Sholé, like an Alexander Haig, sought to be in charge, yet was anything but. Wheelwright, the college president, could not quiet the audience, but Ford Burger, simply the student body president, could direct the crowd.

All watched intently as the regents, president, and dean formed a huddle on the stage. Several times Sholé could be seen to make his point strongly, but it was not evident that the group was accepting his views. In fact, from the ebb and flow of the group's position on the stage—progressively moving away from Sholé, so that he had to step forward to rejoin them—the effect was to intimate that Sholé was not gathering support for his position. Eventually, the

huddle slipped sideways to the edge of the stage, so that two regents were perilously close to plunging off.

I timed the process. After seven minutes, the huddle broke.
Wheelwright and Harold Milligan jointly approached the podium. It was
Milligan, the acting board chairman who spoke.

"While the action, or inaction," he noted with a smile, "of the students today is highly irregular, their thoughtful support of a professor is noteworthy. Here at Masterton College we do seek to teach students to think
independently, to analyze situations, and to stand up, or indeed to sit down,
for what they believe.

"Also, it is true that the Board of Regents does recognize the skills
and contributions Professor Jill Moreland provides at the college. However,
the board has been delayed in its normal proceedings by the loss of Gordon
Munson, the former chair. Therefore, the board has agreed to call a special
meeting to be held this coming Thursday to deal solely with the case of
tenure for Professor Moreland."

With this, Milligan stepped back from the podium and looked
expectantly at Ford Burger. In response, the student body president stepped
over to the microphone. "Graduating seniors," his deep voice reverberated
through the arena, "rise."

As a single wave rising out of the ocean of people in the auditorium,
these students stood. For those on the stage, the body language of dropped
shoulders and nodded heads showed the great palpable relief that swept
there and through the general audience.

However, Burger was not done speaking. "And sit down," he commanded. As one, the students sat. No angry shouts. No fists raised. No questioning looks. Instead, a unanimous silence and seated determination.

Still at the microphone, Burger angled to speak toward the regents,
"Not good enough. We'll wait while you talk some more."

More than one regent dropped head into hands. The essential physical
sense that all would be okay was crushed. Relief shattered into a million pieces.

Sholé now focused his bullish stare at Burger, strode rapidly and
forcefully to him, stopping barely inches from Burger's chest. His entire face

reddened by his emotional response to the unprecedented means and demands, he bellowed, "Listen here, you little bastard. This is a college of higher education. There are rules, there are procedures. You cannot fuck with us and smash time-proven guidelines to bits."

Though Sholé may have intended to speak directly and only to Burger, the student's presence at the microphone and Sholé's harsh voice conveyed most of the verbal assault over the audio system. The tech person at the sound table turned off the microphone a moment after Sholé dropped the f-bomb, leaving that vulgarity as the last word to reverberate around the arena.

Up until this point the audience had seemed unsure of which side should be favored. This outburst swung the crowd fully onto the students' side. Boos, curses, and a variety of verbal messages pelted the stage.

"You're the bastard!"

"Get off the stage, you jerk!"

"Give the students what they want!"

The regents quickly re-huddled. With the crowd not quieted, the regents had to shout to be heard over the din. Several were gesturing forcefully with their hands. Slowly the crowd noise diminished, but still maintained a significant decibel level.

Apparently, this second huddle lasted only five minutes, though at the time, I experienced it as a much longer interval. As the huddle broke, Harold Milligan stepped back to the podium.

"Truly this is an unprecedented situation," he started, "though the circumstances of the murder of Gordon Munson certainly were striking and very unusual for our community. Perhaps extraordinary circumstances merit extraordinary actions. Now though, as prompted by the students, the regents have decided that," possibly unsure of the wisdom of their decision, Milligan faltered briefly before he continued, "we do like Jill Moreland and, anyway," he paused again, taking a deep breath before the climax, "do at this time grant her tenure at Masterton College."

Milligan's last three words went unheard, for they were covered by the roar of the students who rose from their seats. Exultant, they were exchanging high fives, hugging, patting each other on the back. Around them there were different responses. Most faculty members were clapping politely and those near to Jill Moreland were offering congratulations. In the audience people did not know how to respond but were simply standing and watching the students. On stage Marjorie Wheelwright stood woodenly and André Sholé fumed. Red-faced and volcanic, Sholé was taking rapid steps in almost random directions.

New board chairman Harold Milligan remained at the microphone and tried to get the attention of the crowd.

"If I could . . ." but the crowd was not easily overcome.

"Ladies and gentlemen." . . . "Your attention please."

Again Ford Burger came to the rescue. Once more raising his arms for quiet, Burger prompted the noise to subside.

It was Milligan's turn again. "Ladies and gentlemen, it seems appropriate that at this time we ask Professor Jill Moreland to come up to the stage to be recognized."

The students thundered their approval, and Moreland rose and began walking toward the stage. Sholé paced to the back corner of the stage. As Jill reached the podium, the swell of applause seemed to grow even louder. Spectators seemed to catch some of the students' enthusiasm and began clapping too.

Jill tried to speak but her emotions betrayed her. The tears began to flow, and she was able only to mutter a stuttering, "Th-th-thank you." She chose to express her thanks by extending her index finger and pointing to Ford Burger and then to Sandy Green. One hand to her heart, with her other hand she began to point to those in the arena. With rivulets of tears running down her face, she repeatedly pointed out to the crowd of students. From my vantage point, I couldn't tell whether she was identifying individual students or groups of people more broadly, but the response of the students was electric. Even when Jill pointed to the spectators, she got applause. I found that she pointed at me too. I couldn't really be sure, given the number of people in the audience, but I had the remarkable feeling that she had singled me out. I was applauding too.

Finally in her turning and looking in various directions, her eyes lit upon André Sholé staring at her from the back corner of the stage. She pointed at him too. The volume of crowd support lessened somewhat as everyone seemed to wonder why she was beneficially identifying Sholé. To many of the audience, no doubt this seemed incongruous with the emotion of the moment. Most everyone on campus certainly knew that Sholé had been her nemesis, a personally scornful opponent of her tenure case.

Then abruptly the choice of finger changed from index to the adjacent digit. The angle of her extended arm also was altered, from straight out to a more upright position. Recognizing this gesture, the crowd hushed, not expecting this in the socially polite Minnesota setting. Then from the back of the student section, there came a single ringing throaty, "YYEESSS!"

One after another, two volcanoes erupted. The whole auditorium exploded with a ringing endorsement of Moreland's sentiments, with students joined by spectators in a blast of disapproval for Sholé. As this eruption of sound hit, Sholé lost control and broke for Moreland, his violent intent clear. Unaware, Jill had begun to descend the stairs to go back to her seat. Fortunately, Sholé was intercepted by two of the larger regents. In his enraged state, the diminutive Sholé was not easily restrained by these men, but was progressively ushered off the side of the stage. He was not to return.

Marjorie Wheelwright took his place reading the names of the graduating seniors. Not having practiced, she stumbled over Murali Pratik Elbaz and even botched a few of the easier ones, turning Sarah Joy Zeilstra into Sahara Zoe Janeway, but no one seemed to care. After everything had calmed down somewhat, a festive air had descended over the arena. The rest of the ceremony was enjoyed by all.

Postlude

Jill Moreland kept her tenured position at Masterton College. Marjorie Wheelwright struggled to keep her position, but remained president.

André Sholé left Masterton to become associate registrar at a college in Alabama.

Ford Burger went on to graduate school in political science at Stanford.

Lyn King pled guilty to second-degree murder. Her attorney Dallas Blundin expects that she will be paroled after ten years.

The Math Department hired a new professor.

In July a newswire report indicated that a highly decomposed body washed up on the banks of the Mississippi River at Pilcox, Arkansas. The sheriff of Pincon County indicated that the body appeared to be that of Palmer Forsyth, a drifter whose Little Rock family had reported him missing some five months earlier. No documents or ID were found on the body. The decomposition was severe enough that normal means of identification were impossible. A single silver capped molar was visible. The Forsyth family reported that Palmer had such a cap. The ragged fragments of a plaid shirt under torn pieces of a down jacket fit Palmer's known preferences for winter clothing. This completed the identification.

Only I knew that Monroe Wilder had been found.

I sleep in Carole's bed. Every night. In Munson's house. We bought it. Munson's secret room has remained my secret. I'm not sure why.

Sometimes in bed I read my poem to her. She loves it. Fully staggered.